Australian Christmas Stories

by

Mary Grant Bruce

Mia Mia Digital Publishing
Canberra

2022

Published in Canberra by Mia Mia Digital Publishing Pty Ltd
Email: miamiadp@marygrantbruce.com.au

Thirteen of these tales first appeared in *The Leader* newspaper (Melbourne), including 'The Hammock' on 12 December 1945. 'Our Christmas Eve' was first published in *The Daily Telegraph*. 'The Christmas Cook' was first published in *The Woman*.

ISBN 978-0-6480980-2-7

A catalogue record for this book is available from the National Library of Australia

Cover illustration: 'An Australian Christmas' © 2021 Stephanie F. Bruce, a great-granddaughter of Mary Grant Bruce, who has based this painting on the latter's writings.

Printed by: IngramSpark.

Contents

INTRODUCTION

Mary Grant Bruce was born in Sale, Victoria, Australia in 1878. She was so bright that she learned to read by the age of three. She loved writing from the start. She had a career in journalism, mainly in Melbourne, both before and after her first books were published.

Mary's son Jonathan, always known as Jon, was my father. He always maintained that Grannie was a better short-story writer than she was a novelist. About 300 of her short stories were published, many for children and others for adults. A very special group of these writings are the Christmas tales. They were all written before there were any internet, computers or television and — in many cases — even before there was broadcast radio.

I really like these stories both for the strong, positive messages that they contain, and especially for their distinctive Australian flavour and values. You can almost smell the eucalyptus leaves and hear the kookaburras laughing in the background.

Many of the first newspaper readers of these yarns would have come from places where it snows at Christmas. But here in Australia it is usually hot, often dry and sometimes there are droughts, floods and fires to contend with. If you are an Australian in one of those other places right now, you will know just how different that time of year can be. Here is a little bit of home just for you.

But wherever you are, and what ever time of the year it is, my family and I hope that you really enjoy these stories.

Ian Bruce

A GENTLEMAN BY ACCIDENT

It was doubtless ill advised of the burglar, in the first place, to select Christmas eve for the exercise of his profession. Christmas eve, of all nights in the year the one least favourable for that unobtrusive privacy necessary for the most elementary forms of burgling. And this burglar was no novice in his art, he was, indeed, noted among his fraternity for a mingling of astuteness with a certain daring cunning that rendered him at once the envied of the profession and the despair of the police. Every member of the force who was fairly out of the chicken stage knew him, but no member had ever yet experienced the joy of investing his wrists with the insignia of capture. He played "a lone hand" as a rule, for he had a not unnatural distrust of others whose nerves were not as steady or whose resources as many and as swift as his own. And, as his operations were generally planned with consummate art and attention to detail, he had so far been enabled to laugh alike at householders and at the blue-garbed individuals who are popularly supposed to maintain law and order.

Circumstances, and not the burglar's own inclination, had decreed that he should be on the warpath on this particular Christmas eve. For he was in heart a man of peace, and, so far as it could be made consistent with his calling, goodwill towards men. He had his own views of the fitness of things, and they included strict keeping of holidays. No indiscriminate burgling ever found favour in his sight, he liked to choose time, place and occasion with equal judgment. He was, in truth, something of a virtuoso in his art, not by any means the kind of rough and ready housebreaker of melodrama, truculent alike in aspect, attire and intention. To all outward seeming he might have been either a churchwarden or a shopwalker, and his sobriquet amongst his friends "Beauty Bill" was not unmerited.

Indirectly the burglar's little daughter was the cause of his excursion, since it was in romping with her that he slipped and sustained the sprained ankle which had kept him an unwilling prisoner in the house for several weeks. Little Nan had been considerably dismayed at the abrupt termination to the game, and the way in which Daddy's face had twisted as he sat up and ruefully examined his fast-swelling limb, and the consternation of Lou, who was Nan's mother, had been so great that the burglar had affected to make nothing of the injury, and refused to allow it to be doctored, a well meant proceeding which had resulted in so increasing the hurt that it was many a long day before the foot could be used again. Whatever be the trade of the breadwinner, an enforced and lengthy holiday is seldom matter for congratulation, and by the time the burglar was able to use his foot, not only was bread a serious matter in his household, but Christmas cake was out of the question.

Lou was a wise woman and made little of their financial difficulties. But, not so Nan. Nan was accustomed to all that she wanted, and Christmas in particular was to her a season of much rejoicing, and to learn that on this occasion Santa Claus would be conspicuous by his absence and that Christmas dinner would be a feast of dry bread, so upset Nan that she wailed freely, and refused to be comforted. Finally, however, she cheered up, and declared that she knew they were only making game of her, that Santa Claus would never give her the shove, that her leg was not to be pulled, with other declarations indicative of unbelief, and, after hanging up her stocking in the approved fashion, she went to bed and slept with all the confidence of her six cheerful years.

This attitude, which certainly had its pitiful side, greatly disorganised the burglar, a state of mind which became intensified, when, on going in search of his wife a little later, he found her weeping unobtrusively amongst the brooms behind the kitchen door. And when Lou, who had indeed made a very gallant fight for some weeks, at length confessed that she was actually hungry, wrath and determination came upon her husband, and he straightway made ready for the road, against all Lou's pleading. The night might have its dangers, he admitted, but after all, most well conducted households should be soundly asleep by the small hours of Christmas morning. "An' if," said the burglar truculently, "I meet any bloomin' small boys huntin' round for Santa Claus, I'll Santa Claus 'em on the 'ead!"

Strong in this thunderous resolve, the burglar about midnight kissed his tearful wife, told her to go to bed now, an' not be an adjective idiot, kissed her again, and playfully pulled her back hair down, and so set forth.

Most good burglars have in the back of their minds a number of houses suitable for their operations, of which at some time or other they have made a preliminary exterior survey, with a view to future explorations. Quite a number of these were pigeon-holed in our friend's mind, and he had a general working idea of their plans, gained by close inspection during visits to both back and front under pretence of book vending, hawking, begging, and the like. It was to one of these, a large mansion off St. Kilda road, that he now directed his steps.

The house stood well back from the street, hidden in a large shrubbery which the burglar admired exceedingly, both from a practical and an artistic point of view. It was about one o'clock when he finally advanced upon it, after a lengthy period of quiet watching and prowling in the garden, a survey which had revealed nothing but quiet in the interior, and the pleasing exterior fact that no dogs were kept.

The lower windows were all heavily shuttered, so perforce the caller turned his attention to the upper story. A pillared balcony, thickly twined with heavy creepers, was nothing less than an invitation to an athletic man still on the right side of thirty, and in a very few moments the burglar was trying the upper windows, after threading his way through what he considered a far too large assortment of pot plants on the balcony. The windows were locked, and so was the glass door which opened out of a kind of conservatory, but the lock of this was of a most elementary kind, and very quickly yielded to persuasion. The burglar smiled benignly at the ease with which he gained admission.

He waited a few minutes in the conservatory, where the air was heavy with the scent of many flowers, before venturing to turn on his lantern sufficiently to reveal his whereabouts. The faint light showed a door at the farther end and to this the burglar made his way. It was not locked, and an application of an eye to the keyhole showed only darkness within. He shut off the light before he crept in with noiseless footsteps.

Another pause, standing inside the door with straining

ears and bated breath, gave no sound and reassured him that the room was not an occupied bedroom which the fraternity are alike in their anxiety to avoid for an entrance. He felt in the darkness, and his questioning fingers encountered what he made out to be a side-board. "This is ri-buck," murmured the burglar enigmatically, as he turned the slide of the bull's-eye and threw a shaft of light into the room.

It was a long room, massively furnished and hung with large pictures. A dining room evidently, though, the large table was absent. In its place was an unusual object, and the burglar whistled below his breath and then grinned as his glance fell on it.

For it was a Christmas tree. A healthy young fir, that reached to the highly ornate ceiling, growing, apparently, with much vigour in a large green tub, and blooming with all manner of things, such as only the most refined and opulent Christmas Trees produce. It was not finished, only one half bore its load of gifts, and all about the room was a litter of parcels, and paper, and shavings, and string, and cardboard boxes a very saturnalia of unpacking. "They've lef' it in the middle an' cleared off to bed," soliloquised the burglar, and then he grinned again. "Great snakes, why, haven't I got Nan here!" he muttered.

It was really the most magnificent Tree. There was nothing paltry on it, nothing common, and nothing inexpensive. Its gifts, like those of all weddings, were numerous and costly. There were toys of a description which had only previously existed for the burglar in dreams and shop windows. Amazing mechanical triumphs— motor cars, which went by clockwork, dolls for all the world like real babies, only that their clothes were fit for a Queen's drawing-room, models of boats and engines that worked by real steam. There were dainty ornaments, tiny statuettes, gleaming white in the dim light, exquisitely bound books; silver that flashed in a dozen different forms mirrors, vases, calendars, brushes and the like. There were many parcels daintily wrapped in white paper. One, which bore the single word "Agnes," the burglar opened. It contained a tiny leather case, and within was a flashing wonder, a slender ring, set with three great diamonds that danced and winked at him. "Crikey!" said the burglar, and he slipped the little case into his pocket. "That's bad luck for Aggie," said the burglar, humorously.

Just above him was a very exquisite little doll, a tiny French lady, blue gowned, fair haired, very genteel and fashionable. Her the burglar secured, with a view to a certain stocking dangling limply against a little crib he knew, and he followed her up with a most waggish white rabbit that squeaked and ran on proper provocation, and a seal that one could see at a glance possessed unlimited aptitude for diving. They all went easily enough into the specially constructed pocket of his overcoat, which was a garment capable of holding a great deal more than merely its wearer. Then the burglar shut off his light and crept into the hall.

He went into several rooms that were unoccupied and gave no reward to his painstaking search, a prettily furnished sewing room, a great bedroom, a nursery littered with toys that made him long for Nan to luxuriate there. Opening from it was another room. The burglar had grown bold in the dead silence of the house, and he was fairly inside it before he perceived that it already had an inmate. Then he shut off the light quickly and remained perfectly still, his breath coming and going quickly, his hand clenched threateningly. So he stood for perhaps five long minutes, and then, realising with a sigh of relief that the sleeper had not stirred, he turned a narrow pencil of light towards the bed.

It was not a very formidable sight, even for a burglar. The sleeper lay at ease, dainty, pink-flushed limbs tossed carelessly outside the sheet she had kicked aside in the warmth of the summer night. One tiny hand held tightly a battered china monkey; the other was under the little cheek. Her curls strayed here and there over the pillow and across her face, one lock, golden in the dim light, lay on her lips, and scarcely stirred at the faint childish breath. She was very sweet and helpless and little there in her white nest among her soft laces and frills. And the burglar stared at her, at the soft, rounded limbs, the delicate face, the long, dark lashes that swept the cheeks, most of all, perhaps, at the yellow curls— Nan also had yellow curls. They were not quite like these, being of the kind that are kept stiff with vaseline, but, after all, that is merely a matter between Lou and her conscience, and no one else's business. For Nan's sake the burglar had a very soft heart for all tiny maidens with yellow curls.

A few minutes perhaps, he stared at the baby sleeper then the claims of business re-asserted themselves, and half reluctantly, he turned away. In that room he had no desire to explore further. "Kids is not in my line," said the burglar, speaking from a professional and not from a private point of view. He tip-toed gently towards the door.

"Oh, my gwacious!" said a sleepy, startled voice, "dere's Santa C'aus".

The burglar swung round sharply. The occupant of the little bed was sitting up, a vision of dimpling, round-eyed, amazement. He had just time to catch her smile of delighted welcome as he shut the light out and sprang for the doorway.

A long note of woe followed him. "Oh, come back — dat's not fair, Daddy said —" The words melted into a wail, and the now thoroughly alarmed burglar hesitated.

"S-sh!" he said threateningly.

The wail ceased, but the voice continued, injured, protesting,

"Well, it's not fair. Daddy did say if I did catch you I could keep you! Oh, where's dat light done away to?" The wail seemed imminent, and the burglar, every sense on the alert, temporised.

"Well, will you be quiet if I bring the light back?" he growled.

"Course I will," said the small voice obediently hushing to a whisper. "Bring it back, twick. I wants to look if you's done my 'tocking yet."

"S-sh!" said the burglar again. He turned the slide to admit a little light, and increased it on an insistent demand for "more bwighter." "Just you be quiet," he said. "No, I haven't done your stockin' yet. You lie down an go to sleep like a good gel, an' don't wake anybody."

The small mouth drooped ominously.

"But I's twite awake. I touldn't possumly do to s'eep!" asserted the small voice. "Want to watch you do my 'tockin'." A distant note of injury came into her voice.

"But where's your big swag of toys? Why, you hasn't dot anyfing. I don't fink you's a nice Santa C'aus".

"Oh, ain't I just?" said the burglar desperately. "I'm just, the shiny. You look here!" He fished in his pocket and produced the French doll, holding it out temptingly.

How the blue eyes grew round! She stretched out her hands.

"Oh!" she said. "Oh! You is the nicest Santa C'aus! I spec's you did just know I had bwoke my own dear Anna Mawia Betsy Jane. Oh, come here, you booful new baby!" She hugged the doll to her, and crooned a little song.

"There you are, then," said the distraught burglar, who was in a cold sweat of fear. "Now, down you lie — straight off to sleep, and don't whisper another word!"

"But no!" The blue eyes were never more wide awake. "Daddy pwomised I could keep you if I did catch you. 'Twas a twuly pwomise. An' now I's caught you!" She knelt up and laid hold of the reluctant burglar's coat. "Want to see all your toys," she said, confidingly.

"Well, you can't, then,"said the burglar, brusquely. "My toys ain't for little girls to see till tomorrow. You go off to sleep."

Down went the corners of the mouth.

"Well, I's just doin' to cwy an' yell!" she announced; and it seemed probable to the burglar, listening desperately for sounds from the next room, that she would carry out her intention. "You's a nasty, unkind Santa C'aus, I don't love you one single scwap!" The voice rose on each syllable and the burglar, in his anguish of mind, clapped his hand over her mouth. Not roughly — the little mouth was as velvet under his palm. He revolved quick schemes.

"Well, will you be quiet if I show you my toys?" he asked. She looked up into his eyes and apparently liked what she saw there, for she nodded vigorously.

"Come along." He held out his arms, and she came to him joyfully. The round baby arm lay warm against his neck, and gradually the hardness faded from the burglar's face. "Comfy" he asked . . . Nan always liked to be asked that.

Very softly they went along the hall. The burglar blessed the thick carpet that made his footsteps so noiseless. He again enjoined quiet, and she nodded vigorously. "I'll be like one mouse," she assured him in a stage whisper. And then the burglar suddenly became as wax, for there came a marvel of soft lips on his cheek. "You's a kind old Santa C'aus!" she murmured, as she kissed him.

After that there was no further resistance on the part of the burglar. Reassured that no one was aroused, for the house remained perfectly quiet, and, seeing the futility of resisting this small, soft tyrant, he flung dull care to the winds and gave himself up to the pleasure of the moment. And, indeed, she was worth seeing, this spoilt, yellow haired baby, as she rioted over the half-fledged Christmas Tree. The burglar would not allow her to touch anything but one or two toys — of a noiseless nature — but, apart from that, he made no restrictions, and thoroughly enjoyed the moment, taking no thought for the morrow. How she chuckled and exulted, over the great dolls, the wonderful toys! How the sweet eyes sparkled, the gay little voice made music! subdued as it was to a whisper, yet still music. How she clung, too, to the delighted burglar, assured him of her veneration and affection for him; many times flung her arms round his neck in an ecstasy of plcasure. "Oh, my oath, but you are a nice little kid!" said the fatuous burglar — "kiss us agin!"

It was this highly amusing scene which greeted the eyes of an astonished young man who opened the door some ten minutes later. He was in his shirt sleeves, and gave a general impression of being hard at work; his arms were full of parcels, some of which he had put down to open the door; his gold rimmed pince-nez were awry; he looked generally harassed and tired, a look which turned to the liveliest bewilderment at the scene in front of him — the tall, dark fellow with a bulls-eye lantern and a meek aspect, and on his shoulder a most attractive vision in a diminutive white nightgown. The vision was diligently, kissing her prisoner as the door opened. They both seemed entirely happy, and did not observe the newcomer.

"Well, I am damned!" said this latter. "What do you think you'rc up to?"

Like a flash the burglar sprang round, all the softness falling like a mask from his face. The man in the doorway had dropped his parcels, and one hand was in his hip-pocket.

"Stay where you are," he said coolly. "Keep your hands away from your pockets or I'll shoot. What — " But his voice was drowned.

"Daddy! oh Daddy!" cried the vision excitedly. "I've caught Santa C'aus, an' he's just somefing lovely. Oh, just look, Daddy — all the booful things he bwinged to me. Isn't he kind, Daddy?"

"Most kind," said the man in the doorway, grimly, not

taking his eyes from the burglar.

"He's just the dearest Santa C'aus," said the vision. "I kissed him, lots of times. Would you like to kiss him Daddy?"

"Very much," said the man, a kind of grave twinkle in his eye. There was a distinct twinkle in the burglar's eye as it met his. One might almost have detected a subtle camaraderie between the two. They measured each other slowly. In build they were much alike, both tall, both powerful, both clean shaven and distinctly good looking; the aristocrat fair, the man of the people dark. Two goodly men, and each recognised and respected the manhood of the other.

"You needn't worry yourself," the burglar, said at length, "I ain't got no shootin'-iron. You've got a lone hand."

"How am I to know that?"

"You might 'a seen it before this, if I'd had it," said the burglar, grimly. "It's up the spout — popped — went a week ago. So there you are; your trick. You're top dog this deal."

"You've got my child," said the other, slowly. The advantage did not seem to him to lie on his side.

"Good Lord, I ain't that sort," said the burglar, with hasty disgust. He lifted the child from his shoulder. "There, run along to Daddy," he said gently.

But the small maiden had no intention of running along. Instead she protested forcibly, and embraced the burglar's knee.

"No! you's my own Santa C'aus. I's doin' to stay wiv

you! Go 'way, naughty Daddy. Wants to be tooked up on your shoulder adain!" She tugged at his finger, and meekly the burglar picked her up and replaced her, whereat she smiled on him benignly and kissed the top of his ear. He grinned sheepishly, and the man in the doorway laughed outright.

"This is a cheerful party," he said. "I seem superfluous. How did you get in?"

"Balc'ny-plant-house," said the burglar laconically. "Where was you?"

"In the cellar, unpacking things. Heaven only knows why they were put there. I've got to finish this tree tonight. Been round the house?"

"No; no luck. Your nipper struck me first go off. She — I — I've got one something like her. This is a nice little kid."

"We generally try to conceal the fact, in the interests of discipline," said the other gravely. "These things leak out, though. So you've got one, too. I've never regarded burglars as people with family ties. We all have our troubles. How old's yours?"

"Six."

"This is four," said the other, 'this' being at the moment cheerfully engaged in making her doll walk on the burglar's head. He burst into a sudden laugh. "What in thunder am I to do with you?" he asked. "We can't stay here exchanging family secrets all night. I've got to finish this tree."

"I'll help you," said the burglar readily.

The other stared. “And what then?”

“Oh, I dunno,” the burglar said. “You’ve cert’nly got the drop on me, but you don’t hand me over to the cops without a run for my money. I’d as soon be shot as jugged, anyhow. My luck’s dead out.” He smiled as the small person on his shoulder tickled his neck with her toe. “I’ll give you a hand with the tree if you like, an’ you can make up your mind what you’re goin’ to do.”

“Straight wire?”

“Honest Injun.”

“By George, I’ll take you at your word,” Stephen Hallam said. “Don’t know if I’m a fool, but I’ll chance it. And what are we going to do with Dorothy?”

“I’se doin’ to stay wiv mine old Santa C’aus,” said that lady firmly. “He wants me, don’t you dear?” She kissed him decidedly. “Show me more toys.”

“Not just now,” said the burglar.

“Fact is, Dorothy, I can’t finish this ’ere tree till you’re in bed. Say you go there, till it’s done?”

“Can’t you, weally?”

“Not a hope,” said the burglar.

“Well, then, you take me to bed,” said she, acquiescing with, surprising docility. “Wants your nice, funny little lamp, ’an you to tuck me up. Tum along, old chap!”

The burglar looked questioningly at the father, and Hallam nodded with a faint grin. He followed them closely down the hall.

Very gently the burglar laid his little burden down, and

straightened the clothes and tucked her in as carefully as a mother. She flung her arms round his neck. “Oh, I do love ’oo!” she said fervently. “You’s just the dearestest Santa C’aus ever was. Do tum adain soon.”

“Good-bye, little kid,” said the burglar, softly. He patted her tenderly.

“Wants you to kiss me,” she said.

Hallam, watching, felt something like a lump in his throat as the big man bent over the little face. He was so big, yet, so amazingly gentle. When he straightened up, still with one finger in Dorothy’s clasp, Hallam held out his hand impulsively.

“Shake,” he cried. “I don’t care what the deuce you’re here for — you’re a gentleman by accident, if you are a burglar by choice!” And the burglar, fully appreciating the peculiar compliment, gripped his hand readily.

Over the Christmas Tree the two men grew quite friendly. The burglar showed himself a genius for working, and the tree blossomed beneath his touch. As they worked they talked, and before long Hallam found himself in possession of most of the burglar’s family details; knew something of his circumstances, something of Lou, a great deal of Nan. He heard of the empty larder, of the Christmas dinner which was to be non-existent; he heard, too, of that little stocking, so trustfully hung up on the post of the little bed, and his heart swelled within him. The burglar did not expatiate much; it was by judicious pumping that Hallam acquired most of his information. He forgot the burglar’s profession, forgot the cause of his presence in the house. It seemed to him that here was merely, a man and a brother.

It was after 3 o'clock when they finished the tree, and they stood back and regarded it proudly, for it was a marvel among trees. The burglar's hands were in his pockets and suddenly he flushed hotly. With a momentary hesitation, he drew a packet from his pocket and handed it to Hallam.

"You'd best stick that on again," he said, gruffly. Hallam, too, flushed. There was a moment's uncomfortable silence as he tied his wife's ring to one of the branches of the fir. The burglar broke the pause.

"Well, I guess it's time you got that six-shooter of yours to work again," he said.

Hallam laughed. "Six-shooter?" he said, absently. "Oh I never had one!" He laughed at the other's face. "Come along," he said, "we'll explore the kitchen."

From the back regions a considerably astonished burglar emerged shortly after. He bore a huge basket, containing sundry seasonable articles, an uncooked turkey of noble proportions, a ham, a plethoric Christmas pudding, together with smaller comestibles, tucked into the corners. "I don't quite know what they'll say" Hallam laughed. "Cook will make unlimited remarks I fancy. Never mind, it's a poor heart that never rejoices! Come along."

He led the way back to the Christmas tree and stripped its groaning branches of as many toys as the burglar could stow away in his capacious pockets; confining his selection, so he said, to articles especially suitable for small persons of six, with curly hair. Then followed presents of another nature, a silver brush, a dainty brooch, a lace collar. "Your wife might fancy that," he said, and poked them in. The burglar stared at him, speechless.

Finally Hallam slipped a crisp note into the bulging

pocket. "For luck," he said; "a merry, Christmas!"

"No, by Jove, that's too much," the burglar said. His voice shook, something like moisture was in his eyes, for which he was furiously ashamed of himself. He had to turn away his head. "I can't," he said, when he could steady his voice; "you've made me feel a big enough brute already."

"Oh, rot!" Hallam said cheerfully; "this is my party. I've got to take it out of you somehow, you know. Here, keep your hands off that! You've got to have it — you'll hurt my feelings!" He laughed at the downcast face, for at no time before had the burglar exhibited so little cheerfulness. "Shake hands, old man!"

The burglar gripped his hand "You're a man!" he said, shakily.

"You're another!" laughed his host, and then his eyes became grave. "Look here," he said, "it's a bad lay, you know, this game of yours. Can't you chuck it? I'll give you a lift."

The burglar met his eyes.

"No," he said, "no go. I'm too old to change; and besides — well, straight, I tell you, I like it! Every man to his own game, you know. Yours is this — " he swept a glance round the splendid room, "all this — a gentleman's game. I'm a burglar by nature — no gentleman."

"I'm not so sure," said Hallam. He gripped his hand again.

"So long," he said cheerfully a moment later, as he let the laden burglar out of the front door. It was still very dark, but in the east was just a hint of the Christmas dawn. "Mind the step there. My love to Nan, and best respects to

Lou, and wish them a merry Christmas for me. As for you — well, I'm sorry I'm not likely to see more of you!"

"You won't do that, cert'nly," said, the burglar. "Not in any capacity. I reckon you won't have any burglar scares in future. My word, you are a man, an' that's all about it. I'm not much chop at sayin' things, but — "

"That's a mercy," Hallam said lightly. "It's all right, old man."

"I won't forget," the burglar said heavily. He hesitated a moment. "P'raps, you wouldn't mind wishin' the little kid a merry Christmas for me?" he said.

"I'll kiss her for you," Hallam said promptly. "She'll like it better. Well, so long."

"So long," said the burglar. His feet grated on the gravel, and the door closed. As it swung to he turned back suddenly.

"I say," he began, "about that offer of yours — " He broke off, looking a trifle blankly at the closed door.

"Well, it's just as well," he pondered. "It mightn't 'a acted. Once a burglar, always a burglar till you're jugged." He glanced at the faint touch of pink in the dark east. "Wonder if I can get home before Nan wakes?" he muttered as he went down the path.

AN AUSTRALIAN CHRISTMAS

Four a.m. finds dawn creeping through the open windows. The children have not waited for the sun, already small pyjama'd figures are prancing wildly through the house, and the tremendous orgy of unpacking stockings has given place to a saturnalia of possession. Nowhere is Santa Claus more real than with the bush babies of the South. They know that reindeer are no use to him in Australia: but then, they realise that it is only a fair thing that his team should, have a spell while he comes "down below," where it is certain that he uses black swans — intelligent birds, equally able to swim rivers and lakes, or to fly over miles of trackless bush or sandy desert. It is current belief that he stables them in a hollow gum-tree what time he goes back to deal with the cold Christmas of the North.

Out in the paddocks the milking herd is slowly stringing through the wet grass towards the shed, impelled by a smart dog-of-all-work, and a yawning boy on a pony. Steam is up in the engine-room, and the milking machines are ready. The cows come in lazily, and slip into the bails; the gentle throb of the pulsators always seem to soothe them, and they stand motionless save for an occasional flick at a fly, while the milk is drawn from them, to pass swiftly through overhead tubes to the separator-room untouched by human hands until the cream is safely stored away in cans, and the skim milk en route to the pigsties. The dew is hardly off the grass when the cows are again sauntering back to the pastures — a hundred and fifty sleek beauties, milked with less trouble than five and twenty in the old days of hand-milking. Australia has no time to do without machines.

Dew does not last long in a southern December. By seven o'clock the sun is high, and the men, hurrying over the necessary work that they may enjoy the "Christmas loaf", tell each other that the day will be a "fair scorcher". The children are bathing in the creek below the orchard — scamping dressing, that they may have ten minutes among the cherries and apricots on the way up to breakfast. On the wide verandahs running all round the house the sunblinds are down; lashed to floor-bolts, for there is promise of a hot wind — and a heavy Japanese blind, loose in a gale, can batter itself into fire kindling in five minutes. Doors and windows, wide open throughout the night, are carefully closed now. Each fireplace is fitted with a wire screen, since the friendly blowfly, discouraged from entering in the usual way, loses no time in seeking ingress by the chimneys. To grapple with the artifices of the blowfly is the highest point of militant housewifery in Australia.

The north wind is moaning round the homestead by the time breakfast is over. It is breathlessly hot. Everyone discards all but a necessary minimum of clothing. A boy arrives from the township with the English Christmas mail; and for a while there is silence, wistful hearts travelling over thousands of leagues of sea to the land everyone calls Home. The children, failing blankly to realise any Christmas unaccompanied by drought and heat, fling on wide brimmed hats and race outside; the ponies are in the yard, and it is better to gallop over the wide, sunburned paddocks than to sit in the house and dream of the other side of the world. Soon the merry, shouting band, with its attendant troop of delirious dogs, is only a blur across the plain, half-lost in the blue heat-haze that shimmers on the surface of the yellow grass.

Morning is peaceful — housework over, the women-folk settle down in the hall (always the coolest part of the house), and rejoice in unwonted laziness. The mending-basket, and the stocking-bag yawn as usual — but it is Christmas day, and "let everyone be merry!" There is no merriment in darning-bags; and only a busy mother knows the luxurious joy of a day with books and papers instead of heeding the claimant voices of the family rents. Were the day less savagely hot, a drive in the paddocks might be planned; as it is the hall is a haven of rest and coolness, and no one wants to stir outside until sundown.

The men straggle in towards one o'clock. Dinner is a mid-day function, severely cold as hot roast beef and plum pudding are unappetizing with the thermometer at 105°F, and a north wind added by way of unearned increment. Someone says vaguely

"Where are the children?"

The Boss, preparing to attack a: mammoth turkey, says as vaguely,

"Oh! They'll come presently."

They come. There is a scatter of gravel on the path outside, and a high voice pierces through the shuttered house.

"Bush-fire, Daddy!"

The dining-room is empty in a moment — save for Mother, replacing the wire-cover on the turkey. Outside, a small boy, scarlet-faced, is bursting with the urgency of his tidings. The scrub is alight in a far paddock; the big boys, warriors of twelve and thirteen, are already fighting it, the smaller fry scattering to give the alarm.

There are horses in the yard, brought up by an Amazon of ten. Five minutes later, not a man is left at the homestead, and the small boy and his sister, perched on the big water-cart that always stands in readiness, are urging an old Clydesdale mare in the wake of the galloping riders. Water may save miles of fencing — if it gets there in time. In the house the women brew cool drinks swiftly, and load a buggy with them. Presently this also is bumping over the paddock, driven by Mother; and quiet falls on the house, left lonely save for the women who watch for the not improbable trail of fire that may threaten its safety. There is, of course, a strip ploughed all round the garden fence. But a fire with a wind behind it makes little of ploughed strips.

Over in the scrub everyone is working. To fight a fire is simple. Armed with a beater — a green bough, or a sack tied to a stick — you dash at the approaching flames, and beat them out furiously, until you can stand the acrid smoke no longer. Then you fall back, blackened, choking, weeping, coughing, and rub your smarting eyes until sight returns to them. Then you begin again. At intervals, someone apparently an angel from Heaven, though in ordinary life possibly a Chinese cook, brings you a cool drink; and for a moment you are in Paradise. Sometimes the fire comes with a rush, and you are forced to drop your cup, and dash at it. This is the opposite of Paradise.

The day drags on. When the hot wind comes with a howl, the battle grows suddenly fierce to the danger point, and Mother — wielding a beater as steadily as a man —

casts apprehensive glances round for the children. Then it lulls, and the fighters gain on the flames. Now and then a big, blazing tree comes down, the roar, of its fall echoing across the plains. Luckily, a recent shower of rain has left the scrub damp, so that the fire burns slowly — else the battle would long ago have been over, and hundreds of blackened acres an eloquent testimony of defeat.

Towards night, the north wind brings up a violent thunderstorm, and the Boss orders all hands out of the timber. There is no time to think of shelter; indeed, no one wants it, for the rain is cause for thankfulness so devout that thunder and wild lightning are things unheeded, and the drops that put out the fire fall gratefully on scorched faces and burning eyes. A weary procession jogs homeward, to seek baths and boracic lotion.

Somewhere about bedtime, Christmas dinner occurs in a desultory fashion, since people are too tired to eat. The smallest boy falls asleep with his head on the table, and the Boss picks him up and carries him to bed.

"It was hard luck!" says the smallest boy, sleepily.

"It was" says the Boss. "But we saved the grass, Tommy — and we'll keep Christmas tomorrow!"

HOME FOR CHRISTMAS

Small boy Jim hung by his hands from the fence for what seemed a long time before letting go, to fall into the unfathomable blackness below him. He comforted himself with the swift thought that it would not be so very far — not far enough to break any bones, and so spoil all his plans. When the fall did come, it was further than he had thought, since the kindly darkness hid the ditch on the outer edge of the fence. He rolled in it helplessly, and the ground smote him in many places at once, while a big twisted stick, on one end of which he had alighted, sprang up at the contact and dealt him such a savage blow all along his leg that the cry that leapt to his lips was only three-parts smothered by the resolution that rushed to catch it. He bit at his coat sleeve, and lay trembling.

Presently he sat up and listened.

"Wonder did anyone hear me?" he pondered; "yellin' ass!"

Slung round his neck by the laces were the stout boots supplied by a paternal Government to its waifs and strays. He had not dared to put them on before creeping out of the dormitory and down the dark corridor; where, under the Matron's door, a splinter of light yet lay to flash terror into his heart. He sat on the edge of the ditch now, and laced them with hurried, fumbling fingers, listening all the while for some stir in the dark mass of the Home behind him — an outcry that should announce that a little boy had actually discarded his country's bounty of sufficient clothing, ample discipline, and three meals a day. No sound came, but his heart still pounded against the tight little coat. His foot, as he stood up, touched the stick that had dealt him the blow that still felt like a line of fire from ankle to hip. He picked it up.

"You'll do for snakes," said small boy Jim; and trotted off into the darkness.

Behind him along the road that led towards Melbourne a twin line of lamps served to make the darkness more intense. There were none on the road he must go, and he was glad of it, seeing that detection might await him at any moment. Luckily, he knew the way, for in their occasional walks they had sometimes followed it; and it had been pointed out to him as "the Gippsland road." So he knew it would take him home.

He had to set his teeth hard as he went along, for by nature he was not a very brave little boy, and the darkness had always held many terrors for him. Grim shadows sprang, at him out of the night; there were sounds that made his heart stop and then beat frantically, and the very echo of his feet seemed to him like the steps of a pursuer. Always he had that sense of being near someone — something — that makes the horror of blank darkness. He stopped short many times, certain that he was about to encounter some obstacle a fence, a house — some thing to bar his path; and went on cautiously, feeling before him with groping hands. When he did at last run into a sleeping cow he bad no inkling of her presence until he had fallen violently on top of her, and a few strenuous moments followed between the justly indignant cow, struggling to her feet, and a very badly frightened small boy. Jim fell off her at last, picked himself up, and ran as though every policeman in Victoria were at his heels.

Daylight held for Jim worse terrors than the night. He was painfully aware that his tight blue jacket was not like those of other boys, and branded him unmistakably as a ward of the State. He wished that he had left it behind him — to discard it now, unless he could find water deep enough to hide it, was as risky a proceeding as continuing to wear it. There was no water in sight in the grey half light; but there was something else that made him catch his breath and crouch suddenly between two tall hawthorn bushes. He was close to a young orchard, and between the trees he taught a glimpse of a pair of shoulders and a felt hat.

For minutes that seemed hours the little fellow crouched and shivered. Then he ventured to peep again through the leaves, and was reassured that he had not been spied, as there was no movement towards him. So he stayed, watching, until he could bear the strain no longer, and at last decided on making a dash for it. He crept through the bushes and turned to run, flinging a hasty, terrified look over his shoulder. It pulled him up again.

"Well, I am a duffer!" said small boy Jim. "It's only a scarecrow!"

A mighty relief crept over him, with the germ of a mighty idea. His grimy, little face broke into smiles. He dived through the fence, screened from view by the green boughs of trees, and approached the scarecrow that had kept him prisoner for a trembling quarter of an hour. Then with difficulty, he restrained a joyful whistle, for the scarecrow was clad in a boy's coat, and one which yet held possibilities of wear. Jim walked round and inspected it narrowly.

"Well, that's a chuck-in!" he breathed. "Here you go — s'cuse me, Mr. Scarecrow!"

He stripped the coat from the stiffly extended arms. A big black spider started from a sleeve, and slipped into a pocket, whence Jim dislodged it with some difficulty. Other inhabitants having been evicted, he donned his new possession and scanned himself proudly. It was certainly big, even over the blue jacket; his hands were buried in oceans of cuff, and it flapped on his thin little body like a windless sail. One arm was almost torn out, and the rents were as the sands of the sea. Jim saw no faults. It hid the blue jacket, and that was enough. He looked critically at the big felt hat.

"Past prayin' for," he muttered. "Well, I've got me cap."

Out on the road again, fear seized him — the fear of the criminal and he ran wildly, until orchard - and house were out of sight, hidden behind a hill. At his feet a little township lay, the road running through it. No one seemed stirring yet, but Jim dared not risk meeting inquisitive people who might have memories, so he turned aside and struck across a paddock.

A spring gurgled its way along a tiny gully, and the boy sat beside it for his breakfast — one of the few pieces of bread he had managed to smuggle during the previous days — and a draught of cold, clear water. He washed his hands and face, too, and felt better, although it had taken all his resolution not to make short work of the whole store of bread.

"They must know by now," he thought. "Wonder what sort of a row there is!" He grinned appreciatively. "Crumbs!" he said, "won't Matron be dancing!"

The laugh at the thought was checked by the memory that prompt measures would follow, possibly precede, the dance. He rose to his feet and stood hesitating, a queer little figure in his big coat, somewhat pathetic, by reason of the steady eyes in the tired white face. He had not realised until he stood up that he was very tired, and that sleep was creeping over him. Vaguely he had dreamed of running and never stopping until he got to the bush, the friendly bush he knew, that had no time tables and regulations. Now the bush seemed very far off, and his legs were heavy.

"I mus' keep on," he said, doggedly.

Noon found him still trudging, keeping to the paddocks, but never losing sight of the road; so weary, that every step was a struggle. He had eaten all his little stock of bread, and every stream or water hole was an excuse to stop a moment for a drink. Twice he had hidden behind trees from men riding over the grass after sheep. At the sight of anyone on the road he lay flat on the grass and trembled, praying that no sharp eyes were scanning the paddocks for a runaway. It was at one of these times that he had flung himself under a bush in terror at the sight of a policeman's white helmet bobbing above a hedge as he cantered along the road. When the trooper was out of sight, Jim was fast asleep.

At dusk he made for the road, and kept to it for the greater part of the night, a night as full of terrors as the first, through which he kept doggedly on, until at length weariness chained his footsteps, and he began to fall asleep as he walked. The faint moonlight showed him a haystack, and he crept under its lee until broad daylight found him, simultaneously with the farmer's dog — an ill-conditioned brute that would not listen, to reason, and managed to bite his leg before Jim found a stick and beat it off. Its snarl followed him along the road as he ran off, limping a little. He washed the leg in a creek a mile further on, and hoped vaguely that the dog was not mad.

He made fair progress during the morning, but the heat drove him to rest in the afternoon, together with a disquieting foot soreness that sleeping with his boots on did not remedy. The night was hot and airless; but he was amongst the trees now, and the comfort of them helped him through the long hours. You can picture him — a little, lonely figure, groping his way down the rough track, among the ghostly shadows of the trees — limping now, and with dark shadows under the steady grey eyes. He fell asleep before dawn, and rolled luxuriously in a bed of bracken fern, where he dreamed that his father came to him, and held him so tightly that all his troubles fell away from him and vanished utterly. The dream cheered him to press on.

He needed cheering on the third morning of his pilgrimage. He was very tired, for the sleep did not seem to have refreshed him much, and all his food was finished. He begged breakfast from a wayside cottage, and was refused; a little further on he tried again, and this time found a kind, silent man, who fed him well and filled his pockets for the journey, adding at the last a brief word of advice.

"You go home, sonny, like a good lad."

"I'm goin' " Jim said, smiling at him. "I got to be home in time for Christmas." Then, in fear of further questioning, he went off quickly, leaving his silent host to stare long after the little limping figure with doubt in his eyes.

Jim never knew much about the next few days. He had a blurred memory of a struggle that never seemed to cease, a struggle to lift his feet; and then of a terrible heaviness in his head, which was rather worse, if anything, than the other trouble; and across these memories were misty recollections of terrors by day and night, men that he hid from during the light, and horrors of darkness from which there was no hiding. At first there had been hunger, but, to his relief, that trouble left him, so that it really did not seem to matter to him whether he was given food or not. Best of all was the knowledge that he was coming towards his own country. Part of the time he fancied he was asleep and dreaming, but always limping towards his own country in his dream.

There came a hot and stifling afternoon when the sore feet would no longer do their duty, partly because the ground rocked and quivered so that there seemed no place to put them down, even for a moment. He clung to a tree and looked about him dizzily. There were glimpses of a house and cultivation through the trees, and behind him, through all the noises that buzzed and clamoured in his swimming head, a horse's sharp trot sounded clearly. That meant he must hide. The buggy swung round a bend, and he tried to run. His wavering feet carried him forward instead of backward. For a moment he stood tottering irresolute. Then he fell forward on his face and lay still, a little crumpled bundle on the dusty track.

The Widow Lang jerked her horse's head violently, and jammed the brake down with a capable foot, and the amazed animal stopped not a yard from the little figure.

"Did you ever?" said the Widow Lang. "Here, catch hold, Martha." She handed the reins to her companion and jumped over the wheel with an agility that did credit to her six-and-thirty years. "Some abominable little beast of a tramp," said the widow, "and I nearly killed him altogether!" She turned Jim over, and shuddered decorously. "My goodness me, Martha, did you ever seen such a dirty face!"

Martha laughed. "If you'd gone down flat in that dust" she suggested.

"Well, he's quite catamose," said the widow, who probably meant comatose. "What a nuisance!" She drew out a handkerchief and dusted Jim's face. "That's better," she said; "mostly surface dirt after all. He's not bad looking, when you get down to the skin. We'll have to take him home, Martha."

"What bring him into this buggy?"

"I don't see any alternative," said the widow, briskly. "You turn the wheel, Martha, and I'll lift him in." She shuddered a little as she lifted the dusty boy against her fresh print dress. "So dirty," said the widow; "and he does flop so unpleasantly! You drive, Martha, and I will support his 'ead — head, I mean. Go steady now."

Martha went steady — a proceeding which affected Jim no whit, as he knew nothing at all until he woke to find himself in a little bed, very exquisitely clean — he himself, no less clean, apparelled, to his lasting disgrace, in a lady's frilly nightdress. This was all peculiar — so peculiar, indeed, that Jim went promptly to sleep again. Meanwhile the Widow Lang was gently weeping in the kitchen.

"Did you ever see the like, Martha?" she said, between

sniffs. “Curly headed, and as pretty as a picture, and that thin his bones are nearly through his skin. And his poor feet! — raw, Martha; and a beastly bite on his leg, and a bruise right up his leg to his ’ip — hip,” said the widow, with a correction so quick that it sounded like a hiccough, and was accepted as one by Martha, who proffered her mistress some water.

“He’s fair knocked out” said the handmaiden, whisking eggs swiftly. “Food an’ rest’s all ’e wants.”

“You bring that soup when I call,” said the widow, disappearing. Her pleasant face was the first object to dawn on Jim’s eyes when he opened them for the second time — weary and ravenous.

“Bless your pretty eyes,” said the widow hastily. “Martha!”

Jim felt a very baby as they held him and fed him. His life for the next few days seemed a recurrence of sleep and food, and any effort on his part to speak was firmly checked. At length one morning, when food had been administered and sleep did not seem anxious to come, he got four words out.

“Please — what day’s this?”

“This?” said the widow. “Why, it’s Christmas Eve, Jim. Fancy that, now!”

“Christmas Eve!” Jim started up and thrust a skeleton leg and a bandaged foot from the bed clothes. “I mus’ get dressed,” he said, panting. “I mus’ go, really. Oh, please — ” for she was gently putting back the errant leg. “Oh, you don’t understand!”

“What don’t I?” said the widow, truculently. “I

understand you're not fit to get up, my lad." She tucked the blanket in firmly, and instantly melted at the sight of his quivering lips. "Tell me what it is, Jimmy," she said, and, sitting down on the bed, put her arm round the little body. "I'll be able to help."

"I was goin' home," the boy said, forcing his voice to firmness. "Home for Christmas to Dad."

"Where's Dad?" The widow's blue eyes grew hard. She had not reckoned on any Dad.

"He went to the West, nearly three years ago after Mother died. An' he left me with Aunty Lou — an' said he'd sure to be home for Christmas, an' we'd have such a time with all the money he'd get. He couldn't come the first Christmas, 'cause he hadn't found the money; an' the next he was ill, at least he was ill when he wrote in October, and then we never got any more letters. An' this is the next Christmas. Aunty Lou died this year, an' they sent me to the Home. But I knew Dad 'ud come home, an' be lookin' out for me. I just had to come."

"You ran away?"

" 'Twas quite easy," he said. "Last Tuesday."

"That's more'n a week, Jim," said the widow. "Where were you expectin' to find your Dad?"

"At Glendale," he said. "We always lived there."

"And Dad's name was?"

"John Fraser," he said, wearily. "Mine's Jim Fraser, y' know. Do you think I can go?"

"You couldn't walk, sonny," said the widow. "Look here, I'll tell you what I'll do. You got pretty close to

Glendale, I don't know 'ow you did it on them little feet," she added, forgetting the graces of language in the stress of the moment. "I'll send to Glendale, an' find out if Dad's there an' he can come here, if he is. If not, will you have Christmas with me?"

"I'll try," he said, politely. A sob caught in his throat, and he checked it apologetically. "I never reckoned on not findin' Dad," he said. There were stains of tears on his cheeks as he fell asleep again.

"I'll drive into Glendale this afternoon myself, Martha," said the widow, later. She had been weeping explosively. "But you needn't suppose I mean to give the poor lamb up, not to any John Fraser! Not that he's back, I'd have heard of it if he had been, surely. Anyway, men never do come back from the West!"

"D'you mean to keep Jim?" asked Martha, stolidly boning a fowl.

"Certainly," said the widow. I always did want a little boy. He'll be a perfect boom to me about the place! Dear lamb, with his curly hair! Oh, we'll make him such a Christmas, Martha! — better'n any John Fraser 'ud do. I knew him fifteen years ago, Martha before I got married and left Glendale, a big, handsome young limb he was!" There was a reminiscent flush on the widow's plump cheek. "Funny I never heard of him after I came back. I wouldn' 'a liked to think John Fraser's boy was in a horrid Home!"

"Might have been lucky to get there."

"You hold your tongue, Martha Dove. How'd you like to see your boy in a nasty tight blue jacket in a Home?" said the widow, tartly — "if you wasn't a spinster, I mean," as her gaunt hand maiden blushed and bridled. "Anyway, I'm not going to try hard to find John Fraser. And if he comes here, Martha," added the widow, collecting her dignity, "you are to seclude 'im from the 'ouse."

"Would y' call that fair dinkum?" queried Martha. "Jim's his, anyhow."

"I am obliged to you for your opinion, and will contain my own, Martha," said the widow stiffly. "An' anyhow, he won't come. I don't think they grow out of books — these fellers who clear out for years an' then come back like angels in sheep's clothing! I'll tell 'Enery to get the buggy, an' get away while Jim's asleep."

There was no word of John Fraser in Glendale township — so the widow's guarded inquiries resulted; and with a light heart she went about her peculiarly extensive shopping. The stores were gay with gum boughs and tree ferns, and resplendent with Christmas goods; and many and varied were the bundles that filled the hooded buggy to overflowing. The Widow Lang drove home with a light heart, which sank somewhat at the sight of Jim's eager little face.

"Did you find Dad?"

"No, Jimmy, I didn't," said she guiltily "There's no word of him anywhere. I guess he's — he's still in the West, Jim. You'll have to be my little boy for Christmas. See what I brought you." She unwrapped a wonderful pocket knife — a very cornucopia of blades and tools and corkscrews. "That be handy, eh, sonny?"

"Yes, thank you," said Jim soberly. He lay down and drew the blanket over his face. The Widow Lang suddenly found, her tongue bereft of words. The new knife lay outside the blanket, unheeded.

Jim had found his manners and his backbone by the morning. He sat up in bed and received decorously the good wishes and caresses of his hostess, and smiled back at Martha's curt "Merry Christmas." There was a festive smell of much cooking, and dark hints of something wonderful to come after dinner, and the Widow Lang was filling the house with flowers.

He was allowed to get up at noon, and was dressed in a new grey suit, with a red necktie, "to put a bit of colour into his white face" and carried, for his feet were still almost useless, to a big arm chair in the dining room, where presently the most gorgeous Christmas turkey appeared, together with the most opulent of hams, followed by a pudding that blazed most divinely, until Jim could not fathom how anything could possibly be left of it to eat. Afterwards, with a huge orange, which he felt himself totally unable to surround, he was left alone for a while, and there was much whispering between the Widow Lang (who was terribly magnificent in purple silk) and Martha, and 'Enery, and much mysterious running about.

Then Martha came in, all beaming (which was quite unusual for Martha), and picked him up and carried him down the passage to a closed door, with strict directions to shut his eyes — "tight now, none o' y' peepin' " said Martha, sternly. He squeezed his eyes up tightly, and felt himself carried through a doorway, and very gently laid down on a sofa.

"Now you can look," said the Widow Lang.

Jim opened his eyes.

In the middle of the room a beautiful Christmas tree

grew and flourished in a big green tub, looking as though it had been there all its life, and spent the time in producing the fruit that hung on its laden branches. Such a tree! They had darkened the room, so that all the gay little candles it bore twinkled and shone most naturally, and were reflected a hundred times over in the bright coloured balls that bobbed and glittered on the twigs. No one could have imagined a more beautiful tree. All sorts of strange things hung upon it — things most interesting to gentlemen of nine. A big revolver was quite close to him, and so was a dainty bridle — Queensland pattern — which was just what Jim liked; and on one limb there was a cricket bat, and on another a football, the Widow Lang, being a woman and a widow, and naturally ignorant of times and seasons, or perhaps thinking Christmas above all seasons. There were books, and neckties, and gay boxes of sweets, and all sorts of mysterious parcels, done up in bright paper — none of your common brown. Jim looked and gasped; and he looked at the three kind faces. A memory of other Christmases came over him, and a sob rose in his throat.

Martha, who had slipped out in response to a knock, came back.

"You're wanted," she said.

"Bother!" said the Widow Lang. "Wait a minute, Jimmy, dear." She went out into the passage.

A tall brown man stood at the front door. The Widow Lang looked at him and knew him, and rebellion filled her heart.

"They told me," said the stranger, hesitating, "that you've a little chap here?"

"Well?"

He looked surprised. "My name's Fraser," the man said, "I'm looking for my little boy."

"This boy's mine," said the Widow Lang.

"Oh!" His face grew blank. "I — I beg your pardon. I didn't know."

She hardened her heart.

"Yes — oh, yes, he's mine," she said hurriedly. "You made a mistake."

"I did indeed," he said slowly. "I hoped I'd come to the end of my search. Fact is I'm in great anxiety —" He broke off. "Why, it's Fanny Murchison!" he said, quickly.

"I was," she said. "Now Lang — and a widow."

"I'm John Fraser," he said. "Been over West. You remember me, Fanny?"

She nodded, without moving.

"I'm in bitter trouble about my boy, Fanny," he said. "I didn't know. I've been moving about, and all my letters have gone astray, he was in some Home, and he's run away, such a little chap. I've ridden from Melbourne looking for him. God knows what's happened to him — and he's such a man!"

She looked at his haggard eyes.

"You're fond of him?"

"Fond of him!" He looked at her, bewildered. "Why, he's all I've got!"

She paused — a long bitter silence.

"He's here," she said. "Yes, I told you a lie. I didn't

know you cared, and I cared so much, and I haven't anything. Go on." She pointed to the lighted room, and sitting down, rocked herself to and fro with the heaviness the childless woman knows. But John Fraser went down the hall with long strides.

He saw a bright room, and a glittering Christmas tree, and two smiling people. Beyond them, his eyes fastened on a sofa where a little white faced boy lay smiling politely, with a world of weary boredom in his grey eyes. Something held him motionless, with a beating heart.

"Daddy, Daddy, Daddy!"

Jim's voice rang out. He was off the sofa, hobbling, limping, staggering with out-stretched arms towards the silent figure in the doorway. He did not feel the agony in his feet — only his legs would give under him, and the way seemed so long. The room flickered into blackness as his father caught him.

Then he was back on the sofa, with a strong arm round him, and Daddy's cheek was wet. No one else was there, only Daddy and he; and it was Christmas.

"Did you think I'd forgotten — my little chap?"

Jim smiled at him with shining eyes.

"Oh, I knew," he said; "I knew you'd come!"

* * *

The Widow Lang dried her eyes.

"You'll never forgive me, I suppose," she said, sniffing. "You'll never know the temptation — he was such a dear little lad, an' I didn't know if you were any good. I know children are my upsetting sin. But I did love him."

“She was so good to me, Daddy.”

John Fraser smiled.

“There’s nothing to forgive, as far as I’m concerned.” he said. “You saved my boy’s life, an’ that’s enough for me, the bad two minutes you gave me don’t count, when I think of all that. It’s all right, Fanny.”

“An’ now you’re goin’ to take him right away I suppose?” she said.

“Why I don’t think so.” He laughed happily. “Glendale’s good enough for me — an’ I struck it rich over there, y’know. You’ll have to find me a farm, not far off. So you can give me hints about bringing up an unruly son. We were always good friends, you know, Fanny, weren’t we?”

She blushed faintly.

“You’re very good to me, John,” she faltered. “I didn’t treat you well.”

“That’s all right,” he said again. “I’m too happy to care for anything like that. No point in bein’ unhappy when a fellow’s just come home for Christmas!”

OUR CHRISTMAS EVE

"And to think," said I half ruefully, "that we had planned our first Christmas completely to ourselves!"

Mildred laughed, slipping a hand into my arm. "Man proposes — and floods dispose," she answered. "And weren't we lucky that all the boys were able to come!"

I nodded agreement. We were standing in the front doorway of our home, looking out upon what was ordinarily a wide flat below the hill on which the house stood. This Christmas Eve it was a stretch of brown water tranquil in the still twilight. It mirrored faithfully the trees that stood here and there in it, and the long lines of the top rails of the fences. Clear to the river, two miles away, it stretched; such a December flood as none of us remembered. Certainly, no one wished to see it repeated.

We had had a late, cold spring, and summer had been shy of coming; even in December mountain tops still showed a mantling of winter snow. It was a hard season for stock; everyone lost lambs, and the cattle were rough and poor. Then, ten days before Christmas, came torrents of rain that brought down the snows and overflowed rivers that were already brimming. Half the graziers of Gippsland were out, trying to save their stock, for there was little warning, and the flood was as severe as it was sudden.

We, on Warrimoo Downs, would have had a hard time had it not been for our neighbours. Bobby Vereker and Featherstone, who shared Brolga Plains, had George Lathrop staying with them, and they were the first to come to my aid as I struggled to move my sheep to the higher paddocks. Dick Anderson and Carruthers were there almost as soon; and between them all, I had not lost a hoof. We had worked in the water and out of it swimming whenever it was necessary; for two nights not one of us had been in bed. Mildred and Gladys-Amelia, our kitchen deity, had produced meals and hot coffee at all hours of the day and night, as if by conjuring. It had been fairly hectic while it lasted, but I believe that we had had a certain amount of fun out of it; we were all rather young, and then, if the fight had been tough, we had won. The stock were safe, and the flood was going to do the land good in the long run.

For the last two days we had turned from battling with water to slaying snakes. As soon as the river came down the rain ceased, and the sun appeared determined to make up for lost time; we had two days of steamy heat, and the water went back rapidly from the hill on which the house stood, leaving a dense mat of dead reeds and assorted debris to mark the limit of its forward sweep. The rubbish swarmed with snakes, carried by the flood from every hiding place on the flats. Mostly they were small ones, but there was a sprinkling of big fellows; and, since we had no desire that they should find sanctuary in the garden and under the house, there was nothing for it but to fork over the flood-wrack, scattering it thinly and killing the refugees as we went. The boys were Trojans about it; it was evil work, and there was plenty for them to do on their own holdings; but they knew Mildred's peculiar horror of snakes, and one and all declined to go home while a yard of rubbish remained unexplored. We had finished the job at sundown on Christmas Eve, and Mildred had exacted a promise that they should all stay for Christmas dinner at Warrimoo, apologising ruefully for the probable scantiness of the feast, since nobody had had a chance to get to the township for over a week. The boys had accepted joyfully, with no apparent fears. They had great confidence in Mildred and Gladys-Amelia.

They trooped up from the bathroom presently, clean, and cool, and cheerful, if slightly peculiar in appearance, seeing that they were all arrayed in shirts and trousers of my providing; and none of them happened to be my height and build. Lathrop was the only one capable of being worried by misfit garments. He was a person of some dignity, and more than common tall; not at his best in the trousers of a man six inches shorter than himself. There was a gap of bare leg above the top of his socks that gave great joy to the others, who kindly offered to paint it for him after the fashion in which the Zulu rickshaw boys of Durban ornament their sturdy brown calves. Lathrop bore their witticisms with a wintry smile, and was evidently more at his ease when the bell rang and he was able to hide his unclad shanks beneath the table.

We were all pretty tired, but it was a jolly meal, and we made it a long one. The work was over, and it was a relief to be lazy. When we finally pushed hack our chairs Dick swooped on Mildred as she picked up a plate.

"You're dead beat." he said, authoritatively. "Take her away, Jack. Bobby and I are going to clear away the wreck and help Gladys-Amelia wash up. Don't argue, Mrs. Jack; it isn't polite, and Santa Claus won't come to you if you aren't a good girl. We're going to show Gladys-Amelia a thing or two about washing dishes that she's never dreamed of!"

Mildred did not argue much. She was, indeed, dead

beat; reaction had set in after the tense anxiety of the flood, and a hard day of Christmas cooking had left her white-faced, with eyes that looked unnaturally big and dark. There was special need to take care of her just then, a fact of which I had been vividly conscious during the last week, when it had been impossible to spare her at all. I suppose I looked worried, but she glanced up at me with a little laugh as I obeyed young Dick and drew her out on the verandah.

"I'm quite all right," she said; "only a bit fagged. Don't look so miserable, Jack. I'll be quite blooming after a night's sleep."

"Well, you know, what the doctor said," I began, unhappily.

"Oh, doctors always preach," she said lightly. "Think of our grandmothers, poor dears! No one ever worried much about them, and often there wasn't a doctor within 20 miles — or 50. Grannie told me that once a stockman's wife and a black gin were 'her sole dependence' — the stockman's wife was a lady who drank too much, and could only speak Gaelic! We're a pampered set, we modern women; and our husbands fuss!"

"How do you know how your grandfather felt about the matter?" I demanded. "Anyhow, I haven't noticed any special pampering about you this last week, young woman!"

"All the better for me," she said, sturdily. "I'm quite well, dear — only a little tired. If it will ease your troubled mind, I'll slip off to my room now, and go to bed with a book. I'm sure the boys won't think me rude. And I know they will talk snakes, and I do hate them, even to think of a snake gives me creeps."

"Of course they won't think you rude," I said. "We're all going to turn in early."

She blew a kiss to me and slipped off round the corner of the verandah just as the others came out. Except Dick and Bobby, whose dish washing with Gladys-Amelia was in full swing, punctuated with much splashing and with delighted chuckles from the hand maiden. Presently they joined us, full of the consciousness of duty nobly done; and we took deck chairs out upon the buffalo grass and smoked peacefully. The moon was up, and everything was very still. Below us, in the flood water, hundreds of frogs sang their evening song — possibly a chant of joy at the number of their snaky foes we had killed during the day.

Of course we talked snake, just as men who have spent a day on the links can only talk golf; our senses had been keyed to snakes for two days, and we jumped whenever a leaf rustled. Snake stories, old and new, went round the circle. Bobby Vereker told us of the "tiger" that had stretched itself out along the top of a roller blind in the kitchen of his father's station the Chinese cook pulled down the blind just as Bobby's sister Marian came in, and the snake, much astonished, came with it, and landed in the bosom of the cook. That excitable Oriental fled, wailing, into the landscape. Half a mile from home he discovered that the serpent was no longer with him — having, indeed, been left in the kitchen, where Marian Vereker had finished it with a big wooden jam spoon — not a bad thing to kill a snake with, she said, as long as you didn't hit it with the shoulder of the bowl, in which case you would probably miss it. It wasn't over clear, but then, Bobby rarely was. The Chinese artist was discovered with little on but his pigtail, searching wildly for a non-existent bite, and was brought home by a couple of delighted stockmen. They made him —"

"Reminds me of a snake I met up in Queensland." cut in Lathrop. It didn't remind him at all, of course, but it always hurt Lathrop's feelings if anyone but himself held the floor too long. He told us the story of the Queensland snake; everyone knew it was the identical reptile that George Meredith had met in Bourke, but it wasn't worth anyone's while to mention it. We heard him out, or nearly out, in patience, and it was only when he trimmed up the good old story with various little frills of quite extraneous detail, mainly relating to his own heroism, that we began to wriggle under the infliction Lathrop being a chap who would shrink from a bad-tempered Minorca hen. He was a most heroic talker, but boresome.

"'Member the snake you killed in the bachelors' quarters at Myall Lake?" Featherstone asked him. Lathrop said rather stiffly that he didn't, and asked for a match. So we said, as one man, "What was that?" and Featherstone chuckled.

"George and I were staying up there, and one night we went to bed after the other fellows had turned in. It was a hot night, and we pulled the blankets off our beds. George had just turned his down when he uttered a yell like a lost soul, and jumped three feet into the air — there, under the top sheet, was a bulge of dark coils. There was no time to be lost, as at any minute the intruder might think it was time to get up — he grabbed a top boot and fairly pasted it with blows until the sheet slipped off, and then he took a flying leap over the next bed, to be out of harm's way — he was in pyjamas, and barefooted, when one naturally doesn't care to meet a snake. At this point howls of joy came from all the other beds. The innocent young cherubs had carefully coiled an eight foot stockwhip lash under the sheet, and had succeeded beyond their fondest expectations. But you were a hero, all right, George!" Lathrop was understood to mutter something about "idiotic exaggeration."

But Carruthers was already swinging into his pet yarn, which concerned a snake that had got into a little tub of an island steamer, and had insisted on sharing his bunk; assistance from the captain and the mate being hindered by the fact that, being extremely drunk, they looked upon Carruthers's snake as one of a tribe they had just hatched, blest beyond the ordinary run of serpents by having pale blue fins and gold pince-nez; and so they declined to touch it, and were rather annoyed when Carruthers finished it with a revolver.

Dick Anderson followed with a story of a girl of the side-saddle era, who, riding alone in the bush, had put her hand into the saddle pocket in quest of her handkerchief, and had found it tenanted by a lively young tiger snake. She was not bitten, luckily, and managed to fasten the flap of the pouch, much to the annoyance of the snake, which made frantic efforts to get out; after which the girl felt unequal to dealing with the matter any further, and had galloped home at racing speed, finishing by fainting gracefully on her own doorstep. He told it with much circumstantial detail, after which Vereker remarked cruelly that each of his aunts' had had that adventure, and that most of them came home with the snake as a whip-lash. I added my modest contribution — my serpent had been of the carpet snake persuasion. And had done nothing more spectacular than get under the bath and scare into fits the feminine portion of the household. Featherstone, who had been on the stage, and several other things besides, told a jolly little story about a snake in Queensland which persisted in lying on a dead man's coffin, and no one liked either to kill it or to proceed without killing it. That rather finished our keenness for ophidian lore, and as most of the pipes were out, the mosquitoes thereby encouraged to return in full force, somebody suggested bed, and everybody agreed. I sat still for a few minutes to finish my smoke, before going in to the light that beckoned me.

Mildred had gone to sleep as she read. She lay half-turned towards the French window opening upon the verandah by which I entered, and the lamplight fell upon part of her face, and left it partly in shadow. There was a chair near the bed, and I sat down to look at her. I was feeling lazy; and then I had never grown wholly used to the wonder of having her for my own. We had waited so long a time for our happiness of the last year that it often seemed unreal — one had a kind of uneasy feeling that it was not safe to plume oneself too much upon it. Sometimes, when I saw Mildred asleep — like this — I had a quite illogical conviction that it was unsafe to look away, lest, when my eyes came back, they should find her place empty.

So I sat and looked at her.

Presently she stirred a little, as though the lamplight troubled her. It was one of those reading affairs, with a hooded shade, and I leaned across and twisted it to shield the glare from her eyes. As I did so she moved again, and the sheet slipped back gently. Her left arm was outflung on the bed beside her, and as the linen slipped from it something brown came into view; and I sat back, staring idiotically.

The minutes went by, and I sat motionless, my eyes fixed on the head of the snake that lay across my wife's arm. I could see only a few inches of its head; the sheet hid the rest; but those inches were on the blue veining of the wrist, and the wicked head pointed upwards towards the crook of her elbow . . . I had a ridiculous habit, Mildred used to call it, of kissing the crook of her elbow; it was so like a baby's — soft and pink. The brown, obscene head was very close to it, where the silk of her nightdress was pushed back for coolness. The alert, cold eyes met mine, and held them prisoner.

What was I to do? My faculties were never more keenly alive than as I sat there, afraid to move a muscle. One stir on my part might mean the end; the snake was watching me intently, and I knew that if I rose it would move at once — where? It might fancy that the soft folds of silk above its head meant refuge, and glide further up; then Mildred would wake — and if she stirred — ! The sweat broke out on my face. It was scarcely within the bounds of possibility that it would be roused to escape without showing fight, without striking. The cold enmity in the unwinking eyes that stared at me told me clearly enough that I need not hope for it to be torpid or afraid. I had been like all other bush youngsters: had killed snakes from my knickerbocker days, as a matter of habit, without thinking. I had gone in for the bushman's fool tricks of pulling them out by the tail from holes or under logs, breaking their backs with a flick in the air. Now I sat helpless as an old woman, looking at the flat head on my wife's arm.

I had an idea once, as the minutes crawled on, of making a sudden dash at it — trusting to luck to grip it by the neck before it could bite her. I hugged the idea for a few moments, planning just where I meant to plant my grip, my fingers already stiffening to make the clutch. Then my eyes met the wary one's and I knew that it was useless; I would not be on my feet before it would have flashed to attack the nearest enemy — that white, unconscious arm. No; there was just one hope, that it would grow tired and glide away of its own accord before she woke. If she stirred first — then I could make my leap and trust to being quicker than the snake. I watched them fixedly, desperately, every nerve strung to its utmost in the endeavour to anticipate a movement from either. The sweat beads gathered on my face and trickled down, and I dared not raise a finger to wipe them away.

Then, in spite of the hot night, an irrepressible shudder took my body and shook me violently. The cane chair in which I sat creaked in response; and at the sound and the movement the snake's head came up angrily, swaying to and fro over Mildred's arm. Its eyes were unmistakably wrathful, though their bitter coldness never changed. I gripped the arms of the chair, leaning forward; and the eyes and the swaying head fastened on my brain. My head hummed dully; it came to me that I was losing my balance, and a sudden horrible fear caught at my heart — that when the moment came for action I would be physically unable to spring to my girl's rescue. I was slipping, slipping and the eyes bored into my very senses. With a hoarse shout, borne of desperate fear, I sprang across at the swaying head.

"Blessed old ass you are, to go to sleep out here Jack!" It was Bobby Vereker's cheerful voice; and Bobby, in his pyjamas, was shaking me firmly, if kindly. "Told you

you'd be asleep if you waited to finish your pipe; and it's only to be expected you'd dream of the devil and wake in a fright. Wonder you didn't scare the wits out of Mrs. Jack, the way you yelled, her window's wide open."

"The snake —" I muttered.

"It's mighty evident," said Bobby "that you had too much snake this evening. Go in and see if your dying howl woke your wife."

He pushed me gently towards the French window, and I went in, staggering a little, my brain still groping blindly. The light was low, and Mildred lay with her arms crossed behind her head, her breath coming and going quietly. As my step sounded, her eyes opened and dwelt on mine with their look of welcome.

CHRISTMAS AT HENDERSON'S

"I only wish to goodness I could manage it, Polly, old girl," said Jim Henderson, gloomily. "But there isn't a hope."

"N — no," said Polly, his wife, a little unsteadily. "I can see that, of course, Jim. Don't you worry, old man."

"All very well to say that — and, of course, it's no good worrying," her husband answered, rinsing the big meat dish in a snowy froth of soap suds, and putting it carefully on a tray. "Worrying won't alter things; certainly, it won't milk cows and keep a look out for bush fires. But it goes a bit against the grain to make you spend Christmas this way, when we'd planned things so differently."

"Can't be helped," said his wife, with a fine affectation of nonchalance. She dived into the recesses of the dresser to put away a bowl, and took advantage of the opportunity to dry her eyes furtively upon her dish towel. With appearance thus renewed, she faced him again jauntily; a stage effect which deceived Jim Henderson not at all. He sucked hard at his pipe, and a fragment of tobacco ash fell into the dish pan unheeded by both.

"Well, it's too bad, anyhow," he said. "You've always had such jolly Christmas times — such a lot of you to be together and make things go. I never doubted that we'd go over and Christmas with them all — just as if you weren't married at all!" Came a note of indignant protest from his wife, and the big man grinned a little. "Well — partly as if . . . !" he said.

There was an interlude, complicated by the fact that

the hands of the dish washer were wet, and his pipe in his mouth. Order being restored, Jim attacked a saucepan with sand soap.

"You're a real little brick about it, sweet-heart," he said. "I know jolly well that you're disappointed. I guess I know how bad the disappointment is. If only that blessed married couple had waited until after Christmas to give notice!"

"Why, that's the last thing they'd dream of doing," said his wife. "I suppose they thought they were entitled to Christmas as much as we were."

"They shouldn't come down into the bush if they intend to leave people in the lurch — they assured me they would stay six months, and certainly they could hardly have found an easier place," Jim said, gloomily. "Crawlers, every one of them! Loyalty to a decent employer is about the last thing any of them think about. And you were so jolly good to the woman when she was sick — though I believe she was shamming. Just another case of lazy debility. And then they clear out after a bare three months' work — just enough to make me liable for their train fare! Well, I told Wilson what I thought of him this morning, when he was leaving!"

"Bless you, dear, that wouldn't do you any good!" his wife answered.

"That's all you know—it relieved my mind considerably," Jim returned. "But I agree with you, it doesn't help matters on the place." He hesitated. "I say, old girl—will you go down on the coach and have your Christmas at home? I can't leave, of course, but I'd be really happier about you."

"Then you ought to be thoroughly ashamed of yourself!" said his wife, explosively. "I didn't marry you to go off and leave you alone." This time she mopped her eyes with the towel openly and unabashed, and faced him stormily. "How much of a Christmas do you think it would be for me, if I did? It's just a horrible thing for you to suggest, Jim!"

There was a further interlude.

"Well, it can't be helped, then," said the master of the house, presently, as his wife removed her head from his shoulder. "If you won't, you won't, I suppose. But it will be such a shabby Christmas for you, old girl. I can't even go into Burrabong to buy you anything — can't leave the place and the blessed cows. And there isn't time to order anything from Melbourne. I'd reckoned on doing my little bit of shopping on Christmas Eve in the town, with your people. Of course, that part can be postponed — but the day itself will be a real Darby and Joan affair."

"I don't care," said Polly, not very steadily. "We'll be together, and that's the main thing."

"Why, of course, it's the big thing. But we're together any old day," said her husband, practically, "and you've always counted on getting back to your mother's for Christmas. Won't they hate me!"

"That's the part that hurts," Polly answered. "Not that they'll be anything but sorry for you, you silly old thing; but they'll be so disappointed. They've all been counting on it, and planning all sorts of plans. Mother said in her letter that the boys meant to make it so fascinating for me that I wouldn't want to go away with you again! And the little kiddies Beryl and Tommy — they were going to get me to sleep in their room, so that we could all hang up our stockings together, as usual." A large tear trickled unexpectedly down her nose. "Oh, Jim, I'm ashamed to be such a baby!" she faltered. She put her head against the kitchen window and cried softly, to the great dismay of her six months' bridegroom, who became ready to sacrifice his cows and leave his farm to the mercy of bush fires if by doing so he could ease matters.

Emotions were not much in Polly Henderson's line, and she was speedily greatly ashamed of herself. She dried her eyes severely on her husband's handkerchief, and set about obtaining the best artistic effect possible with an array of well-scoured saucepans.

"They do look nice, don't they?" she said, with her head on one side, much like an interested bird. "Mrs. Wilson never did keep them in nice order. I simply wouldn't trust her with my best aluminium beauties! I'm sure she hadn't a saucepan corner in her soul, and I'm always, sorry for the woman who hasn't — there's quite a big bit of mine that's all saucepans and baskets, and it's such a nice part! Jim, if you don't mind, we won't talk about going to Cairnbrook any more, because it's stupid, and we're going to have a lovely Christmas here together, just you and I."

"Bless you!" said Jim, regarding her fatuously.

"Certainly," responded his wife. "But we must be busy to-night because I must pack up all my presents for home. If we catch the coach in the morning with them they'll get home in time, don't you think?"

If a few sighs went into the box of loving gifts packed for her old home, little Mrs. Henderson managed to conceal them gallantly from her husband. It was a little hard, this sending away of the presents she had planned to take with her to the big Christmas rejoicing at 'Cairnbrook.' Nearly all were made by her own hands, for money was not a plentiful commodity on the farm Jim Henderson had carved out of the bush. It was a good farm, and had no mortgage — the 'blister' that poisons a farmer's dreams had been attacked and conquered before Jim had gone to claim his bride. But improvements have an unpleasant way of eating up profits; and there were many things Jim desired desperately to do for his land — clearing, fencing, draining, new cow sheds, and other luxuries. They made quick work of a man's loose cash.

Polly Henderson quite understood the necessity for living economically. She had been brought up in easy fashion on her father's station, a big cattle run where girls and boys alike spent most of their spare time on horseback in the cheerfully inconsequent life of country Young Australia. But her mother, while attaching minor unimportance to dead languages and examinations, had seen to it that her girls were well grounded in the science of house-wifery. Polly was not accustomed to spending money, since hating town and preferring the station continually, she found little to spend on. The allure of shops is not felt in the bush to any extent. She supplied her wants, sartorial or literary, from a cursory inspection of catalogues; lived her simple life, busy with animals, needlework and the domestic arts which are fast falling, alas into the background; and found no great change in her mode of existence when Jim Henderson carried her off to his brand new home. Outsiders considered that she had, perhaps, stepped down a little. Polly, radiant in her new happiness, knew better.

Christmas had meant a great deal to the girl, a little lonely, sometimes, for the crowded home she had always known. Jim was all that was dear and good — a perfect mate, either inside the house or out. But there were days when the nature of his work prevented Polly from accompanying him into the paddocks, and on those days, alone in the house, save for the sour-faced Mrs. Wilson; she had fallen into the habit of looking forward to the day when they should go back to keep Christmas with the dear, noisy, happy throng at home. She had prepared her gifts lovingly—dainty bits of needlecraft and carving and leather work. They fitted cunningly into the great raffia basket she had made for her mother, which, in its turn, packed away into a hat box. It was all very workmanlike and ship-shape — two super-excellent qualities in Polly's eyes. She had pictured putting them all on the plates round the big break-fast table; the little labels for each were ready a week before the day to start on the forty mile drive to 'Cairnbrook'. It was very flat, now, to be getting them ready to send away in a dull coach.

Nevertheless, there was Jim to be considered, Jim, who was so sorry for her, so eager to do anything that could help. The extra work in which the defection of the servants had involved him did not seem to trouble him at all. He hated to see her in the hot kitchen, and was always at hand to aid when the exigencies of the farm and the milking of fifteen cows would permit. It was only the remembrance of the spoilt holiday, and the disappointment for the dear home people, that cast a shadow over the long days. With a lengthy husband always eager to shoulder the burden of work — especially with an expert well versed in the intricacies of 'batching' — it is possible to rejoice in the absence of a Mrs. Wilson.

Yet it was with a little sigh that Polly Henderson greeted Christmas Day. It was six o'clock when she awoke, and already there was promise of heat in the still air of the morning. Jim had gone out noiselessly more than an hour earlier, and, she knew, was already in the cow shed. It was so different an awaking from the one she had pictured — Tommy and Beryl, wild with excitement over their stockings, and gradually the whole household straggling into her room, in various stages of deshabille, to join in the fun. She had not even had time to get letters from them — and they seemed so very far away. Then she remembered Jim, milking doggedly in the cow shed, and hurried to put a match to the kitchen fire before going to her bath.

Breakfast was ready, and a smiling wife waiting on the doorstep, when Jim came over after finishing his work.

"Not a hand's turn of work do I tackle this day — barring cows," he said, when greetings were over. "I'm housemaid — or cook — or whatever you like. But I vote we make a picnic of it and enjoy ourselves."

"Oh-h!" Polly wrinkled her brows thoughtfully. "There's the chicken, Jim — if I cooked it at once it would be cold by lunch time. We could take our lunch down to the creek, and fish, and picnic — I think it would be lovely!"

"First class idea," said Jim, with approval. "The house will be pretty hot before long, and the creek is always a good place on days like this. Just you hurry up, old woman, and we'll get away as soon as we can."

"It will be a beautiful Christmas," said Polly. "You do make nice plans, Jim— I've a good mind to kiss you, only I've no time! I'll pop the chicken into the oven while you wash your hands." She was singing as she ran gaily into the kitchen, and Jim's clear whistle took up the tune, above the splashing of the tap in the bath room. She was filling his porridge plate when he tramped back, still whistling. Then the cheery sound turned suddenly to an exclamation of dismay.

"Jim—what is it?"

"The blessed paddock's alight," said Jim, succinctly. "Never mind my breakfast, old woman — I'll have to run for it." Then the gravel of the yard path scattered under his racing feet.

Polly ran to the window. Across the long, dry grass of the home-paddock came a curling wall of smoke, shot with flame when the fire seized upon a patch of dead bracken in its way. There was nothing between it and the house — the yellow grass came right up to the fence of the garden. To burn a fire-break had been one of the jobs deferred through the unexpected departure of the recalcitrant Wilson. It was a postponement that threatened to be disastrous. Polly turned with a little gasp, and was out at the gate before she realised that she still grasped firmly the porridge-pot. She put it down, and had the satisfaction of seeing the sheepdog advance upon it with amazed delight.

"Well, at least Bluey's having Christmas!" she uttered. Grasping an old sack, she fled after her husband.

Jim was fighting the fire desperately, and endeavouring to solve the problem of being in a dozen places at once. It was a problem that would have solved itself speedily, and to his entire discomfiture, but for friendly patches of green fern that checked the progress of the flames and gave him a chance to beat them out. Realising the presence of his wife, he gave a great shout of anxiety.

"Go back, Polly!"

"Get out!" said his wife, inelegantly, and more than a little breathlessly — the run across the paddock on the dry and slippery grass had been a hard one. She swung her sack, and brought it down on an aspiring patch of flame that came licking towards her over the bracken. "I'm quite all right, dear, and I'll take care." It was regrettable that a smile of the quality of the one she flung at him should have been lost in the drifting pall of smoke.

There was no time for argument. Here and there intrusive tongues of fire crept through the grass, snake-fashion, and to put them out meant hard beating and hard running. Generally, any place once extinguished was safe; but sometimes the fire, apparently dead, woke to unexpected life and blazed merrily across the paddock, with the nearest beater racing to head it off. Luckily, there was no timber to catch, the ground was quite cleared, and only grass and cut bracken, dead and brown, were there to carry the flames. But the smoke was cruel, and to work long in it impossible. Where the blaze was dangerous they could only rush in and beat for a moment, and then stagger out, blinded by the acrid fumes, to rub their smarting eyes for a moment, and then dash in again. There was no wind; but the shimmering heat that lay over the paddocks turned the grass to tinder, and made all effort doubly strenuous. Sparks flew from the fern stalks — more than once Polly found her dress on fire, and was justly annoyed at the loss of valuable time extinguishing it. Twice a snake slipped past her, heading for safety, its usual caution lost in fear. The bag grew heavy to lift, and yet more heavy. She swung it blindly, with numbed arms.

It was a little drain across the paddock that stayed the fire long enough to save them—the grass in its bottom was green, and the flames died down in many places as they came to the edge. A final summoning of strength — a swift rush up and down the drain, thrashing at the momentarily delayed creeping fire — and the danger was over. A long stretch of blackened ground showed where the yellow grass had waved an hour earlier. At its edges, smoke died slowly away.

Polly Henderson sat down on the ground and rubbed her brow with, an exceedingly black hand, producing a fine impressionist result of smears and cinders. Jim, coming to her, cast away the charred remnant of his beater, and sat down also. They looked at each other, and laughed.

"You hadn't any business to come, but I'm jolly well certain I'd never have got it out without you!" Jim uttered. His eyes travelled over her. "Your pretty frock! — ah, you poor old girl!"

"It was my new Christmas frock," said Polly, ruefully, regarding a great burn and many lesser burns down the breadths that had been fresh blue linen. "I did want to impress you — and now I wish I hadn't been vain!"

"I'll get you another, my girl," said her husband. It was a lame expression of many things that he felt at the moment; but his eyes told her more, and had she been a more exacting person than she was, Polly Henderson would have been satisfied. She smiled at him happily — and Jim saw nothing that was not beautiful in her cheerful, if exceedingly dirty, face.

"Well, I'm giving you a lovely Christmas!" he said. "At least, you'll admit it has the merit of novelty — you never had one like it!" He rose, stretching his long form wearily, and held out his hands. "Come on home, old woman — it's high time you had some breakfast."

They went slowly home through the long grass, their feet dragging a little; one does not run wildly and swing a heavy bag for an hour in an Australian December without paying for the diversion. By the gate, Bluey slept the sleep of the replete, the empty porridge pot beside him. He rose, and greeted his owners with hypocritical welcome, tinged with a natural nervousness, and subsided to sleep again with relief, on discovering that they were too tired to note his iniquities.

In the kitchen a sudden smell of burning floated towards them. Polly took her arm from her husband's with a little cry of dismay, and ran to the stove. She flung open the oven door. Within was blue smoke and destruction.

"Oh, Jim!" she cried — "Jim! The chicken! It's a little black cinder!" She drew out the baking dish, and regarded the burnt relic grievously. Somehow it was the last straw — the final blow at Christmas.

"There isn't another thing to eat," she sobbed. "The last of the mutton's gone bad, and even the soup went sour, it's so hot. And the butter wouldn't come — I've been trying to churn it all the morning — and the hens didn't lay a single egg yesterday! And — "

"Ah, hang the hens!" said her husband, very tenderly. He sent the baking dish clattering to the floor, and picked, Polly up as if she were a baby. "You poor little, tired kiddie—do you think any-thing matters —!"

From outside came a sudden "honk honk" and Jim stopped as if shot.

"Wh-what's that?" quavered his wife. She rubbed her face into the grimy shoulder of his blue shirt, still odorous with smoke.

"It's so like a motor that I'm evidently asleep," said he, much bewildered. "By Jove, there's a cooee! Come on, old woman, and see who it is."

He dragged her to the front verandah. A big blue motor was purring gently up the paddock, bumping over the unseen ruts in the grass, since the track was all too narrow for it. So full of people was it that it was not easy to fathom how they did not overflow. They were packed in like sardines — a gay, noisy load of young faces, and summer dresses, and floating veils.

"Good gracious!" gasped Polly. "Jim, I must fly — I'm not fit to be seen! Whoever can it be?"

Round a bend in the track came a cavalcade of riders — tall lads, on well bred horses, racing for the lead. They sent out a mighty shout of greeting. A big man, riding a little to the right, waved his hat with a cheer.

"It's Dad!" said little Polly Henderson, with sudden ecstasy. "Jim — it's Dad!"

The motor pulled up by the gate, and two little figures tumbled out head first, picked themselves up, and raced over the garden beds. They flung themselves on Polly tumultuously. Under the onslaught Polly sat down on the edge of the verandah and was lost to view. But Jim, with a twisted little smile, went forward to meet a tall woman who hurried after them.

"We had to come," said Polly's mother, laughing. "My dear boy, what have you been doing? You look singed!

Father and I have had no peace since your letters came, since none of the family could imagine a Christmas without Polly! And as the motor was my Christmas present, it made our madness possible. Beryl and Tommy, get off your sister, and let me see her. Why Polly, dear!"

"We've been fire fighting," Jim explained. "Had quite a nice morning — and we need a bath horribly. But we're awfully glad to see you, though we don't know what on earth we've got for you to eat!"

"Oh, we brought our Christmas dinner with us," said his mother-in-law, cheerfully. "You poor children! Father! Did you ever see such a pair?"

"Father" gathered his daughter into a capacious pair of arms. In that shelter, with the sudden happiness of greeting round her, and the dear, welcoming faces, Polly suddenly forgot weariness and grime. And not even Louise, who was notoriously a dainty person, seemed to notice the black streaks on her pale face. They were clustering round her, kissing her, patting her shoulders, wishing her a merry Christmas — and nothing mattered.

"Better go and get a bath and a new dress," said "Father," practically. "Who's got a dress for Polly?" He cast a vague glance round his family, evidently expecting to see dresses materialise from the air.

"I've got a beauty for you, Polly, darling!" Louise spoke. "A pink muslin — it's just the prettiest pattern!"

"None of us have had a single present — we waited for you to be with us before we opened them," said Hilda. "And there are millions of bundles for you and Jim!"

"Goodness knows the condition of the hampers, after

these awful roads," quoth "Mother." "But there's enough to eat to leave with a week's supply here, so I expect we'll manage. Can't you boys unpack things?" Her request was vague, and her family treated it vaguely.

"Our present's on the road," chorused Jeff and Alex! "It wouldn't hurry. It's an Ayrshire cow — just the thing for you two old farmers!" The family laughed delightedly — it was a most excellent joke.

"Mulligan's driving her — and I'm going to put him on here for a bit to give you a hand," said "Father's" deep bass. "He s quite trustworthy — you can easily leave the place to him."

"And we're going to take you both back for New Year!" said everyone, happily.

"Beryl an' me, we broughted our stockings wiv us we haven't looked at one little thing 'at Santa Claus put in," said Tommy. "An' we hunged one up for you, too, an' it's bang-full — an' it's in the motor car. An' we're just dyin' to see what's in 'em, but we couldn't wivout you. Oh, Polly, darlin', couldn't you come now, before you has a bath?"

"Oh — you dears!" said Polly. Over their heads she smiled into Jim's eyes.

SANTA CLAUS, JUNIOR

In the hot glare of the December afternoon the long road leading westward from the township of Airedale lay still and dusty—the shade thrown by its fringe of poplars giving grateful relief from the straight ribbon of gleaming yellow track. On either side paddocks stretched away into the dim haze: here and there broken by a farm house, nestling in its orchard, or a bare cottage standing, bald and shelterless, on the plain. Cattle were gathered in the shade of the box trees. A long file of sheep wound across a paddock, making for a rush-bordered lagoon, whence, presently, a dozen wild duck whirred southward. The green of spring had given place to the withered brown midsummer grass.

The road itself was little travelled. A stray spring cart, or a light dray, drawn by sturdy plough horses, jogged passed. A brown-faced girl on a fidgety bay mare kept to the shade of the poplars. Once a motor ate up the yellow distance with a swift rush. Then quiet held the afternoon. Little whirlwinds of dust veered hither and thither, raised by a vagrant breeze that died almost as it was born. The smoke from the farm house chimneys hung awhile on the hot air before dispersing imperceptibly. Under a clump of wattles a big Devon bull swished the flies from his red sides lazily; then even so much effort became too much for him, and he lay down with slow dignity and went to sleep.

In a garden that bordered upon the road, yet was shut out from it by a thick hedge of privet, a woman sat sewing. Her chair and table were set in the shade of a fine old oak that grew in the middle of the lawn, and all about it the smooth grass sward, closely clipped, stretched away to the farthest walls of the garden, broken here and there by gay little beds, bright with phlox and carnations, and gaillardias; and by trellised arches, twined with climbing roses; and by green shrubs, in and out of which birds darted, chattering very busily. The birds, indeed, were the only busy people in the lazy heat. Even Janet Hyde's quick fingers moved indolently; and at length they fell idly on her lap, while she sat and dreamed.

A tall, slender women, with a pale, grave face, lit by brown eyes that held strange depths of sadness and unsuspected flashes of merriment. No one had ever called Janet Hyde beautiful, even in her girlhood's days, excepting one man, who was a lover, and too happy to be a critic; and now that girlhood was far behind her some people who did not know her called her plain. Her eyes and her hair had been "her only hope," she used to say, in those irresponsible days of girlhood. The eyes held all their old sweetness, and about her face still waved the wonder of the soft masses of the hair that had matched their brown depths. Now people spoke of her as "old Miss Hyde"—for it was white.

Janet quite acquiesced in the designation. Old? Yes, she was old. She had been old ever since she had wakened, ten years back, from the fever that had ended a dream—to take up the dry husk of life, and make as good a show out of a sorry reality as might be, seeing that it behoved one to act decently, for the sake of other people, and such "decency" was an integral part of her creed. And because she was a brave woman, the years had helped her, bringing no small share of happiness, and giving her love that had kept her heart and her face young, even though the lustrous white of her hair belied her five-and-thirty years. She had learnt her lesson—the lesson the kind the years teach—that, though the path we mark out for ourselves in the sweetness of youth be closed to us, it need not follow that all the others are bitter—the many other paths that diverge at first, but perhaps lead to a goal not very different. And there will always be comfort in fighting.

A pleasant clatter of cups on a tea-tray made Janet open her eyes as an old woman came across the lawn, laden with afternoon tea.

"Four o'clock, Kate?"

"Yes, an' thim b'ys not home," said the new comer, putting the tray upon the table with a decisive little bang. " 'Tis no good tellin' Master Billy any mortial thing. I was that strict an' pertickler this mornin', gettin' him to promise they'd be home by four——"

"But they never are, Kate, dear! Why do you worry?"

"Worry, is it? Sure' I'm not worryin' over the young rascals. Only—well, the cakes is hot, an' they're afther losin' all their good if they're not ate quick!" said Kate, refusing to meet her mistress's eyes. "Me worry! Not likely, wid all I have to do this blessed day!"

"Now, you shouldn't have baked cakes, Kate," Janet said reproachfully; "and it's so hot, too."

"Now, now, thin—you ate your tea, an' don't you mind me, Miss Janet," said the mendacious hand maid. "Sure, I had lavins av time; more be token, if I bake today, I do not be doin' it tomorrow—leastways, I don't if the b'ys aren't hungry! So it's all the same."

"You spoil them, Kate," said Janet, laughing.

"For you to say that to me!" uttered Kate solemnly. "Me, that's as shtrict an' firm wid 'em as if I was me own shtepmother, an' you that wake, an' Master Paul twishtin' you round his little finger, so he does! Bedad! An' if 'twas me they'd get more shtick an' less shpoilin'; but they have the length av your fut, an' pardon to yez. Whin I was young——"

She broke off as the quick short canter of a pony was heard on the road, and her rugged old face lit up suddenly.

"'Tis them," she said; "praises be to this blessed hour they've got home safe on that misfortunit pony! My, my! Do but listen to that gate bangin'—the darlints! If that Master Billy's not the wickedest little villain, an' more be token the best rider for a b'y of eight annywhere, an' making Master Paul as bad as himsilf! I'll be getting' more hot cakes." She sped towards the house as a black Shetland tore round a turn in the drive, scattering the gravel with his hoofs, and stopped so abruptly opposite the oak tree that is was difficult to tell whether the descent of the two small boys on his back, who fell off in a mass, was involuntary or otherwise. The mass disentangled itself and raced across the grass to fall on Janet.

"Mind the table, sweethearts," she said gently, emerging from the hurricane somewhat dishevelled, with an arm round each small body. "Well, how was school?"

"Not too bad," said Billy cheerfully. He was a dark, handsome boy, with curly hair, cropped to military limits—an arrangement between himself and the barber that had considerably distressed his aunt. "I got caned once—for talking."

"Me too," said Paul sweetly, lifting eyes of heavenly

blue beneath a thatch of fair hair. “I put a gwub into Miss Dixon’s desk—you know, auntie, one of those big woolly chaps. He got on her hand, an’ she scweamed.” He smiled reminiscently. “It was worf it!” he concluded.

“Oh, Paul!” said Janet.

“Well, she paid me out,” said Paul sturdily. “She had her fun—six cuts ’twas. So ’twas fair. She shouldn’t be afraid of gwubs; you aren’t. Wimmen are such silly hens!”

“But I’m a woman, Paul.”

“But you aren’t a silly hen one,” said her nephew, comfortably. “I guess Billy an’ I have taught you a heap!”

“You!” said Billy, with the scorn eight years feels for six. “I like your cheek, young Paul. Glory! Here’s Kate! Are they hot, Kate?”

“Sure, they’re just afther comin’ out av the oven,” said Kate, dispensing cakes with regal prodigality. “ ’Tis hungry you’ll be then, darlints. Ate plinty—they’ll not hurt yez. Did you say she caned yez? Ah, ’tis the harrd woman you sind thim babies to, Miss Janet! I’d cane her!”

“Now, didn’t you deserve all you got, Billy?” said Janet, laughing.

“ ’Course we did,” Billy grinned; “and Miss Dixon’s not a bad old sort either. I say, auntie, I saw the new doctor—an’ he’s going to take me for a ride in his motor.”

“That’s lovely,” Janet said. “But I hope you don’t worry him, Billy.”

“I don’t,” Billy affirmed. “He pulled up himself and yarned to me. I hope old Dr Featherstone stays away a long time. I like this doctor.”

"Well, I like my own old Dr Featherstone," Janet said, laughing. "I'm afraid, Billy, I'll be glad when he is back."

"Auntie! But he hasn't got a motor!"

"No, but I've known him since you were a baby, old boy," said Janet; "and you see, I don't know your new man—not even his name."

"I don't know that either," Billy said. "But he's just a splendid chap himself. You've no idea how int'rustin' he is —he knows about everything, an' specially about boys. That's why I like him."

Janet sighed faintly. It was a source of trouble to her that there was no man's influence over these little orphan lads who made her world.

"I told him about you, too," Billy said, "an' how splendid you were, an' he was very int'rusted. He's coming tonight—he's goin' to sound his hooter on the road at our gate. Will you come down an' see him, Auntie?"

"I don't think I will, old chap," Janet said. "I don't know him, you see, and he'll be going away when Dr Featherstone comes back. But if you're going motoring you must hurry up and unsaddle Pickles first. Is Paul asked, too?"

"Well, if I am, he is," said Billy. "Come along Paul-oh, an' we'll let Pickles go. Hurry up—are you eating cakes still?"

"There aren't any more," said Paul, regretfully. "Why didn't you make a lot, Kate?"

"Sure, it's the lovely appetite he has, bless him!" said Kate, regarding him with fatuous admiration. "Arrah now, what's that?"

The "honk-honk" of a motor sounded beyond the trees.

"Oh, by George!" said Billy, ruefully. "There's the doctor—and this blessed pony isn't let go!"

"Give him here," said Kate. "Sure you'll not lose a minnit while I have these two hands an' nothin' to do wid 'em."

"Bless you, Kate, darling!" said Billy, fervently. They flung themselves briefly, if heavily, upon their aunt. "So long!" They raced across the lawn, disappearing behind the shrubbery.

Janet laughed.

"And you don't spoil my babies," she said. "Oh, Kate!"

"Faith, I do not," said Kate, sturdily. "Will you have thim miss a treat like that, just for lettin' this blessed image av a pony go. 'Tis harrd you are!"

"We're both hard!" said Janet. Their eyes met, and they laughed at each other.

In the motor excitement had calmed to quiet ecstacy, and the gentle art of conversation began to flourish. The new doctor was a companionable fellow—a big man, with a beard streaked with grey, and kind eyes, and he was certainly "int'rusting." The talk veered naturally to Christmas.

"Hope you hang up your stockings," said the doctor.

"Well, rather!" said Billy, wide eyed. "What else could we do?"

"Oh, that's all right," the doctor said, "I know some boys

who don't—but they miss lots of fun."

"Do you hang yours up?"

"Well, no, Paul, I don't," admitted the doctor. "I'm too old to bother Santa Claus."

"That's what Auntie says," Billy observed. "We don't believe it, you know. I think it's awf'ly rough not to give old Santa Claus a show. Auntie doesn't have half such a lovely Christmas as we have. She says Santa Claus doesn't come to grown ups. But he brings Kate things.

"H'm," said the doctor. "I fancy that auntie of yours must be a pretty good one. Can't you act Santa Claus for her?"

"How?"

"Well, plan something nice for her," said the doctor, plainly puzzled. "You'd have to think what she'd like; you see, I don't know her. It's not half bad fun to act Santa Claus."

"Does anyone act him for you?"

"No, Billy, old man; I'm a lonely sort of fellow, you know," said the doctor. "However, I'm too old to matter—but they say women never get too old for that sort of thing, so you're safe to try it for your Auntie."

"That's a jolly good idea," said Billy to Paul later, as they trotted up the drive through the scented dusk. The motor was throbbing away into the distance. "I'm going to plan like mad, an' you can, too. I'd love to give Auntie a decent sort of Christmas."

"Wather!" said Paul.

"An' the doctor, too," Billy said, " 'cause he's no end

of a brick. I say, Paul, can't we plan to give 'em a party?" An' then they'd both have fun! There's always stacks of cake on Christmas, and we could fix things up somehow."

"Let's start plannin' 's hard 's we can," said Paul, solemnly. The dark head and the fair came close together and "planned" ecstatically.

An air of dark secrecy enveloped them, that thickened as the days went by. Janet, mildly puzzled, tried to solve it, but was met by such bland lack of comprehension that she gave up the attempt, and occupied herself in her own plans for the time she loved to make joyful for her boys—to whom, indeed, all times were joyful. Kate, lost in an aroma of much cooking, made awful preparations for undermining the digestions of her darlings. School ending, and the boys were left free to their conspiring, which was mainly carried on in a disused shed. The "Christmas feeling" was in the air.

Janet, returning one evening from the township, parcel laden, heard behind her the throb of a motor, that slackened and stopped. A courteous voice hailed her.

"May I offer you a lift?"

She turned with a smile, knowing it was Billy's friend, but at the sight of the man in the motor the smile suddenly changed to amazed horror. Silent, white to the lips, she stared at him, watching his friendly face reflect her own astonishment, and grow drawn and old under her gaze.

"Janet!" he said.

"You!" Her voice was almost inaudible. She put up her hand vaguely to ward off the thronging ghosts of the bitter, dead past. "You!"

"Janet! Janet!" he said, heavily. "I didn't know—I—"

She struggled for composure. In the quick anguish of seeing him again, of finding her heart alive after ten years' burial—her brain reeled.

He came towards her with quick strides. "Tell me—"

"Don't." She shrank back from him, her face quivering. "I will not speak to you—I cannot. There—there is not anything to say."

"But I will know——"

"No!" she burst out, with sick anger. "Can't you see I would rather be dead than speak to you. Go back—go!" She fled away into the dusk, and Roger Byrne, walking as an old man walks, went back blindly to his motor.

To Janet, hurrying along the dusty road, there was but one idea possible. She must go away. Not again must there be this awful chance—the risk of meeting him—the blank shame of knowing that this face had yet power to make her heart leap wildly. In the bitter ten years she had struggled against her womanhood, she dreamed that Roger Byrne was dead to her—now she knew that he was vividly alive, must be so always; and the knowledge spelt agony. There was nothing for her but flight. She must take the boys away—quickly—until he had gone.

At the gate, suddenly, weak and trembling, she leaned against the post, panting. A tall, old watching figure lifted the latch and came to her, and she felt the old servant's arms holding her fast.

"Kate—you knew?"

"Wid these eyes I saw him—a wake ago—an' bad luck

to the day! Sure I hoped he'd go widout you knowin'—me little lady—dear heart!" There were tears on the wrinkled cheeks.

"I must go away, Kate."

"It might be better. Come on, into the house. Ah, the divil's in the men, so he is!" said Kate, fervently, leading her up the path. She looked keenly at her mistress's white face, and fell back on one sure comfort.

"Don't be goin' into your room, darlint," she said. "Sure I'm up to me neck getting' tay, an' thim b'ys is no one knows where. Could you be findin' thim for me? 'Tis in some owld shed they are, wid a great secret on."

"I'll find them," Janet said, eagerly.

She turned down a side path, calling as she went. There was no answer, but a light glimmering from a shed guided her. She opened the door softly and peeped in.

A battered lantern lit the interior dimly. The shed had been roughly cleared, as testified much debris piled up in corners, and in the centre a very marvel of a Christmas tree reared itself proudly in an old tub. It was a stout, young sapling, its leaves a little drooping now—but who would criticise withered leaves on a tree so laden? The boughs bent beneath the strangest medley of adornments. There were numerous bundles and parcels, mainly done up in newspaper, with a great superabundance of string, and the tree was gay with fruit—big oranges and apples, bunches of cherries and golden apricots, and even an odd cucumber or two. Then there were candles—the stout unromantic candles used for the buggy lamps, and purloined with much difficulty and derring-do; and a final touch of highest art was lent by several twists of colored paper that gave the tree a very frivolous and gay appearance. Below, cross-legged on the floor, sat Paul, rapt in an excess of silent admiration, while above, on a somewhat shaky rafter, Billy struggled with a rope which was supposed to be assisting to hold the tree upright, but was somewhat failing of its high purpose.

"Bust the rope!" said Billy.

"She's all shickery," said Paul, casting an anxious glance aloft. "You'll just have to pull her straight. Gwacious, she is lovely!"

"I guess they'll be pretty pleased," Billy said, hauling away vigorously. "Wish we'd had a bit more money, to buy him that hat. This'll be the rippingest Christmas we ever did have." His face suddenly fell. "Oh," he said. "Oh! There's auntie! Oh, you meany, to have come! Now it's all spoilt!"

"Oh, Billy, dear, I'm sorry," Janet said. "I'll go away and forget all about it. You see, I don't know anything. Only, you mustn't sit on that old rafter, it's not safe."

"Safe be hanged!" said Billy, with a groan. "It'll never be the same now. Oh, why did you come? Paul, if you hadn't sat there like a silly image, you'd have had your back against the door!" His lip quivered. "There's no good planning anything!"

"We did want it for a s'prise," Paul said, miserably.

"Oh, I do hate myself!" Janet said. "Sweethearts, I'll never think of it again until I get the surprise. I'll go away now. Only, Billy, dear, do get down."

"All right," said Billy, dolefully.

He swung his lithe little body over the rafter, hanging an instant by his hands. There came a little sound of cracking wood, and, simultaneously with Janet's cry—with her quick spring, that yet was not quick enough—the old beam crashed down into the gay little tree. It missed Paul by a hair's breadth; under it, his back across the tub, Billy lay very still.

* * *

The house was dark and quiet when Roger Byrne let himself in two nights later. It was Christmas eve, and the township he had just left was gay with flags and ferns, and crowded with happy people; but on Janet Hyde's house, where for two days they had fought for the little quiet body, the shadow of death hung very near. They had sent for him quickly—there was no other doctor within many miles—and, indeed, Janet seemed altogether unconscious of his identity, as she worked over her little lad, save that he knew she would never touch him—never be near him if it could be helped. She spoke but seldom; the question in her eyes never failed, but she did not put it into words. And Roger, watching Billy's white face, could not answer it.

Just at the door of the sick room, where a wet sheet hung straight and cool, Roger stumbled over something that sobbed softly.

"Why, Paul!" he whispered.

The little figure in pyjamas crept into his arms.

"They won't let me in," Paul said, choking back tears that might make a noise. "But Kate's gone to sleep in the chair, so I crawled here. Please let me sleep here, so's I can hear Billy if he speaks. I won't make any row!"

"Sonnie, you can't sleep on the floor," Roger said,

pityingly. “It’s eleven o’clock, and you’re stone-cold.”

“Billy might call me.” The sobs were very close. He turned his face into Roger’s breast, and caught his coat in his teeth, shaking. But when he felt himself carried along the hall he fought silently, desperately, to be put down.

“Let me go!”

“Listen, old man,” Roger said. “You can’t sleep there—see, we want all the air for Billy. Paul, I promise you I’ll bring you the moment he calls you.”

“Even if I’m asleep?”

“Yes, I’ll wake you. I promise you faithfully.”

“If he calls!” Striding through the dim hall, Roger Byrne knew how little chance there was that the call would come. The night would end matters one way or the other. He had used the utmost resources of his skill, and now Billy must do the rest himself. Billy, who tossed helplessly, or else lay in a stupor that was very like death itself—and very near.

“There is no change?” Janet’s questioning eyes were black-ringed, and her face absolutely colorless. She bent over the bed, keeping the iced cloths adjusted on the restless head. Not once in those terrible hours had she left her post. Now it seemed to her that there was a difference, a little more weakness, a grey shade in the pallor of Billy’s face. Hope, that had buoyed her up unconsciously, began to leave her.

She tried to make herself face it—life without Billy. He was her very own; he had come into her life when it was hardest and his little fingers had smoothed out many of the worst knots. They had always been chums. She had taken him from her sister’s weak arms, and in all his glad little life they had not spent a day apart. How could she do without him?

The slow hours crept by as they watched. Once or twice, looking up with that terrible, unspoken questioning, she caught the pity in Roger's eyes, and read in it her answer. It brought her own gaze back quickly to Billy—she could not lose a moment of his time.

The night-light was paling sickly in the dawn when she found Roger beside her.

"Take this," he said.

She motioned the glass away, but at his gently insisting gesture drank its contents with a little impatient movement. How stupid it was to think she mattered—as if anything could matter but Billy!

"You must rest," he said.

The compassion in his whisper seared her heart with sudden fear. What was it?—was Billy——? She could not speak. Unconsciously she caught the little hand that lay on the sheet and turned agonised eyes to the doctor's face, as if by that desperate grasp she could keep her boy from slipping away from her.

"Billy!" she gasped. "Sweetheart!"

She felt the doctor's hand grip her shoulder, suddenly, roughly.

"Look!" he said.

Billy's eyes had opened slowly. He was looking at her, not with the dreadful glassy stare she so dreaded, but—oh, blessed relief—with consciousness. His lips tried to smile.

"Don't speak, sweetheart." She slipped an arm under

him as Roger held a glass to his lips. Billy smiled sleepily, turning to her, and holding her dress with weak fingers, his head nested into her arm. The next moment he was asleep.

It was real sleep at last. The merciful certainty gave her strength, while dawn merged into summer daylight, and the Christmas sun mounted higher, and Billy slept like a log upon her breast. Once or twice the doctor mentioned to her to lay him down, but she smiled faintly and shook her head—not for worlds would she risk one instant of that life-giving sleep. She scarcely felt that her own limbs were growing stiff and heavy, and that her cramped position meant torture—whatever it was, it was good to bear it—for Billy.

It was with a feeling of helpless anger against herself that at length Janet realised that she could hold out no longer. She was swaying a little in her utter fatigue—struggling vainly to keep upright and hold Billy still. Then she heard Roger's voice in her ear, and felt his touch.

"Lean against me," he said.

He drew her against him, supporting her gently, and allowing her cramped limbs to relax. The relief was instant, and though her pride struggled, she knew for Billy's sake she must give in. Yet it was almost more than she could bear—the tender touch, the nearness that was so terribly dear to her. In the profound stillness of the room she could feel the hard beating of his heart, his breath stirred the white splendor of her hair. . . . It seemed to Janet that they had stood so for years, when at length Billy woke.

He smiled up at her, and his eyes were bright and clear—there was even a hint of color in his pale lips. She put her face to his, sinking down on the bed beside him, and Roger left them together.

He came back soon with nourishment that Billy took meekly, one hand fast in Janet's. Then he lay back and smiled at them. A sudden, bitter self-consciousness came upon Janet—pride, outraged and miserable, flooded her white cheeks and kept her head bowed. Billy's weak little voice broke the silence.

"It isn't Christmas, is it?"

"It is, then, old man," Roger answered.

"How'd I get sick?" Billy demanded—then, without waiting for an answer, "I was plannin' such a lovely Christmas for Auntie—an'—an' you were comin' too!"

"Was I, old chap?"

"I was Santa Claus," Billy said, sleepily. "We were goin' to have a lovely party for Auntie—an' you, 'cause you were lonesome."

"Well?" said Roger. There was a strange quiver in his deep voice. "I came, Billy; can't I stay, now that I'm here? Ask Auntie."

"But you can—can't he, Auntie?"

Janet's head went lower.

"You might tell Auntie, Billy, that I've been waiting for this Christmas for ten years—that I listened to a lie, and broke my heart over it—and only old Kate told me yesterday it was a lie." The deep voice suddenly stopped; for a moment the room was very still.

"I'd like you to stay for Christmas," Billy murmured, drowsily.

"I want to stay more than anything else in the world" Roger said. "Will you ask Auntie to forgive me, Billy?"

"She always forgives us—when we're sorry."

"Sorry!" he said—"Sorry! Oh, Janet, Janet—God knows I am sorry!"

He knelt down and hid his face in her dress. There came the terrible sound of a man's deep, stifled sob.

"Don't!" she said, brokenly. "Do you care so much?"

"I have broken my heart for you all these ten years," he said. "Janet, can you forgive?"

"I want him to stay for Christmas, Auntie!" Billy's drowsy voice, faintly puzzled, broke in, and Janet smiled at him—but the smile faded. She dropped her face upon her hands.

"Ah," she said, "I am old. My hair is white"

"It is the most beautiful hair in the world," Roger said, with his lips upon it. "Janet—let me stay for Christmas—for always. Be merciful, and forgive, Janet—take me back." He felt her tears upon his face as he drew her, unresisting, into his arms.

IN GREAT WATERS

Dawn on the lake. Across its glassy water stole the first pink flush, rising from its mysterious sea bed behind the long, dark ti-tree shore line—never so dark as in that first hour of the morning. The dim horizon brightened, showing clear-cut in the faint glow. Above it the clouds receded slightly, leaving a lurid space below, while their lower edges became tipped with palest gold. Gradually the space brightened, until it lay a flawless line of amber, lustrous in purity. The breeze stirred gently. Then, rising from the unseen, came the golden ball of the sun—at first a thin curved line, scarce seen above the sharp silhouette of the ti-tree, yet gradually widening, and ever brighter and more clear, until, with a sudden leap, the whole glowing disc was revealed, lighting all the dim scene into radiance and beauty. The first long rays shot across the surface of the water, and the little wavelets, stirred by the breeze, rippled in answer, until each tiny crest caught the new light and flung it hither and thither in a shower of opalescent foam. In the thick scrub that grew down to the very edge of the lake the birds called to each other to greet the morning; the far off chime of the bell bird in the gullies, heard faintly through the full-throated carol of the magpie, the plaintive call of the mynah, and the twitter of a hundred little songsters. From a great dead gum tree rang out the wild peal of the laughing jackass, and another strident burst of mirth echoed in answer from further inland. All the myriad inhabitants of the bush sprang into wakefulness, from the big wallaby, that paused, half suspiciously, before plunging into a tangle of bracken, to the tiny white butterflies, dancing in and out of the twining clusters of supple-jack yet glistening with dew. From afar came the low boom of the breakers. The sullen clouds rolled backward before the sun's triumphal march, and the path of light across the lake broadened and grew brighter.

Into that shining path came a vessel—a heavy fishing boat, its sails set to catch the fitful puffs of wind, which, however, were not sufficient to keep it on its course. There was but one occupant, and he was rowing with long, easy strokes that told of lifelong practice, yet with a weariness in his movements born of the long night's vigil. Before him, in the sterns, lay his net in a tangled heap—a mute witness of failure. A few small fish were in the bottom of the boat, their scales shimmering against the dark mass of the net. The man's eyes rested on them, and he laughed grimly.

"A bright sort of Christmas box, you are!" he said bitterly; "I reckoned my luck might ha' turned on Christmas Eve, and it did—turned a little worse. By Jove, I hardly thought it could!"

He pulled savagely for a moment; then he paused, and shipped his oars with an impatient movement—what need was there to hurry home with his renewed tale of failure? He lit his pipe, and taking the tiller, stared hopelessly across the lake. The sunlight fell on his tired face—a boyish, handsome face it was, with brown eyes that had in them something of a dog's look of wistful fidelity. Just now the boyish aspect contrasted sharply with his worn look, and the lines of care across his brow. The boat drifted slowly on as he sat with bent eyes trying to work out the problem of life that was weighing him down. It was no unusual one—the sordid details were ordinary enough, and yet they meant all his life. Neither was it hard of solution. Given an early marriage and a sickly girl wife; losses of nets and fishing gear; doctors' bills and, finally, a long run of bad luck, when night after night saw only fruitless toil, morning after morning the same empty-handed home coming—there could be but one result. The result was imminent now; but in the Christmas morning Phil Merton sat with knitted brow, trying vainly to find a way out.

The wind rose slightly, filling the big sail, and the boat began to slip through the water more quickly. Over the lake, a mile away, the roofs of the little cottages gleamed white in the sunlight; beyond, further down the shore, the long piers stood out boldly, jutting far into the sea that foamed into the passage between them, sending its turbulent waters far over the sheltered lake within. Phil shifted the tiller, for the wind had dropped somewhat, and made a long tack across the lake, running in this time until the boat grated on the smooth shore. He leapt out and drew her up the beach, driving her rusty anchor deep into the sand; then he took out the net, straightened its apparently hopeless tangle, and coiled it in the stern with mechanical deftness. Taking up the few poor fish that represented a night's hard work, he set off through the sand towards his home.

A few minutes' walk brought him to the door of the cottage, and lifting the latch softly, he entered the kitchen. No one was astir, and the room was close and airless. Phil, fresh from the morning sweetness and the clean sea breeze, felt as though he would stifle inside; he opened the door wide, and threw up the little square window. Then he tiptoed to the door of the inner room, and looked in. A girl lay on the low bed, her face half hidden in the masses of disheveled dark hair; one arm was flung across the coverlet, and she was sleeping soundly. With a sigh Phil closed the door, and turned to the kitchen. The room was littered with an untidy accumulation of odds and ends. On the rough table were the unwashed cups and plates from the evening meal of the preceding evening; the fireplace was choked with a week's ashes; dust lay thick on every poor piece of furniture. The whole room bespoke neglect and carelessness; it was alike cheerless and comfortless. Phil glanced around, and sighed.

"Poor little woman!" he said aloud. Then he set to work upon the chaos, and soon returned it to something like order. In half an hour the fire burned cheerily in the well-cleaned fireplace, the litter of untidiness had disappeared, and beneath the vigorous onslaught of a broom the floor once more assumed an appearance of self-respect. Heating some water, Phil washed up the dishes and scrubbed the table with all a sailor's handiness. Finally he dusted vigorously with an old sock, and was regarding his handiwork with pride, when a peevish voice came from the doorway behind him.

"So you're back!"

Phil started, and turned to greet his wife.

"How are you, lassie?" he asked quickly.

"Oh, same as usual," she said fretfully—"an' that aint much. I couldn't sleep all night, an' now you've woke me with your row just when I did drop off."

Phil flushed painfully under his tan.

"I'm awfully sorry, old woman," he said, "I was only tryin' to get things a bit straight for you."

"I don't see what you want botherin' round," she said, "things are well enough without always fussin' about with a broom an' a scrubbin' brush. Did you have any luck?

The tired look was back in full force on the man's face.

"No luck, dear," he said "only a few little 'uns."

She sat down on a broken chair, a limp, untidy figure, squalid even in that poor room, yet with the remains of prettiness in the fretful face. Meeting his sad eyes, she began to cry weakly. He put his arm round her shoulders and tried to comfort her, even in his own hopelessness, but she shook him off impatiently, bewailing—as she so constantly bewailed—that she had ever married him. His face grew drawn and pinched as he tried to soothe her. At length she dried her eyes, and sullenly set about the task of setting the meagre breakfast table, while her husband prepared the fish. As they finished their silent meal, a cheery face looked in at the window, with a merry greeting.

"Mornin', Mrs Merton—Mornin', Phil," said the visitor. "Merry Chris'mas to you both!" Then he disappeared.

Polly Merton laughed bitterly. "Merry Chris'mas!" she said, with a sob; "there ain't much merriment round this hole, I guess. Here we owe nearly £20 to the store, an' can't get no more credit; there ain't hardly a thing to eat in the house, an' we're both pretty near barefoot, an' me needin' med'cine, an' you can't get no fish. I'd like to know what you think we're goin' to do!" She laid her head on the table and began to sob.

Phil rose abruptly and walked to the window; then he came to her side and stroked her rough hair gently. "Cheer up, my girl," he said, trying to infuse courage into his own sad heart; "luck may turn any night, an' if we get a little ready money we can easy pay off the debt by degrees."

She interrupted him angrily.

"Oh, what's the good of talking like that!" she exclaimed: "you've been sayin' that since the winter, an' things gets worse and worse: I don' know what's goin' to become of us—go beggin', I suppose, an' starve. I wish to God I'd never married you! I don' know why I was such a fool. It ain't worth bein' alive to be like this!"

He winced as though something had stung him.

"It 'ud be a jolly sight better for you if I was dead," he said bitterly; "at least you'd get the insurance, an'—you'd be rid of me."

She sobbed more loudly.

"You just say that sort of thing in spite!" she wept; "if you'd only go an' try to get some money —"

"Try!" he said—"try!—oh, my God, how I try—!" His voice failed him, and, flinging on his cap, he dashed out of the house.

Rushing on, blind with hot tears, he ran against a little child and knocked her over. The child's sharp cry brought him to his senses, and he picked her up gently, played with her for a moment, and brought a smile to the little mouth that quivered uncertain whether to laugh or cry. Then he kissed her, and watched her toddle away along the narrow path, until she was safely at home. Turning abruptly to where the big sand hummocks rose at his right hand, he climbed through the shifting sand, and presently found himself on the wind-swept ocean beach.

Far as the eye could reach the grey sea heaved before

him, the dull expanse broken here and there by the white cap of a huge wave far out. Upon the beach at his feet the surf roared and seethed as the great breakers came dashing in, long walls of water advancing in resistless majesty until their crested summits reared, curved and toppled over with a mighty crash, sending their hundreds of tons of water high up the shelving sands. To right and left the bare hard line of the beach stretched away until the white spray clouds hid the view. Before him stood out the long grey walls of the twin piers, through which the current now ran rapidly out to sea. A fishing boat was moored in the smoother water of the channel, the net coiled high in the stern; but the owner was nowhere to be seen—probably keeping his Christmas, Phil thought, with a sigh. He walked to the end of the pier, and looked down through the green water on the jagged rocks below, their brown surfaces coated thick with mussels. Here the sea raged furiously, boiling up amongst the rocks as if from some vast submarine cauldron, dashing against the huge piles with a force that made the great timbers quiver, and sent flying showers of spray high up into the watching man's face. Overhead the gulls circled ceaselessly, and ever and anon the hoarse cry of a sea bird was heard above the din of the waves. A steamer was coming in, tumbling about among the billows, yet making good headway. The spray half concealed her funnels as she neared the entrance, fighting against the rapid current and the big seas that fought and struggled in the narrow passage, but she came on steadily, until at length she was in the sheltered water between the piers, and gliding onward to the lake within. One of the crew, a man he knew, caught sight of Phil and waved his cap. "Merry Christmas, old man!" he called cheerily.

Phil turned away with a harsh laugh, and walked with long strides along the pier, the boards echoing beneath his tread. He swung himself down on the beach and set off rapidly on the smooth wet sand, walking with no purpose except a desperate longing to leave thought behind him. His foot struck something soft, and he looked down to see the body of a great black swan lying with twisted neck and draggled feathers. Pity for the splendid dead creature surged within him, and then a wild wish that he were lying on the sands as calmly and peacefully, with the certainty of no waking. Leaving the big bird on the shore he strode on.

For nearly two days he had not slept, and his very brain throbbed with weariness. The beach seemed to rock beneath him, and the long roar of the breakers beat in upon his tired mind with a dreadful reiteration. He would go home, he thought, turning backwards; but there was no rest at home. A groan burst from his lips, and he flung himself face downwards on the sands, burying his face in his arms to shut out the roar of the sea. The dull booming still came to him, but more faintly, with something soothing in its sound. Then his weary frame gave way, and he slept.

When he awoke the chime of the Christmas bells was floating over the lake from the little church in the hamlet on the other side. The sun was high in the heavens, but the dull cloud masses were creeping up, and the wind wailed fitfully. He dragged himself to his feet, stiff from his cramped posture, his mouth dry and parched. It must be time to go and help Polly with the scanty cooking, he thought, and he struck homewards over the beach.

At the top of the hummocks he turned to gaze at the sea. The tide was slack, and the water beneath the piers was still, except for here and there a little eddy. Further out the sea was calmer, the long line of the horizon unbroken save for the heavy clouds. He turned to go, but almost in the act swung round again and stared fixedly at a certain spot in the sea, to the west of the piers. Over it the gulls were circling, but otherwise it bore no outward signs to distinguish it from the rest of the heaving grey expanse; and yet there was something in its aspect that made the man on the hummocks turn white and then go crashing down through the low bushes and out on to the pier. He ran along to the end frantically, and shading his eyes with hands that shook with an emotion he could not control, strained his gaze upon the water. Yes, there was no doubt—it was salmon, a big shoal, and coming slowly towards him, the presence of the fish only discernible by a darkness in the water that none but a trained eye could detect. Salmon! And salmon meant money—a big cheque that spelled freedom from care, and the very thought of which drove away the sense of impending ruin. But he must get help. He turned and sped rapidly back to the village.

As he passed the fishing boat, moored in the channel, an idea struck him. It was Jack Trewin's boat—he would get Jack to help him; there was no time to bring his own boat round. He raced to Trewin's cottage and explained his errand; and then both men dashed off for more assistance.

But for once that was not easy to find. Most of the fishermen were Catholics and had gone across the lake to attend the special Christmas service which a priest had journeyed 60 miles to hold; others were out in their boats; the cottages were almost deserted. They found one lad who was willing to pay out the net from the shore, but at least three others were needed in the boat and to help to haul in the catch. As they met and paused, half desperate with their want of success, a voice hailed them from the lake.

"Hallo, you chaps!" it said; "what on earth's the matter?"

A boat was coming slowly in to the jetty, bearing four men, merry looking, lighthearted tourists, enjoying a week's freedom from the city heat. Two were rowing, with more vigor than accuracy of time and stroke; a third held the tiller ropes, and invariably pulled the wrong one; the fourth sat in the bow and directed operations with an indiscriminate use of nautical terms, weird in its prodigality, but evidently very soothing to his mind. He had twisted himself round and hailed the anxious fishermen in a stentorian tone.

Phil's heart bounded with relief. They were new chums in a boat, true; still they were men, and surely they would lend a hand to drag in the net, where only strength was needed. He called back loudly—

"We want someone to help with the net," he cried, "will you come?"

"By Jove, yes!" said the youth in the bow, "no end of a jolly lark! Pull in chaps."

The others bent to their oars with a hearty good will than sent a shower of spray in the air from the blade of one, and stretched the other on his back in the bottom of the boat. The leader in the bow anathematised their clumsiness.

"You blessed land lubbers!" he said cheerfully, as the crabcatcher regained his seat with a scramble, nearly losing his oar in the attempt. "Pull, now—dip—yeo—heave—oh!"

The stroke oar missed the water altogether, and a vigorous pull from his companion brought the boat half round. Phil and Trewin nearly danced in their impatience.

"Oh, you sea-asses!" said the leader. "I'd like to rope's-end you. Look out there, Stevens. Starboard your hellum, can't you!"

Stevens promptly put the tiller over to port. At that moment one of the oarsmen caught another crab, and lost his oar in his excitement. A chorus of dismay rose from his companions, while the boat drifted round a hundred yards from the jetty.

"Good Lord!" said Phil, desperately, "the fish'll be in kingdom come while we wait for them to get that oar back. Here, look out. I'm goin' in."

He kicked off his boots as he spoke, and dived off the jetty with a clean, quick plunge. He swam with long hasty strokes to the floating oar, which all four occupants of the boat were endeavoring to reach, in imminent danger of being upset. They stretched out their hands to take the oar, but Phil had no intention of giving it to them. Reaching the boat, he caught hold of a rope that dangled from the bow, and swimming with one hand, towed the vessel to the jetty, where Trewin was waiting to secure her hastily.

"By George!" said the steersman, with respectful emphasis; "you are a hummer in the water! Makes a chap feel small. What's your game with the net?" And he looked at Phil as if he suspected the net to be concealed about his person.

Hastily Phil explained the situation. The visitors were eager to help, and Phil turned to Trewin.

"They can easy manage it ashore, with young Bill to show 'em the way, Jack," he said.

"Yes, but what's the good of talkin'?" asked Trewin impatiently. "We can't go without more hands in the boat."

Phil drew a long breath.

"If we wait for more hands, we'll lose the shoal!" he said, desperately. "Can't we chance it on our own, Jack? I'll row if you'll pay out the net."

Trewin looked at him rather blankly. "You couldn't do it," he answered, after a moment's hesitation. "I reckon we'd be mad to try."

"I'll go mad if I don't try!" Phil exclaimed. "Good Lord, Jack. It's salvation for me to get those fish. An' I'm not goin' to let' em get away! We can swim, even if we do get pitched out. For God's sake, old man, let's chance it."

Trewin looked pityingly at his haggard face. He was no coward, but this was indeed a mad enterprise, and he did not believe in the possibility of success. Still, there was a chance, and knowing how desperate was his friend's position, he hesitated to refuse. In the little hamlet every man knew his neighbor's affairs, and just how hard was each individual struggle to keep the wolf from the door. Where all were poor, differing only in respect of the degree of poverty, there was a lively fellow feeling between the men who daily and nightly risked their lives in the long strife against wind and wave. Out of that danger loyally shared together year after year, grew a comradeship more binding than any tie of blood. The fishermen were brothers in arms—made kin by the sharp fight for existence; and that bond could withstand any test.

"Jack!" Phil's voice was sharp with suspense. "You can have my boat if yours gets hurt," he said rapidly. "I know I can do it—stand by me, old man!"

Trewin made an impatient gesture. "Oh, d— the boat!" he said, half angrily; "I wasn't thinking of the blessed boat. But you've got your wife to think of—remember that, old chap."

Phil's face grew set.

"Yes," he said. "I remember. I've got my wife to think of. That's just it. Jack, will you come?"

The stony face told Trewin more than any words could have done. He hesitated no longer. "Come on, then," he said briefly; and turning, he led the way over the hummocks. The two fishermen sprang up through the deep soft sand, with the ease and swiftness born of long habit. Phil had not replaced his boots after his swim, and he dashed on, unheeding the sharp twigs and branches that strewed the sand on the summit of the hummocks. After them came the visitors, with the boy whom they had pressed into the service, the city men floundering and slipping back, and encouraging each other with jests and chaff. At the top of the rise the fishermen paused.

"See them?" Phil asked quickly.

"Yes, by George!" his friend exclaimed. "We'll be only just in time. Run for it, Phil!"

They raced down the slope. On the beach they paused to direct their helpers. The work of the latter was simple. They were to wait at the edge of the water while the fishermen pulled the boat from the channel round the end of the pier, and brought to them the line that held one end of the net, and this they must hold while the boat was pulled out to sea again and round the shoal that was coming now very near the end of the pier. Then, when the fish were enclosed, the boat would be brought in through the breakers and beached, after which all hands would unite in the task of pulling in the net, with its leaping, struggling haul of fish, half maddened with their sudden imprisonment. The plan was simple enough, and easy to carry out had they possessed sufficient assistants; but for one man to bring the boat in through the surf was an undertaking little short of madness. Now, however, there was no time to think of that.

Rushing along the pier, Phil let himself quickly down the slippery steps that led into the deep water of the channel, where the boat was moored. Trewin followed him, and in an instant they had cast off the rope and were pulling out between the piers. The tide was still slack, and they had not much difficulty in reaching the open sea, save where the surf formed a bar across the channel's mouth. There it took all the strength of the two men to bring the heavy boar through, and they each breathed more freely as they rounded the end of the pier, rowing out wide to avoid the sunken rocks. They pulled in towards the beach. As they came nearer the boy Bill ran out along the pier, and they directed the boat towards him until they were near enough for Trewin to fling him the end of the net line, while Phil managed to fend the boat off the huge worm-eaten piles. Bill ran back until he was able to swing himself down upon the sand, there to hold the line while the boat went round the shoal.

Hastily Phil seized both oars and commenced to pull out to sea again, while Trewin took up his position in the stern and began to pay out the net. Suddenly a woman's scream sounded above the roar of the sea, and looking up, the fishermen saw an agonised face. It was Polly Merton. From her cottage door she had seen the rapid conference of the men on the lake side, and their hasty disappearance over the hummocks towards the sea; and, fearing she knew not what, she had followed them in time to see her husband commence his single-handed pull. Only too well she knew the peril of the task. In that moment she forgot all their troubles; the rain that an hour ago had been all-engrossing was as nothing beside the danger that menaced the man she loved—loved, despite the cruel words that had made him desperate. Her whole heart went out to him in her cry of fear.

"Phil! Come back!"

Her husband's face had darkened at the sight of her, but at the appealing cry it brightened. He hailed her cheerily.

"It's all right, lassie," he shouted. "Salmon—a big shoal!"

Little she cared for that consideration now. Her voice grew desperate. She ran along the pier, keeping level with the boat, now swiftly moving out to sea.

"Phil!" she cried again; "you mustn't row alone. Wait for help—oh, you mustn't try!"

His voice came back across the tossing water. "No time for that, lassie," he called. "I'm going to bring you a Christmas box back from the sea!"

The wind took his last words, and the roar of the water almost drowned them as the great waves split themselves against the gigantic framework of the pier. She shrieked again to him, but he was out of earshot, and she was utterly powerless to do aught but watch the boat as it tossed hither and thither among the big seas. Now, it was out in the open, beyond the piers, where the water was calmer, and for a moment she breathed more freely as she saw how ably Phil managed the boat, pulling with long, powerful strokes that seemed to make light of the ocean's might. But the worst danger was to come.

Overhead the clouds had crept up gradually until they had concealed the sun's face, and now were spreading over the blue summer sky. The first heavy drops of rain fell, but she heeded them not as she strained her passionate gaze on the little vessel among the billows. Phil felt them, and between his strokes muttered that Polly would catch cold again. Why on earth didn't she go in? Trewin grunted in reply as he crouched in the stern, paying out the hundreds of fathoms of neatly coiled net. He had little sympathy for the woman who could bring to his friend's face such a look as it had borne that morning.

Phil did not notice his mate's failure to respond to his fear. In truth his task demanded all his energies. They were abreast of the shoal now, and he strained fiercely at the oars in his efforts to take the boat past the fish, until all were surrounded in the net. Harder—harder! till the beads of sweat mounted on his brow, while with every movement the great muscles stood out under his wet, clinging jersey like rigid bars of iron. On—on; till a deep word of relief broke from Trewin.

"It's all right, old chap; we're round 'em—pull in!"

Like a flash Phil obeyed. A few fierce strokes with his right arm, and the boat's nose pointed towards the shore;

and then he bent to his oars, and pulled as he had never pulled before. A moment, and they were in the breakers, the huge seas dashing after them, curling around the boat, and threatening to swamp them a score of times. On he struggled. The great waves bore them forward, but the net was a dead weight astern, and seemed to haul them backwards resistlessly. Still on, with failing muscles and loud throbbing heart—with panting breath and eyes before which spots gathered and danced in mad, bewildering circles. The seas tore past them, bearing the boat on their hollow backs; they burst and crashed about them, engulfing them in clouds of blinding spray. The net was drawn closer now, and he could see behind the boat the dense masses of the fish as they darted to and fro in their bewilderment, leaping out of the water in vain efforts to escape from the sudden imprisonment. Trewin had made the net fast in the stern, and was hauling fiercely on it to relieve the strain on the boat. Behind him, Phil could dimly hear, through the loud drumming in his ears, the shouts of the men on the shore. They must be nearly in—he tugged at the oars with the last remnant of his strength, and drove the boat forward—almost home now!

A great green wave came curling in behind them. It caught the boat on its crest, and dashed forward, bearing it like a cockle shell on its towering height. The might of all the shrieking sea seemed concentrated in one fiercely rushing wall of water. It mounted beneath them, until to the watchers on the shore the boat seemed tossed high into the air. A moment it paused—and then, with a roar that shook the heavens, it crashed down.

Flung from its breaking crest, the boat plunged down—down through the yielding sea. The water poured into her.

With a desperate strength, a last mad effort that seemed to burst his heart, Phil strained at the oars. For a moment it seemed that the boat would right itself—and then a huge billow overtook them, roaring beneath the stern. The boat lifted and plunged forward on its nose, and for a moment stood almost upright amidst the swirling seas—a woman's despairing scream rang out, and they were gone.

Flung clear of the boat and unhurt, Jack Trewin struck out for the shore. The next wave lifted him, and raced inland with him, leaving him lying on the beach, bruised, breathless, but uninjured, while not far from him lay the stranded boat, the line still fast to the stern. He staggered to his feet.

"Phil!" he gasped.

There was no answering voice, no sign in the boiling surf of the dark head over which the waters had a closed a moment before—or was it a year? Wild with fear, they searched the water with their eyes, the woman's face grown grey with dread.

What was that coming towards them? Borne on the advancing wave, an inert, helpless figure. The water played with it in cruel mockery, tossing the limp arms aloft, as if in piteous signals for help—matting the crisp curls on the broad brow. Nearer it came. A cry of anguish broke from the frantic wife, and she dashed into the water to meet her husband, followed by the white-lipped men.

They took him from the sea with gentle hands, laying him tenderly down on the yellow sand. The sun shone out from the clouds, throwing into pitiful relief the slight form that lay so still. On his temple was a blue mark where the boat had struck him; but the boyish face bore no pain—

only a look of peace, perfect beyond earthly dreams. There was no fear in the brown eyes gazing upwards with the straight, steadfast look they knew so well. The dead lips parted slightly, as if to break their awful silence.

Overhead the scream of a gull mingled with the dull ceaseless roar of the surf. Trewin put out a reverent hand, and drew the lids gently over the wide eyes.

SANTA CLAUS, MEDIATOR

Tannibar township—where the coal comes from—lies in a bleak range of southern hills. There was no definite idea about its planning; each man built where it seemed good to him, and some of its streets meander through gullies, while others run boldly to the top of precipices, where a sheer drop gives only footing for goats. One looks from the summit of the main street across ten miles of swamp and plain, seeing on a clear day, the sun glint on the hummocks and the foam of the breakers that roll in beyond Clam Bay. It is not known, however, that the inhabitants of Tannibar ever trouble ever trouble about that view of cloud and shadow—dim scrubland and far blue gleam. Their outlook focusses on the heart of the district; the gully in the midst of the town where the mine belches its ceaseless black smoke across the face of Mount Despair.

Mount Despair rises sheer from the mine. Its name defines it—stubborn, and steep, and grim; scarred with the Golden Stairs, cut in its face where the scarp is most perpendicular, and with the uncounted huts of the people of the mine. There are no roads on Mount Despair; the huts lie irregularly, as though some giant had shaken them helter-skelter from a mammoth pepper castor. Between them wander tracks that the winter rains have cut into ditches. Goats wander there, too, browsing on the heaps of old tins outside every house—for when things are brisk in Tannibar the grocers do an amazing trade in every canned delicacy produced in or out of Chicago. "Saves cooking," say the miners' wives. "Give us one miner before six farmers!" say the grocers.

Such is Tannibar—always bare and grim, bleak and dripping and cold in winter, and in summer an inferno of heat and flies and dust that lies in deep drifts sufficient to smother the unwary cyclist. Its manners are its own—or those of most coal mining towns. So are its morals. Missionaries are not found in its secret places. They find China a safer hunting ground.

And the strike lay heavy on the people.

When the men "went out" first no one looked upon it as a very serious matter. Times had been good for a long while. Shifts were light, and skips easy to fill, and the heaps of tins outside the houses waxed fat and multiplied. The grievance was nothing very much. Some of the more careless of the men hardly bothered to know what it was. There was plenty of money, and the leaders said, "Go out." So they went out, and, much to their amazement, the mine, after a few preliminary throes, went on without them, bringing in men in guarded trains that ran express, with policemen to shepherd the passengers from the station to the pit. It was hampered, certainly; crippled and delayed in its contracts, and the output dropped with a decisive thud. But the main point—the harrowing certainty—was that it went on. Not for a week had its black smoke-drift ceased to trail across the huts on Mount Despair.

From their vantage ground on the hillside the strikers—and their wives—watched the mine unceasingly. There was, in fact, nothing to do but smoke and talk and watch the mine, all of which profitable employments could be prosecuted simultaneously. The new men—the "blacklegs"—knew perfectly well why they watched it. For themselves there were quarters rigged up at the pit mouth, and from that guarded precinct a non-union man strayed at his own risk. That a man is a coward is not necessarily inferred because he hesitates to meet three or four hundred men who are thirsting to make things unpleasant for him. Though the blacklegs affirmed that they were not afraid of the men. "A feller can fight a man," they said. "But—them women!"

There would seem to be a special quality of endurance given to the women of a strike. Nine months now the men had been out, and for six months out of that nine privation had gripped the town cruelly. Strike pay, albeit regularly doled out, does not go far in providing even the necessaries of life. Under its rule some necessaries become luxuries—such as boots, and meat, and winter clothing. They are relegated to the limbo of things forgotten. To one section, even satisfied hunger grows to be a luxury. The men—somehow—are always fed; the children come next, and though they look pinched and sallow the mothers contrive to satisfy them—after a fashion. But the women come last.

Their cheeks fall in, and their hair loses its lustre. Gradually the clothes hand in looser folds and looser on their shrunken bodies, and into their faces creeps the blue, hunted look that cold and hunger give. The "worry lines" deepen round their dark shadowed eyes. Their little vanities go—when one's clothes will no longer hold together, it is not easy to make a brave show. And the miners' women are not good at patching. Walk about Tannibar in a strike time, and you will see many a red elbow and shrunken shoulder peeping through the rags of summer clothing. Here and there you may meet a girl whose bristling fringe of curling pins testifies that she has not altogether forgotten youth's idle hour. But for the most part the women are idle, fierce-looking slatterns, staring down towards the mine with a world of resentment in their heavy-lidded eyes.

Curiously enough, it was the men who sickened of the strike first. Most of them would have returned to work months before the end, seeing plainly enough that there was no prospect of victory for their side, and that each week brought in more non-union men, and lessened their chance of work in the future. But the women fought desperately against the growing inclination for peace, and the men quailed under the lash of their tongues. One only dared to break loose and go back to the mine, and he became, in the women's eyes, a lower thing than a blackleg. He was forced to leave his home and take up his quarters under guard at the pit; his children were afraid to go to school; the women hooted his wife in the streets. Finally they caught him—a band of fifteen women—and when the police rescued him he was in rags, with a broken collar bone, and his nerve gone. It has never been contended that the manners of Tannibar are those of gentler places.

So the months crawled by, sapping strength and courage and hope—all but the dogged obstinacy that the men called "self-respect." It needed only one shadow more to complete the gloom. And it fell—the shadow of Christmas.

It was the children who brought it into the homes—children have such a happy way of ignoring the obvious, and turning back to pleasant old traditions; and most of the children of the Mine had known none but good Christmasses. It came on little Dick Glynn like a thunderclap, as he came through the main street on his way from school, walking slowly, because nowadays he seemed to have no inclination to run. The storekeepers of Tannibar had suffered badly enough, but still they, too, clung to tradition. Winton's window brought Dick up with a jerk.

There stood Santa Claus—a poor enough figure, surely, perhaps eighteen inches high, and rather shabby, seeing that Winton worked him hard each December. But still Santa Claus—his faded coat spangled with what were certainly icicles, and snow bordering the hood that framed his kind old face—and who would ever grumble that he was shabby, at all events in Tannibar? Hc bcnt his benignant gaze on a window full of delights—toys, sweets, gilded balls, and boxes of raisins with almonds marking "XMAS" on their glossy surface. "Seems like pokin' fun at 'em—an' it's downright cruel for the kids," Winton's wife had said as he put them out.

Dick gaped. So long the shadow of the Strike had darkened his little life that he, with the other children, had forgotten that there was such a time as Christmas. When one is seven years old, and hungry—hungry for the "burgoo and spuds" that form strike diet in Tannibar—one does not think of almonds and raisins and other delights. But now he remembered, and with the remembrance came a sudden flash of happiness, more vivid than he had known for months. Christmas was coming—and everything in the world was right at Christmas! He turned from the sorry splendour of the window, and ran, panting, up Mount Despair.

It was Jim Glynn's night to act as picket, and his wife was giving him his tea early. He sat at the kitchen table in silence, eating his bread and treacle slowly, so that it might go further—the ration was not a large one. There was no milk in the thick cup of tea beside him, and the tea itself was a pale shadow; the Glynns had two milch goats, but Jim insisted on their milk being kept for his wife and boy—and did not know that Mrs Glynn's share went to a woman with a month-old baby further up the hill. She sat by the table, patching a little coat of Dick's; Mary Glynn had not been brought up in a mining town, and she clung passionately to the ways of her youth. She was still neat, though her blue cotton frock was threadbare; and Jim's clothes were whole. The Glynns were not popular—they savored too much of the aristocracy, for the People of the Mine.

Dick's little flying figure came in helter-skelter. He rushed up to his father, panting for a moment too much to speak.

"Daddy!" he said—"Daddy!—"

"What on earth are you tearing like that for?" Glynn asked, noting the flush on the thin little face. "What's up sonny?"

Dick found his tongue.

"Daddy—did you know it was Christmas?"

Jim Glynn put his cup down into the saucer with a clatter. He looked at the boy silently. Then, over his head, his eyes met his wife's, and lingered there.

Dick was too full of his news to notice anything in the silence.

"Santa Claus has came!" he said, breathlessly. "He's in Winton's window, Daddy—an' all sorts of things. Everything 'll be all right now, won't it, Daddy? We'll have Christmas dinner, an' stockings, an' things. He'll make it all right, won't he? My word, I'm glad he's came!"

There was silence still, and the boy looked up wondering. And then Mary Glynn suddenly gave a curious little sob, and, getting up quickly, went out of the house.

Her husband put his arm round the boy.

"I wouldn't talk of Christmas this year, old chap, if I was you," he said slowly. "Times aren't too good, you know; an' it hurts mother. She—I'd—like darned well to give you a good Christmas, son. But —"

"But I thought Santa Claus fixed all that up, Dad," Dick said. "Mother always told me he did—an' why would he come if he didn't mean to? I got some stockings yet—I can hang one up, can't I? I bet he'll find it!"

"D'you think this looks much like Christmas?" asked the man, half savagely. He thrust his hand towards the bare squalor of the table.

"N—no," Dick said. " 'Course I know 'bout the strike, Daddy. But Santa Claus doesn't worry his head 'bout strikes, does he? I don't see how he'd have time to. An' if he does——" He grew eager again. "Daddy, I bet if you an' Mother hung up your stockings this time he'd find them 's well 's mine. Mother always said he was an awfully knowing old cove!"

"Good Lord!" said Jim Glynn under his breath. He put the boy aside, and strode out of the kitchen, his hunger gone.

"Mary—what's a man to say?" He faced her miserably, where she stood looking across the trailing smoke below.

"I don't know," she said slowly. "I've been wondering

for weeks. I knew it was bound to come. He believes so, you see—we always made it real to him—and—" Her voice trailed away into silence. "There isn't any hope of a change?"

"Hope! Not a scrap! The men are madder than ever since that last lot of non-union chaps came through. I b'lieve there'll be murder done if they catch one of 'em—there's tar and feathers waiting in three different places."

"Jim—you wouldn't—?"

"No, I'm damned if I go in for any of that sort of game," he said. "I'm too sick of the whole thing—I'd go back tomorrow if I dared sling the others over."

"No, you can't do that," she said. "You've got to stick to the others. There might be a bit o' bush work, Jim."

"There's mighty little of that—an' only tucker to be made at it, anyway. An' the strike pay stops if a fellow's earning wages. It's only the single man as have a chance there," Glynn said. "You'll have to tell the little chap, Mary—can't you fix it up somehow?"

Mary Glynn laughed hardly.

"I do think Santa Claus is a deal more real than God to a kid like Dick," she said. "And you're the sort of chap that 'ud hate me to tell him there wasn't any God. No, I can't—not yet, anyhow. There's three weeks yet, Jim—let's hang on an' see if the luck'll turn."

But there were other children in Tannibar—and other fathers. Larry Murphy's merry face was almost savage when Jim Glynn relieved him on picket duty.

"Seen Winton's windy?" he asked. "Sure, I'd like t'

wring the little man's neck—what's he want with his onreasonable decorations? There's the three kids been prancin' up here at me t' know what sort of a Christmas they'll have. What sort! We know the sort, don't we Jim, man? An' I looked at 'em dumb-like—till I swore—an' they wint away cryin'. The divil take all strikes, I say!" Larry crammed his cap down over his eyes and turned heavily to climb the hill.

There was crying that night in more than one cottage on Mount Despair. It is not easy to contemplate Christmas glories, even as interpreted by Winton, when you are small and hungry; and when thin, unsweetened porridge is all you have to steel you to the contemplation. Crying, too, among the mothers—for the Tannibar women are much the same as other mothers when a matter touches "the kids." Winton suddenly became the most unpopular man in the township, which was somewhat unfair, since he had given credit as long as he dared. And the men began to cast looks of distrust at Benjamin and Forth, who were the leaders of the strike, and to whisper in groups among themselves. Someone said there were queer rumors about the money that was coming in. Benjamin looked uncommonly sleek, in that starved town, and there was a report that Forth's wife, who lived in Melbourne, had bought a piano. "If I thought 'twas true," uttered Larry Murphy, "I'd shpile his music f'r him!"

The days crept by, yet not so slowly now to the men, who would have been glad to put further off that shadow of Christmas. Most of the elder children—they acquire wisdom early in a mining town—had learnt the uselessness of talk or pleading; but the younger ones refused to be comforted, and the fathers and mothers sickened at their chatter, their questions, their entreaties, and, most of all, their certainty that the good time would come.

Polly Hunter was supposed to have the heaviest hand and the sharpest tongue in Tannibar—no mean distinction; but Bill, her husband, found her quietly sobbing over the tattered sock little Bill had carefully pinned to his bed a week before Christmas, with the worst holes tied up with string; whereat Bill swore luridly, and afterwards kissed Polly for the first time for seven months. And Mary Glynn, looking for her man one day, discovered him whittling with a broken knife at a bit of flawed lightwood, out of which he was endeavoring to make something resembling a horse. "I thought it'd be better'n nothing," he said, jerking his head towards the corner where little Dick lay.

For little Dick Glynn was sick. Not worse at first than many another child who had sickened as a result of the wretched food and insufficient clothing through the hard winter. There had been many sick children in Tannibar, and not a few mounds in the cemetery behind the hill. Mary had not troubled over much about Dick—at first; he was a happy-souled youngster, and would generally fight down quickly any childish ailment. But this time he did not come round as usual. It seemed to his mother that he did not care to fight. He would lie quite still all day, seldom speaking, though always good tempered, turning away listlessly from food, though she racked her ingenuity to tempt him to eat. He was tired, he said, and his head ached—that was all. But Mary Glynn, watching him with the fear that grips so easily at the mother who has but one child, grew silent and haggard, and Jim would look at her with troubled eyes, fearing to shape his anxiety into words. Old Mrs McLeish, who was popularly supposed to know more than three doctors, was less constrained.

"The bairn's no' richt," she said. "Happen he'll slip away on ye, Mrs Glynn, ma wumman, if ye're no' careful. A doctor? Hoots! What'll the puir body tell ye? Feed him up, he'll say—an' it's easy to say that. Aweel!" She paused expressively, and then waddled away, leaving Mary Glynn trembling and speechless. Jim, coming in later, found her kneeling by the bed, her head buried in the coverlet beside her boy.

Dick was asleep, with a smile playing on his lips. He muttered occasionally, and his father leant to catch the broken words—"Santa Claus." Glynn straightened with a jerk, and turned away.

It was the weekly meeting of the men two nights before Christmas, and dusk found them stringing slowly down the tracks of Mount Despair. There was something new on their faces—a weariness, a hopelessness, that the sufferings of nine months had failed to trace, had made deep marks in the last few weeks. They muttered among themselves in twos and threes, though no one dared openly to voice the growing unrest.

Benjamin and Forth, quite alive to the spirit lurking in their followers, moved here and there among the men crowding into the dimly lit room. They were shrewd men, with a certain lofty contempt, well concealed, for the miners. They were nearly all so many children in the leaders' eyes, easily swayed by a little windy eloquence. Personally they found the game a good one—a far easier and better living than labor at the skips they once had helped to fill. It would not do to allow the men to think for themselves. They dropped pieces of information like oil on the troubled waters.

"McLeod's weakening," Benjamin said. "Heard today from town—he's about full up. A week or two more, an' he'll be asking our terms."

McLeod was the principal mine owner, a dour man, popularly credited with a cast iron will. This was good news, if true.

"How j' know?" growled a big Cornishman.

"Got a letter today," said Benjamin, easily. He tapped his breast pocket. "Read it to you presently."

He mounted a kerosene case and read it presently. It was quite a good letter—it had cost him and Forth some hours of laborious composition, but it seemed by no means labor lost. The men received its cheering prognostications with murmurs of satisfaction. If McLeod weakened they might indeed hope. Benjamin came down from the kerosene case with a satisfied smile.

There rose a murmur near the door, and Jim Glynn came quickly up the room, threading his way roughly and without apology through the throng. He sprang up on the box and looked round at the upturned faces of the men, clearing his throat once or twice. There was a mutter of surprise—a silent man, he had never been known to speak at the meetings.

"Didn't think he'd be here," a man whispered—"their kid's nearly gone, poor little chap."

"Wh—what I want to know," Glynn said, stammering in his nervous energy—"What I reckon every one of us want to know, is, what's the good of it all? If McLeod is weakenin'—an' I guess we want more proof o' that, knowin' McLeod—even if he is, how long's it goin' on? Ain't we weakening too? Ain't we starved and sick an' wretched—clothes in rags an' spirits gone? An' what's the damn good of it all?"

There was a murmur of grim assent. It seemed to roll round the room.

Benjamin's squeaky voice rose in protest. He elbowed his way through the men until he reached Glynn's side.

"Come down, you fool," hc said.

"No, I won't come down," Glynn answered. "We've danced to your pipin' these nine months, an' what's it done for us? You—you're fat and well dressed. Forth's all right—so's his missus. But what about our women—an' our kids?"

The last words broke from him almost as a cry.

"There's half of us don't know much about it," Glynn went on; "three parts never wanted to go out. But we went out—an' look at us now! I never asked no man's help in my life—nor I never had no cause to grumble. I'm not the only one as could clear his five-an'-twenty bob in a shift many a time. It's you, an' men like you, as done it all—you blokes as never worked—never had no heart or muscle to work." He laughed savagely. "I ain't got much muscle either—now." He held out his great arm, the shirt sleeve falling loosely round it. "It's gone in this blasted nine months I've been a gentleman!"

Benjamin and Forth were on either side of him now, trying to pull him down. It was a bad move. There was a growl among the men.

"Leave him alonc!"

"Leave me alone, or I'll break your neck, Joe Forth!" said Glynn, stiffening. "I'll speak now I'm here, if I never do again. I don't care if I'm killed for it. I want to go back! I'm sick for work—men like us aren't built to loaf! Say we got all we've asked for—say we got it tomorrow—would it ever pay us back for these nine months? Y'know it wouldn't, don't you, boys? D'you think there's one man among us as is going to forget what his missus come to look like—or how his kids cried to him? His kids——"

Something choked his utterance. And, knowing what his cottage held, they could not meet his haggard eyes.

"My kid's cried to me these three weeks for Christmas," the hard voice went on. "Christmas—an' we've burgoo and spuds to give 'em, an' little o' that. An' my kid's dyin'—just as yours died, Andy Walker; an' your boy, Gowan; an' your little baby, Jack West—'cause we'd little damn grievances, an' we went out. I guess a man knows what's a grievance when his kid—when his kid's dead."

The hard voice broke and ceased. He stood, staring blindly at the men, and a low, ominous growl ran round the room—a sullen assent to the rough words that voiced every man's secret heart. Then came a new voice.

"Let me up there, lad."

They looked at the newcomer stupidly, scarcely believing their eyes. Benjamin's shrill voice came first.

"McLeod! Hold him!"

"Ay, it's McLeod. And you've no need to hold him—he's an old man," the mine owner said calmly. "They told me I was chucking away my life to come, boys, but I reckoned I knew you better. Will someone keep that little

Jew chap quiet? And let me speak."

"Go on!" It was a shout from every throat.

"I was a pit hand once, as you know," the old man said, speaking slowly. "I've worked and sweated—yes, and I've struck. And much good that ever did me. And my wife worked with me, and—there were kids. I guess I've known the meaning of these months. And I thought if I came and spoke a fair word to you we might fix things so as not to spoil the kiddies' Christmas."

"Go on!"

"I'm not going to crawl to you, boys," McLeod said. "The mine's there. I'll give work to every man—save those two curs that have fattened on you—who'll go back. And we'll talk over the grievances fair and square once you're working. And—it's my own risk, and no bribe—I'll fix an advance of so much credit at the stores for every man who gives me his word tonight he'll start work the day after Christmas! Is it a bargain?"

"There's my hand on it," said Jim Glynn.

There was an uproar then—men talking roughly, crowding round the old man, shaking his hand—and one or two that sobbed weakly. Behind it Forth and Benjamin slunk away. Above the excited crowd old Andrew McLeod beamed happily.

"We'll make a mighty Christmas of it, boys," he said.

* * *

But Jim Glynn, slipping from the room, made his way with slow steps up Mount Despair. There was little room in his heart for gladness—relief from the tension of the weary months was swallowed in the realisation of what lay before him. The strike had ended too late for him and Mary. Their sacrifice already lay upon its altar.

At the door of his hut he stopped, listening, in physical fear of going in. It came to him that he could not face it. Throughout the evening he had carried with him the vision of Dick's still white face as he had left it—so like death itself that the final struggle could not have made it very different. But to see it—to know the boy was gone —! He leaned against the door post, shaking.

"Jim!"

The door was open. Mary's hand was on his sleeve.

"Don't," he said; "don't lass. He's—he's —." The words died in his throat.

Mary caught at his hand.

"Oh, don't look like that!" she cried. "He's better—truly he's better, Jim. An' Mr. McLeod's been here—only he told me not to tell you—with brandy for him, an' soup. Soup, Jim, lad! An' the strike—."

"The strike is over," Glynn said, stupidly. "Then he isn't dead?"

"Look; he wants you!" She dragged him in.

A pale little shadow of Dick smiled up at him—but there was life in the blue eyes.

"Santa Claus has come, daddy," he whispered. "Tole y' he would. It's all right now, isn't it?"

Glynn was on his knees, one arm out-flung across the bed.

"It's—all right, son," he whispered.

A NEW YEAR'S DAWN

CHAPTER I

It was Christmas time at Barindah—Christmas time, but by no means Christmas weather—not the still, burning days that one instinctively associates with an Australian Yule, but bleak, wintry weather, with piercing winds and biting rain storms, that drove the cattle across the paddock to the furthest limits of the fences and back waters. Summer had never really come, at the close of that year, in the early seventies. Old John Woodward, casting weatherwise glances at the distant mountain tops, said there was snow yet on Mount Misery, and predicted a lively flood on the ever lively Wangong River when eventually it should come down, dislodged from its winter resting place by one of the sudden storms. "A mighty good thing the drays are home," he added, thinking of the heavily laden bullock wagons that had returned with their six months' supplies but ten days before. The half yearly journey was long and hard enough in any case, without the added danger and discomfort of flood and tempest.

Within Barindah Homestead on Christmas night was mirth and light, and warmth enough to banish all thought of the bleak winter out of doors. Even the ceaseless howling of the wind was lost in the big dining room, where huge logs blazed and spluttered in the great open fireplace, which, unlike your poverty-stricken modern grates, stretched its welcoming width right across one end of the room. Rain was falling in torrents, but the sound did not echo from the bark roof or the homely walls of wattle and daub—bush architecture, but none the less comfortable and secure. And even had the spirit of the storm been more intrusive, it is doubtful if he could have prevailed against the spirit of laughter that held sway within.

It was a large party that had gathered around those roaring red gum logs. The Woodwards themselves were no inconsiderable contingent, from the white-haired father and mother to small boy Dick—the baby and the pet of his swarm of big brothers and sisters. There was the eldest girl, Lizzie, who had married Tom Haviland, and had brought him with her to celebrate Christmas in the old home—which, perforce, necessitated bringing Tom's brother, Harry, newly arrived from England; and frankly ignorant of the ways of the bush, but willing to learn, especially, from such a teacher as pretty Nell Woodward. Nowise backward as a teacher was Nell, and the lessons progressed apace. There was another Englishman, a colonial-experience man, named Farquhar, who had been touring Australia for over a year, making Barindah his headquarters; and with him Miles Vernon, a squatter from Queensland; and in the heart of the merriment was long Lynn Mason, the engineer, who, being engaged to Mary Woodward, the second daughter, had ridden a hundred and fifty miles to spend Christmas week with his betrothed. Then there were the Truscotts, a newly-married pair from a neighboring station—that is to say, one thirty-five miles away; and a merry trio of maidens from Sydney, old schoolmates of the Barindah girls. And, considering that they all talked at once, and most of them laughed in addition, it is not wonderful that the wind's howling fell on deaf ears and the rain slid unheeded from the bark roof.

They had played all the Christmas games and cracked

all the time-honored Christmas jokes, which in such a gathering are as much a matter of course as the Christmas dinner. Then there came a lull, during which the host was called upon for a yarn, and spun them a tale of old Monaro days that kept them quiet as price, and led somehow to his wife's slipping her hand into his, and forgetting to take it away. After that there was a general outcry for a song, and some of the girls sang. Songs by 'Claribel'—quaint ballads with generally a laugh or a tear in them, this being before the enlightened days of comic opera and coster ditties. Then Farquhar gave them a little French song, which fell somewhat flat, and was nervously pronounced "very pretty" by the girls; but everyone was relieved when Tom Haviland struck up *Wrap me up in my Tarpaulin Jacket*, and trolled it forth in a lusty baritone. They all joined in the chorus, even to quiet Mary, who was playing the accompaniment, with Lynn Mason's hand on the back of her chair The long notes rang out wistfully—

> And say a poor buffer lies low—lies low.

"I don't like that—it's not a Christmas song," Nell said, with a petulant shrug of her pretty shoulders.

"What's wrong with it, Miss Nell?" Harry Haviland spoke.

"Oh, I don't know—it's too true, I think," the girl said. "It might be any one of our own boys."

"Australia's full of poor buffers like that," Mr Woodward said, half sternly. "They're everywhere—on the wallaby track, in the shearing sheds, anywhere—all of them working towards the last place of all—the bush shanty. I can't say I like hearing you sing about the 'six brandies and sodas,' myself; it's a good deal too near real life. How those dogs bark!"

"'Possums," Farquhar said laconically.

"I don't know," Lyn Mason put in; "they've been at it a good while. Might be dingoes; but I fancied I heard a horse whinnying just now, not far off."

"Can anyone be there, John?" Mrs Woodward asked anxiously.

"Not likely, mother; who should it be?"

"Well, you never can tell," his wife answered. "Travellers come from here, there and everywhere to Barindah. Besides, I've had a queer feeling all day that Gerald isn't far off." She spoke almost shamefacedly.

"Gerald! Why, old wife, didn't he write specially, saying he couldn't possibly leave Melbourne? I wish he could, indeed, poor lad; it's against the grain to think of him moping through Christmas by himself in that unhomelike place."

"I don't think he'll mope over much," Farquhar put in. "Gerald's a fellow with many friends, and he's not likely to be left to himself."

"Perhaps not," his host said; "still, I don't know that I altogether care for Mr Gerald's friends. Might be better for him to be on his own. Still, wherever he is I'll bet he's not within cooee of Barindah!"

"Listen!" Lynn said quickly; "there's old Lassie barking, and she never barks for a false alarm, does she? I think I'll take a stroll round, Mr Woodward, and see if there's anything about. The dogs wouldn't bark so persistently for nothing. Come on, Jim!" to the eldest of the Woodward boys, and putting on their overcoats the two sallied forth into thc rain.

Mrs Woodward sighed somewhat anxiously. Not many knew how near to her heart was the handsome scapegrace nephew—her dead sister's only child. He had been her first care, before ever any of her own babies had come to share the love she had lavished on him for his mother's sake first, and then for his own. There was that, in him that made her specially tender to him—a lack of stability, of steadfastness, the more conspicuous by association with her own sons, all like their father, unswerving of purpose, and incapable of anything but straight going. Gerald Carr had always been something of an anxiety. Too easy-going to resist temptation, he had made several slight lapses from the straight path, until at length his uncle had been glad to send him to Melbourne to enter the office of a big shipping firm. There young Carr seemed at last to have found his niche, for nearly a year had gone by without any complaint of him reaching far away Barindah. But in his aunt's heart there was always a fear and a longing—such a feeling as many mothers know—how well!

Lynn and his companion pulled their hats down over their eyes as they splashed their way down the slippery path to the front gate. It was very dark, and the stinging, wintry rain cut like a knife. The air was full of the sound of the dogs' outcry, each, to the smallest terrier, doing his best to drown the roar of the gale.

"Quiet, you brutes!" Lynn shouted, and flung a stone among them. There was a yelp, and silence for a moment, then the barking broke out again more fiercely than ever.

"I'll swear there's someone there!" Lynn muttered

"that's no 'possum or dingo. What's that at the gate? By Jove, Jim, it's a horse—and saddled!"

They ran to the gate and flung it open. There, indeed, was a horse, utterly knocked up, with drooping head and quivering nostrils, too weary to move from the hand laid on its bridle. But the rider?

"He's been slung, somewhere," Jim Woodward said; "can't be far off, the horse wouldn't have come any distance in this state. Let's coo-ee!" and a long shout rung out from him, and his companion. For a moment there came no answering signal, then a faint sound came feebly to their ears.

Lynn was the first to trace it to its source. A few hundred yards away a man lay, half hidden in the long wet grass; a man whom the effort of shouting had taken the last remnant of strength. Lynn knelt beside him, and struck a match, sheltering the tiny flame for a moment with his hand.

"Good God, it's Gerald!" he said, "Gerald! and hurt!"

Between them they raised the unconscious form and bore it to the homestead, where the cheery light through the open door of the hall showed Mrs Woodward standing on the threshold. She started pitifully at the sight of their burden, but in a moment commanded herself, and was the quiet, resourceful mother, giving low words of advice and gentle orders to one and another that presently had all her helpers busy at their different tasks—preparing a bed, getting hot bottles, warm flannels, stimulants—all that was necessary. Very gently the bearers laid the still form down on the big sofa in the dining room.

"He's not very much hurt," Lynn said, a quarter of

an hour later, going out to the little anxious group which had been banished, perforce, to the kitchen. "His ankle's broken, and there's a nasty wound on his head—looks like a kick. Mr Woodward says he should be pretty right in a few days, barring the ankle. I'm going to sit up with him—he's inclined to be a little off his head."

Through the long night Gerald Carr tossed uneasily in the merciful unconsciousness of delirium. Lynn sitting beside him with a grave face that grew ever graver and sterner, heard, bit by bit, a story that sent blood ebbing from his heart—a story of shame, and disgrace and flight. "Money, money, money!" moaned the hard, senseless voice, it was the one note that never varied throughout the incoherent jumble from which the listener could scarcely piece out a connected tale. But what he heard was enough. "Money, money!" and then a pitiful cry, "I'll put it back!"

The night was waning when a soft footfall made Lynn turn his head. Mrs Woodward was beside the bed; and at sight of her Lynn sprang up and tried to lead her away anything rather than that she should hear those miserable ravings. But one look at her set face stayed him.

"It doesn't matter," she said. "I have heard enough. I came in some time ago."

She sat down by the pillow and looked long at the weak, handsome face. Gerald was quieter; delirium was giving place to the heavy slumber succeeding fever and utter exhaustion. Now and then he started up with a hoarse cry—always a cry for mercy; but gradually all movement ceased, and he lay inert, his heavy breathing the only sound in the quiet room. From the foot of the bed Lynn watched the anguish deepen on the face of the woman sitting motionless by the still form until at length he could no longer bear the silent strain. The atmosphere of the room seemed to be choking him. He turned on his heel and went out into the grey twilight of the dawn.

For two days Gerald lay in that heavy stupor—never wholly conscious, but mercifully free from delirium. At length, there came an evening when he opened his eyes and asked a feeble question. He struggled obediently to take the nourishment tenderly forced upon him, and immediately sank into a refreshing sleep, that lasted until the sun was high next morning. Then he awoke to complete consciousness, and, with the return of memory, to haggard misery.

Bit by bit the wretched story came out—the old miserable tale of youth's temptation and fall. Betting had brought him to grief; he had run through his own money, and then it had been so fatally easy to take—only as a loan—some of that which passed through his hands daily. Of course it had not been repaid; one 'certainty' after another had failed him. And then came the chance of using a large sum the unexpected tip that seemed such a sure thing for the Cup. It, too, had been beaten; and then had come—discovery.

"They weren't bad to me," he said, wearily. "They gave me a month to pay it back—for Uncle's sake. I tried, too—God knows I tried. But what chance had I? Five hundred! It might as well have been fifty thousand!"

"Why did you not come to us, dear?" Mrs Woodward asked gently.

The boy's face hardened.

"No," he said, shortly. "I'm low enough, but that I

couldn't do. I know Uncle's been hard hit by the drought, and I'd die before I asked him for money—for that. So when the month was nearly up I felt I must see you all again, and I started up here. I reckoned I'd just be with you for a few days, and then—finish things."

Mrs Woodward shivered. "Don't!" she said, sharply; and then she turned to her husband with a long, beseeching look. John Woodward shook his head.

"I'm like Gerald," he said, curtly. "I might as well try to raise fifty thousand as five hundred. You know what my overdraft is now, old wife. If I'd had time——" He turned to Gerald. "When's your month up, lad?" he asked.

"On the thirtieth of December. They said if the money was paid in by 9 o'clock that morning——"

"That settles it," Mr Woodward said; "I can do nothing."

"My money's all locked up—what there is of it," Lynn Mason said ruefully. "If only I had known——"

"Oh, what's the good of talking about it?" The sick lad moved impatiently. "I know you can't help me, any of you. I wouldn't take your help if you could. There are a few days yet before the warrant's out for me. I may as well have them in peace, and then—well, I won't go to gaol. I'll kill myself first!"

"Don't talk like a cur!" Lynn said, with a movement of disgust. "Surely there's a way out—if—"

"Can I help?" Gavin Farquhar had come in quietly.

"I couldn't help hearing that something was wrong," he said, half apologetically. "I don't know what it is—and I don't want to. But if money's any good—well let me take a hand!"

There was silence. Farquhar turned to Gerald's tell-tale face.

"How much is it, old man?" he asked, curtly.

"Five hundred—oh, but I can't——"

"That's all right. You're not strong enough to talk. Will my cheque do now?"

The sudden hope that had flashed into the boy's weary eyes died out as quickly as it had come. "I forgot," he said, dully. "It's no good, Farquhar, thanks. The money's got to be in Wangong on the morning of the thirtieth. It's no good."

"What's today—the twenty-eighth! Oh, by Jove!" Farquhar's face fell.

There was dead silence in the room for a moment; each set face dumb with the stress of great anxiety. Then Lynn Mason spoke slowly, as a man speaks who says no light thing.

"If that is all," he said—"if it will make things right to lodge Farquhar's cheque in Wangong the day after tomorrow—well, I'll undertake to get it there!"

Hope sprang once more into Gerald's eyes. John Woodward shook his head.

"You couldn't do it, lad," he said; "it's useless to try. Today's more than half gone—there's only tomorrow; and the roads are awful. It's not possible."

"I can do it," Lynn said quietly. He was not looking at the old man. All he saw was a girl's white face, where fear and hope struggled against each other.

"Oh, if you'd try, old man!" The words broke despairingly from the sick boy.

Lynn gave his long form a sudden shake, as one who shakes off doubt and irresolution. "Try—why, of course!" he said, cheerfully. "I'll do more than try—I'll do it." His eyes sought his sweetheart's wistfully. "You might come and help me run the horses up, Mary," he said; "I'll get away as soon as I can."

They were very quiet as they drove the horses up to the yard—these two who had not seen each other for so many long months—whose little season of joy was so rudely cut short. The girl had said not a word except to encourage him; but there was that in her eyes that made Lynn Mason in his heart curse with whole-souled vigour all hare-brained boys and careless employers.

"I'll come back, of course, dear," he said. He had sent the sliprails home behind the horses and they were walking up to the house while Tambo, the young station-hand, caught and groomed his mount. "It won't be for long, but I reckon in the circumstances I can take a day or two. And it's worth it—isn't it?"

"To me; but Lynn, it's too much for you," she said. "I can't let you knock yourself up for my sake. You should, rest, once you get down to Wangong."

"Should I?" He laughed lightly. "You can expect me back in time to wish you a happy New Year, my girl. And don't go worrying—there's nothing for you to trouble about. I won't be long away; there's only one inducement more pressing than to get down in time with the money, and that's to get back to you. We won't have all our time spoilt!"

Then there was saddling in haste, hurried preparations and farewells mostly omitted; and in a very little time Lynn was ready for the road.

Mrs Woodward put her hands on his shoulders. "My boy, my dear boy, I know what this means to you," she said brokenly. "How can I say what I feel?"

"Bless you, mother, don't try!" Lynn said cheerfully. "It always upsets you to say what you feel. Don't worry about me, I'm all right. Now then, you women, get out of my way, and find something useful to do!" He pushed Lizzie gently into a verandah lounge, and piled Nell and Amy casually on top of her. "Too many of you to kiss," he said, looking at the heap. "Good-bye all. You can let me out of the sliprails, Mary." He put his arm through his bridle, thanking Tambo with a friendly pat, and they went down the path together.

Lynn was wise in his generation, and his leave taking was short. "Don't be downhearted, dearest," he said; "look after Gerald and keep busy, and be sure I'll be back before New Year's day." Then he was gone, only pausing at the first bend in the track to wave a cheery farewell to the slender, motionless figure by the sliprails.

CHAPTER II

Lynn Mason made the best use possible of the daylight hours that remained to him after leaving Barindah homestead. The outlook was scarcely inviting. He had rather less than a day and a half to accomplish a journey which generally took three full days, and all the conditions of travel were against him—the weather bad, the bush tracks seas of mud and frequently barred by trees that the recent gales had brought down. Lynn, however, would not allow himself to feel doubtful. He knew that he: could obtain relays of horses on the way, and that in itself was a tremendous advantage; also, the country was all familiar to him—he had worked over it, and knew both the tracks and the people of the district through which he had to pass. If help were needed he could depend on getting it—though perhaps after delay. For Lynn, like many another Irishman, had "a way wid him," and his kindly heart and cheery tongue generally made him remembered, as well as he was liked, in the districts where his profession led him.

There was a somewhat unpleasant idea in Lynn's mind that the Wangong River would be in flood, and accordingly he pushed his horse over the miles that lay between Barindah and the ford. Never a very safe river was the same Wangong—turbulent and stormy, broken by rapids, liable to sudden floods and cold as are all rivers fed by the icy mountain streams. In after days the representations of the Woodwards and other settlers led a tardy Government, to establish a punt on the river, but at that time the only means of crossing was by the ford, which, except in the height, of summer, when the river was low, was by no means safe. Many a time had cattle been lost in bringing them across, and once, when crossing a rowdy mob of steers, Mr Woodward had seen his favorite stockman swept away and drowned before his eyes, while he was powerless to help him. Lynn had no thought of fear for himself; but he recognised the certain delay if the river were 'up'. It was with very distinct relief that he saw, on sighting it at last, that though it was fairly high the crossing could be made without much difficulty.

Once over the river, Lynn gave the chestnut mare her head, and, as far as the roads—or what passed as roads—would allow him, made the pace a good one, until the hills compelled him to slow down. A big range confronted him, impassable in most directions—his track lay directly across a frowning hill known—and known adversely to most travellers—as Mount Misery. Many a weary journey had Lynn made across that bleak, scrub-grown hill, where the winter snows lay until long after summer had brought warmth and growth to the valleys and plains. He recalled with a shiver one bitter night when, worn out with illness, he had lost himself on a snow-clad spur of the hill, wandering aimlessly until hope of getting out had almost left him. His horse had saved him on that occasion, but it was a near thing. Many a time he had camped alone on the bleak slopes; so steep they were that the majority of the few women who journeyed that way made the ascent by 'hanging on' to their horse's tail. For a woman it was reckoned a day's journey across Mount Misery, and a hard day at that.

Lynn pushed quickly through the foothills, knowing that when the real ascent came it must necessarily be very slow. He had hoped, rather against his conviction, that he might cross the mountain before night, but soon he realised the futility of the hope. Night came down before he reached the summit, and though he struggled on until he was at the top, even his daring did not carry him to the length of foolhardiness required to attempt the descent in the darkness. Besides, the mare was blown, and needed all the spell he could give her. He unsaddled and tied her up, afraid to let her go, lest, even with the hobbles on, she should stray down the hillside. He had taken the precaution, however, to bring a feed for her, and she was enjoying it before he had succeeded in the darkness in collecting enough wood for a fire.

He boiled the billy, and revelled luxuriously in the warmth of the fire and the milkless tea. It was not long before he had finished his meal, and then, wrapping himself in his blankets, he lay down. He could not sleep, however. A vague uneasiness, a very real fear lest he should not be in time, kept his nerves strained too much to relax. Every sound of the dense bush around him made him start a little; faint rustlings in the undergrowth, the sudden crash made by a wallaby, the far-off cry of a curlew—all the bush signs that custom had made so familiar that it was amazing to him to find himself noting them. Overhead the moon peeped out feebly now and then amongst black, sailing clouds, racing across a dim sky. One faint star twinkled at him—in a friendly way, it seemed. He wondered, dreamingly, if it was looking down at Barindah, too—at the warmth and light and life that he had left behind him in the quiet plains. The thought brought a waking dream of Mary, and, unconsciously soothed, he fell asleep.

Before dawn he was up, not waiting to boil the billy, for he knew he could breakfast at Gidgee, a tiny hamlet where his second horse awaited him. To kindle his fire now would take too much. The mare looked fit and well, showing no signs of the hard journey of the previous day. Lynn felt more light-hearted as he mounted her, and commenced the descent.

Through hazel thickets, dense with musk and tangled with a hundred creepers, he pushed his way. The heavy dew of the night burdened every leaf and bough, falling in showers as the passage of horse and rider shook the scrub. Long trails of wet convolvulus and clematis brushed his face, leaving in his nostrils their faint, sweet scents, half lost amidst the sharper, acrid odors of the bush. The sarsaparilla flung a purple glow across his path, where dainty orchids nestled, almost hidden in the heavy undergrowth that knew no disturbing human touch. There were birds all round him, yet seldom did he catch sight of them; only faint rustlings, twittering notes, now and then the clearer whistle of a lyrebird, told of the life about him. The sounds fitted into the dim twilight with no disturbing influence; they could not break the hush of the bush dawn.

Underfoot the going was treacherous, stone boulders, half concealed in the grass, gave scanty foothold. The chestnut mare stepped daintily, planting her feet with caution, now and then gathering her legs under her as a sudden slip carried them several feet down the steep descent. Once or twice a hole, its mouth concealed by bracken, nearly brought them to grief, but the mare was active as a cat, and the steady hand on her bridle never slackened; the watchful eye of the rider never relaxed its vigilance. But the way was hard, wearing alike to horse and man, and it was with a long sigh of relief that Lynn found himself at length in the plain below.

Thence he pushed, on rapidly. It was many miles yet to Gidgee, and the mare covered them in good style. The track was rough enough, most of the way through scrub only less dense than that they had left. Lynn did not spare her any more than himself, and they were both weary when at length the scattered township roofs seemed to spring out of the scrub, as a sudden turn brought them into view. The landlady of the little shanty ran out at the sound of hoofs.

“Saints above, it’s Mr Mason—gerrls, do be lookin’ now!” she cried. “An’ what is it that’s bringin’ ye back so soon? Not a shplit wid Miss Mary, thin, surely?"

Lynn laughed as he swung himself to the ground.

"Not much, Mrs O'Shea. Only business, and I'm in the very deuce of a hurry. Can you give me something to eat while Patsy catches my horse?"

"Is it Patsy, thin?" demanded his mother. "Sure Patsy's gone to Wangong, Christmasing, to a dance—dance is it, an' me an' the girrls here alone. Sure I'd break his legs from undher him if I cud only lay me hands on him! But don't you fret—Biddy'll run the little horse up, an' be thankful. Biddy, thin!" and a shrill scream induced the appearance of a lanky girl of fifteen, whose lean, bare legs made surprising time across the paddock, at the further side of which Lynn's fresh horse could be seen grazing.

"Come in, dear," the landlady went on, leading the way into the bar parlor, while another of Mrs O'Shea's 'gerrls' took the saddle off the chestnut mare, and led her to the rickety stable. "Sit ye down, an' the best the house has is yer own, an' ye know it. Sure there's no one hereabouts as has that selfsame twinklin' eye of yours. It's aisy seen ye was raised in green Ireland!" She flung a cloth on the table as she spoke, following it up with sundry comestibles, at which the eyes of poor, hungry Lynn gleamed. "There's a good pickin' on the turkey yit, poor bird. Biddy's he was, an' she rose him from a chick, an' he weighed two-an'-twinty pounds, no less, widout his feathers. It fair broke the heart of her to hear his dyin' squawk—it was on'y the wishbone pulled her round. Ah, Mr Mason, it's that gerrl has the feelin' heart! An' the 'am—if ye'd known that pig ye'd have known what a pig was!" Mrs O'Shea always became most oracular when most moved. "Sure he was like one of us; he loved us that much it seemed on'y fittin' he should have Christmas along wid us!" Lynn, cutting generous slices, fully agreed with the conclusion, if not the reasoning. "The puddin's done—Patsy's death on puddin'—but there's a poy here as Norah made, wid gooseb'ries; thry it now, Mr Mason, dear—" and only a quick movement on her guest's part saved his turkey from a plentiful deluge of pie. "What! ye won't! well, prisintly, thin. Norah, gerrl, is that tay wather iver goin' to boil? It's fair ashamed I am, Mr Mason, to keep ye so long waitin' on' yer tay!"

Lynn laughed.

"Sit down and take things easy, Mrs O'Shea," he said. "Any news in your part of the world?"

"No—leastways old Mick Mornane's dead, rest his sowl. Boxin' day he died, and we've woke him these two nights."

"Two nights?" Lynn said; "isn't that unusual?"

"Well, p'raps. Ye see, 'twas this way—the wake was the night before last, and Father Nolan was to come up to bury him yesterday. But the roads is bad, and p'raps the father wint to the races at Wangong an' couldn't get back, an' anyhow he didn't turn up till this mornin'. So, seein' last night that the corpse was still there, an' the whisky not run out, an' nothin' else on to amuse the bhoys, we reckoned we might as well have another night—'twas a pity to waste it!"

"I see," Lynn said, attacking the pie. "And is the funeral to-day?"

"It is, thin. A good show 'twill be, too—iveryone from

these parts will be goin'. Jim Daly's goin' to drive me an his mother, an' I tell ye, Mr Mason, I'm that stuffy, wid the two nights of it that I'll be thankful for the jaunt. Ye couldn't stay for it I suppose?"

"Thanks—I'm afraid not," Lynn said, regretfully. "Can I have some more tea? Thanks. No, I'm in too much of a hurry, though I'm sorry to miss it."

"Now, I'm rale sorry," said Mrs O'Shea, sympathetically. "We could aisy have squeezed ye in—Mrs Daly's not that fat. I mind the time whin I wint to ould Gran Clancy's buryin', sittin' all the way on Terry O'Brien's knee. Thim was good days!"

"They must have been," Lynn answered with conviction. "I'd almost stay for the funeral to-day if you'd promise to sit on my knee, Mrs O'Shea!" Whereat that highly flattered dame bridled, and said delightedly, "Go along wid the soft tongue of ye, now do!" while she aimed a destructive blow at him with her apron.

"Well, I must be off," Lynn said, rising, amid protests from the family that he'd never call that a meal, sure. Mrs O'Shea added a warning terrific in its solemnity.

"'Twould take the inside of a ostrich to stand boltin' good food like that," she said. "Sure, the overcoats of the stummick won't stand it. I mind the time whin my first husband died just through that. 'Twas peritis of the lungs, it was, an' him as fine a man as iver I saw. O'Shea wasn't a patch on him !"

"Was that Terry O'Brien?" Lynn asked.

"Terry O'Brien!" said his hostess, with a blank stare; "no, why shud it be? There was niver more than unrequoited friendship bechune me an' Terry O'Brien. No; 'twas Billy Rourke, honest man—me second he was, an', take him all round, the best of the batch. A foine, upstandin' man, save an' except for the whisky. Ah, well, it's a quare world!"

Lynn gasped.

"I thought you said he was your first?"

"Did I? Well, perhaps he was!" said the dame, tranquilly. "Wan gits mixed at times, an' there's no relyin' on me memory since I was a widdy. Well, if ye must go, good-bye, an' good luck to ye, Mr Mason, an' be sure ye pay us a longer call nixt time. We'll look afther the little yeller mare for ye. Biddy won't be sparin' the brush on her. Good-bye!" And with the hearty farewells of the whole family in his ears Lynn found himself riding down the track.

The horse was very fresh, and, the track being (for a wonder) good, Lynn struck into a hand gallop, which soon left Gidgee far behind him. Such a pace, however, could not last long, and he was forced to slacken speed when the road again became a mere bush path, overhung with a mass of creepers. There was no fast going then—often, indeed, he had to make a detour to avoid some insurmountable obstacle or a belt of scrub too dense to force a passage through without delay that might be fatal to his plans. There was a better track than the one he pursued. He had chosen this one because it saved a few miles, but there were times when he doubted the wisdom of his choice. At length, after hours of toilsome progress, he came out into the open plains again.

Mile after mile he left behind him at a steady pace.

The horse was good, as 'game' and plucky as its rider, and answered every call he made upon it. Mile after mile—till his brain reeled with the dizzy monotony of it all. He knew every yard of the way—how happily he had ridden over it on his way to his sweetheart only a week before!—and there were often times when he was able to save a mile by wary short cuts—wary, for in the bush the short cut is often the longest way round. And yet how slowly he seemed to be going on! Fear was upon him; would he be in time?

Night fell and found him still riding hard. His horse was tiring rapidly; he himself was so weary that he could scarcely keep upright in the saddle. The dense bush was nearly ended now; but with the advent of darkness he was forced to slow down into a walk. It seemed to him, wearied out, that the scrub had never been so lonely, so full of strange weird noises. The moon rose, pale and watery, casting dim, mysterious shadows about him. Was that a face peering at him from the shadow of a clump of dogwood? No, it was only a sapling, its trunk white where the bark had fallen. He laughed at himself for his fancy, scarcely realising that weariness and anxiety had weakened even his strong nerves.

At last the scrub ended, and he came out upon the clearer plains that told of civilisation at last. He urged his tired horse into a canter, for there, not four miles away, were the twinkling lights of Longfield, the last stage of his journey. Once there he knew he need not fear, for but fourteen miles lay between Longfield and Wangong, and, by starting early in the morning, on a fresh horse, that fourteen miles could easily he covered before 9 o'clock. The sudden realisation came to him that he had won his race—and with the knowledge came quick reaction—once the urgent need was gone the power to answer it seemed to leave him, too. He swayed in his saddle, but recalled himself quickly.

"Hang it!" he said aloud. "Hold up, Lynn—you're only half through!"

The sound of his own voice seemed to steady him. But afterwards he admitted that no part of all that weary journey was as long as that four miles that lay before Longfield.

Lights gleamed from the shanty as he rode up, and the tuneful notes of an accordion issued from the open door. There was a sound of many feet, a great noise of voices and laughter of a heartier kind than city ballrooms know. The landlord poked a bald, perspiring head out of the bar door.

"By George, you're pretty late, Mr Mason," said he. "Twelve's gone sometime ago. It's a blooming wonder if you'll get a partner." He mopped his damp brow. "They've had me at it," he said; "made me dance a darned varsoviana, if you'll believe it. I never sweated so much in me life. Caperin' about like a dashed poddy-calf. Well, you want somewhere to put your horse, I reckon?"

"I do, and another at 5 o'clock, Barnes. Can you manage it? I've come from Barindah since yesterday afternoon."

"Barindah," the landlord gaped. "Oh, you're stuffing me; it couldn't be done, and I hear the roads is that bad. You can't fool me, Mr Mason—we all know your jokes!"

"Well, it's true," Lynn said wearily, propping his long form against the verandah post. "I'm a jolly sight too knocked out to try and fool anyone. Give me a feed and a bed, Barnes, and whatever you do, have me pulled out at 5—not a minute later. I've got to make Wangong by 9 o'clock."

"Oh, I guess we can manage that," the landlord said, looking at Lynn with respectful admiration. "By George, that's a great ride. I don't believe there's another man in the district could do it." He led his guest into the supper room, and turned him loose on the sandwiches. "By George, you're pretty hungry, aren't you?" he commented. "I'm blessed if I know how you'll sleep, there's such a devil of a row goin' on."

"Sleep!" Lynn said. "I'd sleep on an earthquake—twenty hours in the saddle doesn't leave you needing rocking." A stupendous yawn interrupted him.

"By George, you must be tired," said the landlord sympathetically; "there's no blooming fun about a ride like that, by George, there isn't! Come along," and he ushered him into a tiny room less remarkable for cleanliness than attributes not so desirable. "I won't make any mistake about 5 o'clock, and you can ride my little bay mare in—she's in the stable, and as good as you'll get, by George!" Lynn did not hear any more for though he sat down on the bed to take off his boots, he fell asleep while fumbling with the first legging.

Now, the landlord was a man of his word, and accordingly he did not forget to direct Jim, the groom, to call Mr Mason at five. He would have gone himself, but that somewhat earlier in the night his legs and his head had given way simultaneously, and before the dance ended he was slumbering peacefully, his feet on a form and his head on the floor, in a pool of spilt beer. Jim was not too steady himself as he went to Lynn's room at five o'clock.

"Wake up," he said, vaguely, sitting down on the edge of the bed. He bent over and shook the sleeper, who never stirred. "Wake up!" he repeated, more energetically, pummelling him with a hard pillow. "What—you won't? Well, the boss said I 'ad to pull yer out!" He laid laborious hold on Lynn's legs, and pulled ferociously.

Lynn was dreaming—a queer dream of scrub and mountain and unseen enemies. There were snakes about him, and suddenly one coiled its horrid length around his legs and strove to drag him down. He kicked out furiously, with a muffled shout.

The heavy boot caught Jim in the waistcoat, and he dropped Lynn's legs. He sat down and groaned, rocking himself to and fro, gasping and holding his hands to the injured part of his anatomy.

"Oh—h!" he said feebly; "oh-h-h! Fair in the wind. Oh-h, you measly, long brute! Catch me tryin' to pull yer out—yer ought to be caged!" He sat on the floor, looking wrathfully at the unconscious Lynn for some time; dreamily, as one on whom many potations have done their work. Finally he lay down with care, and snored peacefully, and Lynn slept on.

The sun rose higher and higher, streaming in across the quiet face on the bed. There was no sound—everyone had long gone, after the dance, and the shanty lay silent in the December morning. Not a breath of air stirred—no warning came to tell the sleeper that the time that meant so much was racing by. It was nearly three hours after Jim had made his ill-fated efforts when Lynn suddenly stirred and woke.

Half asleep, he started up. The sight of the bright sunlight told him all, and with a groan of dismay he felt for his watch. It was 8 o'clock.

"Oh!" he said; "oh, what a damned fool I've been!" And he started for the stable at a run.

CHAPTER III

Barnes's little bay mare was looking dreamily into her empty feed box when the whirlwind burst upon her. Someone raced across the yard to the stable and flung the doors wide; then a saddle was thrown upon her back, the bridle slipped on, almost before she was aware of it, and she was outside, with a wild-eyed rider on her back, galloping for Wangong.

"I don't know if you can jump," Lynn said, as he jammed his felt hat over his eyes, "and I don't much care. All I know is, I'm not going by the road."

The little bay mare flattened her ears slightly and tore on. She did not know what this strange, tall man said; but she knew the way she was going, and that fences were an integral part of it. And fences were as meat and drink to the little bay mare.

A big log fence rose out of the long grass. It was big, but it was honest—no lurking barbed wire made traps for the unwary in those good days of the seventies. Lynn steadied the mare slightly, and took a shorter hold of her head. He had not the least idea whether she would jump it.

He was not left long in doubt. There came to him that

flash of sympathy between rider and horse, when the rider knows his mount means business—when he feels that quick gathering of the muscles telling that all the horse's powers are concentrated on the leap. Lynn gave a quick sigh of relief—he knew it was all right, even before the little mare had tucked her legs beneath her and taken the fence in a flash, as a swallow skims the stream.

"Good, old girl!" he said, and patted her neck.

Paddock after paddock was flung behind them. The going could not have been bettered—the ground was fairly soft, springy beneath its mat of grass. Once the mare stumbled badly over a log, lying hidden, and nearly came down, but Lynn's hand held her up, and she recovered herself cleverly. After that Lynn held her in somewhat. "No use breaking my neck just at this point," he said. "And I'll want all she's got to give me."

Which was true. Every few minutes his watch was in his hand, and the passage of the flying hands made him terribly afraid. It seemed to him that the hands galloped faster than the little bay mare. Only half an hour more! He did not know how far he had come, but he knew that a long stretch of road yet lay between him and Wangong. Could he do it—could the racing mare?

Afterwards, in calmer moments, Lynn marvelled that he had been in such a hurry. If the money had been lodged at 10—at noon—at any time that day—it must have been in time, for all practical purposes. Gerald's honor would still have been safe. But during his wild ride these thoughts never came to him. Gerald had said "nine o'clock," and to the letter of those words his messenger felt bound, to keep. As far as his mission was concerned, everything after nine that morning was blotted out before him.

Twenty-five minutes! The road swung round in front of them, and Lynn put the mare at the last fence. It was a stiff three-railer. She went, at it bravely, but she was tiring, and it was only with a hit and a scramble that she got over. The top rail hung in splinters as Lynn glanced back. He glanced apprehensively at her—he must not knock her up too soon.

They were on the main road now, and the going was harder, while the dust rose in a cloud around them. Steadily, at a hand gallop—but how the hands flew over the dial! There was no sign yet of Wangong. The steady thud of the mare's hoofs beat and re-echoed in the rider's brain. He set his teeth hard.

And then the road turned abruptly, the scrub that grew on either side seemed to part in front of them, and the roofs of Wangong flashed into sight. They were far enough away yet—a long straight stretch of road yet intervened—but it was the goal at last. Ten minutes!

The little mare rolled slightly in her stride. Lynn, in sudden terror that she might, after all, give way, eased her, spoke to her, patted her neck, leaning forward to shift his weight. The roofs came nearer. Could she do it? His haggard face whitened beneath its dust.

The main street of Wangong opened before them. Shopkeepers, setting out their goods for the day, looked up curiously at the clatter of hoofs, seeing a little mare, drenched with sweat, swaying as she galloped—a tall rider, leaning forward, his nervous hand firm on the rein. But Lynn saw none of them. He pulled up before the bank, and slipping off held the mare's head against his coat as she panted. They were just opening the bank doors.

* * *

"You look due for a rest, Mason," Garth, the bank manager, said. Business had been transacted satisfactorily, and they had adjourned to the neighboring hotel. "Come across to my place—there's a quiet room there, and you can sleep all day if you want to."

"Thanks, old man, but I've no time," said Lynn, gratefully, putting down his glass. "I've got to get on the road again going back to Barindah."

"What? Not today?"

Lynn nodded.

"Oh, you're stark mad, Mason!" Garth spoke almost angrily. "I never heard of anything so absolutely insane. You've done a ride sufficient to knock up any two men; you look thoroughly dead beat, and here you are proposing to do it all over again. It's enough to kill you."

"Oh, don't fuss, old chap," Lynn said, a trifle wearily. "I wouldn't dream of staying. I can assure you I'm quite able for any amount of riding yet. Besides, I promised to be back at Barindah before New Year's day." He flushed ever so lightly, and met Garth's keen gaze with a laugh.

"Well, I know to my cost it's no good arguing with you," said the latter. "If you will, you will, and I can't stop you—though I give you my word, I would if I could. But as I can't stop you, I can do the next best thing—I can lend you a clinking good horse."

"Now, that's really kind of you, old man," Lynn answered heartily. "I was at my wit's end to know where

I could get one, and not much inclined to spend half the day looking about. I'm leaving Barnes's little mare in the stable here—she deserves the best treatment they can give her. I'll buy her if he'll sell."

"Oh, Barnes'd sell anything he's got—at a price," said the other. "Well, if you're anxious to be on the road, come round and we'll see about my nag now."

Lynn followed gratefully, and half an hour later found himself cantering down the dusty track along which he had galloped so madly that morning. He was only beginning to realise how tired he was now that all excitement was over. His very bones ached with weariness. The few hours' sleep he had snatched had hardly served to refresh him, for he had fallen across the bed in an uncomfortable position, and besides, sleep taken fully dressed, and with heavy boots and leggings, is not calculated to banish fatigue. But his work was done—ah, the relief, the steady comfort of that thought! He pictured his return to Barindah—he should be there next night, he thought, hopefully. How they would run out to meet him, to hear his news. He fancied he saw Mrs Woodward's face as she would strive to ask with trembling lips if he had been in time. The joy of being able to tell her that everything was right—that was worth all the ride! There was another face in his day-dream that, he knew, would meet him earlier. She would be watching at the sliprails, knowing well that he would be there, her welcome ready for him. His heart sang at the prospect—forgetting the scores of lonely miles that lay between.

* * *

The twilight of evening was falling on the plains, next evening when Lynn Mason came to the Wangong

River. Things had gone hardly with him. The first stage of his journey had been easy. Garth's horse was good, the roads better; he made good time, and felt satisfied with his progress when, after a refreshing bath at a wayside 'traveller's rest', he turned in for the night. He had not slept well, and waking, heavy-eyed and weary, had ridden out again in the grey dawn. From thence misfortune had dogged his footsteps. His fresh horse was a rough, half-broken brute, which had made the journey a misery; once he had reared and fallen backwards, and Lynn had narrowly escaped with a severe shaking—thankful, as he picked himself up, bruised and aching, that it was no worse. The journey across Mount Misery had been a fearful struggle. The horse, unused to hill work, had taken to it unkindly from the first, and at length had knocked up altogether—whether it was really exhaustion or aggravated jibbing Lynn was too weary and disheartened to find out. He had left him at length and finished the descent on foot.

At a settler's in the foothills he had succeeded in obtaining another horse, and though it was a sorry enough steed, he was too thankful to get any mount at all to cavil. By this time he began seriously to doubt whether he would reach Barindah that night. His fall had shaken him more than he had at first thought, and his head was aching so intensely that he was scarcely conscious of his surroundings. The horse jogged—jogged—jogged; he could not get him to walk a yard. The ride was torture.

The Wangong came into view, and his first sensation of relief at being so near home was checked by one of dismay. He pulled up and stared blankly at the river. It was in flood.

From bank to bank was a tumbling stretch of broken

water—swirling past hidden logs, eddying, dancing, sparkling, as the level rays of the sinking sun lay across it. The ford had long since disappeared. It was as old John Woodward had predicted: the storms had brought down the long-delayed snows of winter from their mountain beds.

Lynn rode to the bank. Not far away were the rapids—always dangerous, now a mad tumble of water. No human being could live in them. The river raced down to them, bearing on its eddying breast a hundred trophies of its progress—logs, trees snapped off by the sudden weight of water, dead sheep, portions of fences—all the pitiful debris of a flood. The rapids yawned, hungry, for them.

Lynn had swum the river many times, but never like this. He had crossed it in time of floods often enough, but then he had been strong and fit, and with a good horse; and now he was weak and worn out, with a wretched mount. His heart failed him for a moment. But what could he do? If he remained on that side where could he go? There was no house within twelve miles, and besides things would be no better to-morrow; the river would not be down for a week. And on the other side was Barindah, with its warmth and welcome—and Mary.

"Oh, I'd cross while I'm thinking about it," he said.

He rode up the bank for a quarter of a mile; no use to court destruction by crossing near the rapids. Coming to a place, where the bank shelved down he did not pause to think again. "Thinking won't warm the water," he thought as he forced his unwilling horse into the river.

From the first he saw that the horse would go near destroying them both. Taken by surprise by Lynn's sudden turn he was in the water before he had time to resist, and once in it was swim or drown. The water was icy, so cold that it struck to the man's bones; he was afraid that it would numb him, and he worked his limbs as much as possible, shouting encouragement to his horse—words that were lost in the splashing water. It was all he could do to prevent the animal from turning round and making back for the bank. The current carried them downstream, the horse scarcely seeming to make any headway against it.

They were in midstream when the horse made a sudden attempt to turn round. Lynn checked him with an angry spur thrust, and then, he knew not how, the horse suddenly turned completely over, and in a moment they were fighting under water. Lynn realised from the first that he could never swim out alone; his strength was too far gone. He struggled to reach the bridle, keeping himself afloat amidst the plunging, kicking hoofs. Something struck him hard on the face, and for a moment he winced; but the icy cold numbed the pain, and he forgot it in the sternness of the moment.

The current bore them down, tossing them hither and thither like corks, playing with them in cruel jest. It seemed ages to Lynn—ages of icy misery—before the horse righted himself, and he somehow managed to catch the bridle. With one hand on the saddle, the other as best he could steering their course by the reins, he supported himself while the horse struck out for the bank. The animal was a feeble swimmer, and the current bore them downstream relentlessly. Lynn felt his strength ebbing; he could not hold on much longer. Water surged round his mouth and ears. The roar of the rapids, appallingly near, came to him.

Then, as consciousness was slipping away, he felt

a sudden tug at the bridle in his hand—a frantic lurch forward from the horse—and his feet touched the ground. Breathless, spent, he allowed himself to be dragged, passive, up the bank, and there at last he let go the bridle. A mist came over his eyes and blotted the world out.

The cold brought him to himself, and he struggled to his feet. A few yards away the horse stood, trembling, his head drooping, his legs planted wide apart. Lynn dragged himself into the saddle and urged him slowly forward.

Pain forced itself upon him—a dull pain in his cheek—a slow trickle. Mechanically he put up his hand, scarcely realising that he was injured. Then he started, with a stifled cry of pain—for his fingers went through his cheek and touched his teeth! The horse's hoof had laid his face open as a knife slits an orange.

He rode on, unconsciously, holding his soaked handkerchief to the injured cheek. The numbing effect of the water had passed off and the wound spelt agony. Slipping and stumbling on the rough track, the horse went, unchecked by any movement from the drooping form in the saddle. Night came down.

* * *

In the grey, mysterious dawning of the New Year Mary Woodward came slowly down the track leading from Barindah. She had passed a sleepless night, starting at every sound. Never before had Lynn failed to keep his lightest promise to her; her heart told her that only grave reasons had prevented him now. Unable longer to bear the suspense she went out—telling herself hopefully that she was going to meet him.

Three miles from the homestead she found him. He

was still on his horse—a strange pair, in the shadows of the scrub. The horse, utterly exhausted, had come to a standstill beneath a big gum tree: Lynn was lying where he had fallen forward on the animal's neck.

"Lynn!" Her voice rang sharp in its terror.

He lifted his ghastly face, smeared with blood, and with difficulty she repressed a cry at the sight. For a moment she thought he did not know her; but gradually a faint smile dawned in his eyes.

"Dear—I'm back—in time," he whispered.

She put her arms round him with a choking sob. He slipped downwards, and, putting out all her strength, she lowered him to the ground, taking his head in her lap. He put out a weak, uncertain hand, groping pitifully as in darkness, and she took it in her cool, firm clasp. The smile came back into his eyes for an instant before the tired lids closed in sleep.

A CHRISTMAS PEACEMAKER

Out in the open of the yellow withered paddocks the sun still beat fiercely. The sheep, clustered under every sheoak and light-wood, panted with distressed heaving sides. They seemed to look wistfully towards the green line of bush that showed through the shimmering heat haze. Over their heads, winging slowly westward, the black swans sought the cool, still places of back-water, and their camping ground in the rush-fringed lagoon. The horses were clustered round the big water trough—a listless group, with hanging heads and ever switching tails that swept lazily to and fro against the ceaseless warfare of the flies, droning, buzzing, maddening. A flock of white cockatoos chattered and screamed in the dead branches of a giant gum tree.

Within the old garden of the homestead the sunlight was softened. It filtered and trickled through the leaves of the trees—grevilleas, peppers, stately old pines—and fell softly on the green of the lawn. In the orchard at the side, it found its way through the thick foliage of the fruit trees, making a delicate tracery of light and shade on the long grass; a pattern that shivered and rippled like a kaleidoscope, as a vagrant breeze stirred the tall soldier heads in the grass and set the dandelions nodding and curtseying to the bluebells. The flower beds drooped sadly, but in every corner where shade lurked, brave bells of nasturtiums clung and climbed and laughed, peeping from their screen of flat green leaves. The dogs lay on the verandah, panting, with lolling tongues; but under the pyramid tree the great grey Persian cat crouched and watched, steely eyes fixed on the branches above her, whence came the twittering of countless sparrows. The big red house lay silent, dreaming in its setting of gay flowers and green trees.

On the lowest bough of a gnarled old apple tree, Joyce swung lazily to and fro. Everyone knew the Bargilla apple tree. Never anywhere else grew such great red apples as it bore. Generations of children had played and quarrelled and made friends beneath it, and climbed in its wide flung branches; generations of lovers had trysted there, and blessed its kindly screen of leaves. It had listened alike to childish confidences and vows of faithfulness; its leaves had rustled in sympathy over more than one parting that seemed endless; over some endless in stern reality. How well Joyce knew it! Every twist of the hoary trunk, every knotted bough. All her life she had made it her special retreat; the place where she brought all the joys and sorrows of her childhood and girlhood—sorrows so few, joys so many and innocent and careless. Someone else had learned to come there too; there had been a time when she was never lonely there. But that was long ago. So long the short months seem when wistful eyes strain backwards to glimpses of a dead time.

Across the lawn a small boy was laboriously practising the goose step. For a long time the girl's listless gaze had rested on the little figure in the white sailor suit, as again and again he planted himself on one sturdy leg, and endeavoured to use the other in a way unsanctioned by any drill sergeant. Again and again he overbalanced. Occasionally he sat down abruptly on the short, thick grass, and paused to wipe his heated brow on his sleeve. Then he returned to the charge.

"Never mind the old goose step, Clyde," Joyce called

out.

Clyde looked across at her and laughed, showing two rows of astonishingly white teeth in his brown, handsome little face. He set his jaw in a way worthy of more than his six years.

"I'm going to do it or bust, Auntie Jo!" he cried; and Joyce, laughing for a moment had watched him renew his efforts at balancing. Then she fell into a reverie, and forgot him, until a sudden joyous shout roused her to behold a proud little figure waving one leg in the air in a series of complicated evolutions.

Clyde raced across the lawn to her, only pausing on the way to turn a somersault. He flung himself upon her.

"I've got it at last, Auntie Jo!" he cried. "I can do the—the duck walk!"

"The duck walk?" said Joyce, bewildered. "Oh, I see. Yes, old man, you can, and very hot you've got over it."

"Oh, bovver the hot!" said her nephew. "I fought never I would do it, but I did. Won't Captain Alan be pleased, Auntie Jo?"

At the silence he glanced up quickly to meet the pain in the girl's eyes. His bright face fell.

"Oh," he said blankly, "I did forget. Please Auntie Jo, don't mind so much—I'm sorry."

She kissed him. "Never mind, dear old boy," she said, though her lip quivered. "It's all right. Why, there's the tea bell, Clyde. Come along, or we'll be late." She put her arm round the little shoulders, and they went in together to the broad verandah, where the table was set in a corner screened by a trellis covered with jasmine and honeysuckle. Her sister was already seated, and her brother-in-law made his appearance simultaneously with that of Joyce and his little son.

"You look provokingly cool, Joyce," George Langdon said, with an approving glance at the tall, slight form in the white linen dress. "How do you manage it?"

"Well, I haven't been dragging dying sheep out of the mud, for one thing," the girl said.

"No—and I certainly have. By Jove, it's something heartrending to see those poor brutes," said Langdon, dissecting a chicken rapidly. "A fellow feels that he can't work hard enough, and yet much of it is quite hopeless work. We'll have a bright Christmas at this rate—mine will certainly be spent out in the paddocks."

"Won't Santa Claus come, Daddy?" Clyde's face was full of anxiety.

"I daresay he'll manage to remember you, at any rate, old man," his father said, laughing. "But it would be no good for me to hang up every sock I've got this Christmas, I'm afraid. A big fall of rain's the best thing he could put in, and there doesn't seem much chance of that."

"Santa Claus hasn't always time to remember the big people," his wife said, looking at the downcast, childish face. "There are so many little chaps, you see, my laddie. Last Christmas he gave Daddy a very good time, so we mustn't grumble too much this year."

"What about Auntie Jo?" queried Clyde. "She had a somefing lovely stocking last year!"

"All the more reason I shouldn't have much this time,"

Joyce said. She was looking straight in front of her, her voice a little harsh. There was a moment's awkward pause: each of the "grown-ups" was remembering vividly how very good had been Joyce's last Christmas day—what gladness had been Santa Claus's portion for her. Now—

"Auntie Jo's stocking will be all right this time—don't you worry, old chap." George Langdon said quickly. "Joyce, eat something, or I'll punch you. Have some raspberries?"

"No thanks, dear—it's too hot to eat," Joyce said. "I think, if you'll forgive me, Nita, I'll go back to my apple tree—there's an attempt at a breeze there."

"If you've finished your tea," Clyde said, earnestly, "you might look for my turkey chicken—he's lost. I've looked in the stables, an' the fowl yard, an' the garden, an' lots of places, an' he must somewhere, 'cause there's no dead smell! Say, you go an' look in the pigsty, nice little Auntie Jo!" Joyce made her escape under cover of the general laughter.

"George, I can't bear it!" Nita Langdon's eyes were full of tears. "She says nothing, and she's always cheerful and bright and busy, but she's breaking her heart. Just look at her!—white and thin, and those pitiful circles round her eyes. I know she scarcely ever sleeps. Can't we do anything?"

"My dear girl, what can we possibly do?" Langdon asked. "Hume's no better off—he's no more like the man he was than I'm like Clyde's turkey. I've never seen a chap so completely altered, and for the worse. He looks wretched, and no one can get a word out of him. But what can you do? They're equally proud, and equally certain of being in the right. I tried mediation once, and only burned my fingers, and made things worse, if possible, than they were."

"Yes, I know. One can't interfere. I'd give anything to bring him back to her, but one is so helpless. Did you ever see a girl so miserably altered in four months?"

Langdon nodded.

"I'm as worried about her as you are," he said; "but, as you say, one is helpless. We're the very best of chums, Jo and I; but I know there's one subject I mustn't touch on. I can assure you, old woman, I'd give half I'm worth to bring Hume back, but what's the use of wishing? Wishing can't do it."

"Could Santa Claus?" asked a small, intensely interested voice.

Langdon started.

"Good heavens!" he said, "I'd forgotten the existence of the small pitcher. You mustn't speak of what mother and I said, you know, Clyde."

"I won't repeat," Clyde nodded gravely. "But I want Captain Alan back, too—just dreffuly, Daddy. I'm forgetting all my drill what he taught me. An' p'raps if he came back Auntie Jo would be laughing again. Don't you possibly fink that Santa Claus could bring him back?"

"No, old chap. I'm afraid Captain Alan won't come. Santa Claus hasn't time to bother about long asses who don't know what's good for them. You run and look after Auntie Joyce, and don't let her feel lonesome," said his father.

"All right, I'll keep company with her," said the small man seriously, slipping down from his chair. They watched his lithe little form as he raced along the verandah and over the lawn. "I think Joyce would have broken down altogether by this but for Clyde," his mother said; "there is wonderful comfort in a little child."

Clyde found his aunt on the grass under the apple tree. He pitched upon her, and she rolled him over, smothering him in the soft grass till the parents smiled at each other as the peals of childish laughter floated to them. When she let him go, Clyde sat up with several dandelions in his curly hair.

"Want to race with you," he said.

Joyce shook her head.

"Auntie Jo's a bit tired," she said. "Do you mind?"

"'Course not," said the small boy. "Well, tell me stories."

"About Santa Claus?"

"Yes, please. About him and his reindeers."

Joyce thought a moment.

"You know, old man," she said at length, "I don't think Santa Claus ever brings his reindeer to Australia. They wouldn't be much good, would they? I always have an idea that the old fellow has a different turnout altogether for this country, especially for the bush, where there are so many rivers and creeks and lagoons to get across. Don't you think he might carry all his things in a kind of boat, with wheels to it, and, instead of reindeer, drive a team of black swans?"

Clyde gave a delighted little shout.

"Oh, that's a lovely idea!" he exclaimed. "Tell me more, Auntie Jo."

"I think he has six swans," Joyce said, musingly. "He feeds them very well all the year round, and in winter he stables them in a big hollow tree, and all the Bush Fairies have to find grubs for them. When they are moulting he has them rugged, and if they get roup he gives them eucalyptus. And his boat is just the bark of a big tree, like the blacks' canoes, only he has wheels to it. I think he took the wheels off an old perambulator. His harness is made out of supple jack, but he doesn't use much, the team knows his voice so well. He hasn't any whip, but he carries a whip-bird on his shoulder, so that he can start the swans."

"And where does he keep all his fings?"

"Oh, down in his big cave under the roots of an old gum tree. Nobody knows the way but the Bush Fairies, and they never tell anyone. But all the year round he is busy there, collecting all the toys and presents, and storing them away; and in December he is extra busy putting numbers and names on different parcels, so that nobody may be forgotten. Poor old chap, how tired he must be by the time Christmas morning comes!"

"Oh, I do hope he's putting my number on an air gun!" Clyde said fervently. "What do you s'pose he's going to put yours on, Auntie Jo?"

Joyce shook her head.

"I don't think he'll bother about me this time," she said gently. "Sometimes he forgets; he's very busy, you know.

And then sometimes he mixes people up, and brings the wrong things—not so much to little chaps, Clydie, but to grown-ups. Sometimes they want to be very merry, and he only brings them the saddest little song; or they may have poor, cold, starved hearts, that only want one dear voice, and he brings them Christmas crackers. And, oh, Clydie, the hardest part of all is that they have to laugh over them!"

He looked at her wonderingly.

"Why, Auntie Jo?" he asked.

"Because they must," she said. "Someday, dear little chap, you'll know why." She paused, and caught him to her suddenly. "Oh, but I hope you won't!" she cried. "I hope you'll never know. I want you to laugh always, because you want to—not when it is the hardest thing in the world, and because you must laugh if you want to keep from crying. And when you're big it's cowardly to cry."

"Isn't it the straight fing?" he asked.

She shook her head.

"No, it's not the straight thing," she said. "The straight thing is to set your jaw—hard, like you did when you were trying the goose step—and go right on. Never to whimper, no matter how deadly tired you grow. Only, you can hope that the end will come, and put in your prayers that please God it won't be long."

She stopped, and looked at his anxious little face.

"Auntie Jo's no good at all," she said, with a sudden change of voice and face. "It's not the straight thing to talk to my boy like that, any way. Never mind, Clydie, I was only dreaming. Come and I'll race you!" and the next moment the pair were flying down the leafy orchard lanes, scattering the old brown hen with her brood of half-grown chicks, which flew wildly, and uttered profane protests as they flew. "That old hen looks just 'zackly like Daddy does just before he says 'Damn,' " Clyde said, laughing. "Do you s'pose hens ever says damns, Auntie Jo? I guess their little chicks makes them pretty mad, like the old Leghorn got when her duck-chicks went into the water, and she could do literately nothing with them!" But Joyce felt herself unequal to the problem, and chased him up to bed through the twilight shadows.

It was a very wide awake little boy that his aunt tucked up, kissed, and left, half an hour later. The brown eyes stared obstinately into the dim light. Clyde had said his prayers, but he had another and a private petition. He knelt up in bed to offer it.

"Please God," he whispered, "Auntie Jo said she prayed it wouldn't be long. I don't know what that means. But if You could send a wire to old Santa Claus to bring Captain Alan back and put him in Auntie Jo's stocking, I fink she would be more better. Please do!" And Clyde lay down, satisfied, with the infinite faith of six years.

Next day was Christmas eve, and early in the day Mrs Langdon and Joyce drove off on mysterious errands to the township, ten miles away. It was very hot, with a bush fire haze hanging about—thickest over Merindah, Alan Hume's station, four miles from Bargilla. Nita Langdon saw the anxious look in the girl's eyes as they dwelt upon it, and sighed that she could offer no words of comfort. Four months had dragged by since the day that Alan had galloped fiercely away from Bargilla, and since that day his name had never been mentioned between the sisters—not from lack of sympathy, but from deepest comprehension.

Four months—even to Nita, how long they seemed!

Clyde stood at the gate to say goodbye, a rather wistful little figure.

"If you see Santa Claus," he said, "you might tell him there's a little chap that wants an air gun!"

"Never!" said his mother, firmly.

Joyce smiled down at him as she took the reins.

"You forgot, old chap," she said, "we're leaving Santa Claus behind in the bush! Don't worry, he'll know the best thing to bring." The ponies were fighting for their heads, and the buggy whirled down the dusty track.

The day seemed long to Clyde. Daddy was away with the sheep, and there was nothing to do, for small boys. It was too hot for carpentering, too lonely for toys; the big kitchen, where he was generally welcome, was in a bustle of preparation for the next day, and he was hunted out. Mary was making ham frills and pie collars all the time he was eating his lunch, and nothing seemed satisfactory. He looked out a new stocking and hung it on the end of his cot, afterwards performing a like kind office for the rest of the family. Then there seemed nothing at all to do.

About three o'clock he wandered outside the yard gate and into the home paddock. Mick, his little Irish terrier, came with him, highly delighted to be out for a run, and the pair chased ground-larks until they were tired, and had come some distance from home. They rested in the grass a while, and then came a moment of brief, delirious joy for Mick, for a hare started up beside them, and in an instant master and dog were in full cry. When at length they pulled up regretfully—the hare a vanishing speck in the distance—the house was quite a long way away, the line of scrub much nearer. Mick was evidently impatient to go further. He yapped insistently at his silent little master.

Clyde was thinking deeply. The bush was so near—and Auntie Jo had said that Santa Claus was there. What if he could see him? If he could tell him to bring Captain Alan back to Auntie Jo? Wouldn't it be a glorious thing for a little chap to do—all alone, with nobody to help him!

He thought very wistfully. Santa Claus would do it for him, he knew. He was such a kind old chap—everybody knew that. And if he only guessed what a difference it made to Auntie Jo that Captain Alan never came now! Clyde knew perfectly well that he had only to hear of it to set everything right at once. It would be so lovely to see Auntie Jo happy again—"not just talking happy, but happy in her eyes," Clyde said aloud. It was that thought that decided him—the longing to see those dear eyes glad as they used to be. And then he was so sure of Santa Claus. So he set off.

Mick trotted gaily beside him, a highly-delighted dog. He knew those bush places, where there were snakes to be barked at and wild things to chase—so different from the tame, uninteresting lambs that no one would allow him to have games with. Here it was very different, and he sprang at darting swallows and pursued ground-larks to his heart's content, his little master joining in the chase. It did not seem to take them long to cross the flat grey plain that finally merged into the green shadows of the bush.

A little breeze blew the scent of the trees to them as they drew near the scrub. Clyde threw back his head and drank it in greedily—the sharp, sweet, aromatic scent that brings almost a stinging delight to the nostrils. Clyde loved the bush. He was always perfectly at home in its densest places, and his greatest pleasure was to accompany his father in a long ride through the scrub. Sometimes Joyce would drive with him in his tiny pony cart across the paddocks, and they would spend the day together among the trees—following the creek through its twists and turns; hunting in the damp gullies for maiden hair and dainty fringed orchids. So it was with no feeling of strangeness that the little lad left the open plain and plunged into the shadows.

Now, where was Santa Claus? Not far off, Clyde supposed, for he would not want to be further than he could help from the houses where little folk lived. So the boy wandered in and out among the trees, looking always for that great big gum tree where the old saint might have his home. He wished that he might see some of the little bush fairies that knew all about the place. But the bush fairies kept their secret well.

Very cool and sweet were the mossy gullies and the long, leafy alleys where the sun scarcely seemed to peep. Sometimes for sheer joy of living, Clyde threw himself down on the soft green and rolled luxuriously, while Mick, who thought it was all a game for his benefit, rolled likewise and licked his master's face affectionately. Sometimes Clyde forgot his quest, and only remembered that he was a merry little boy with a gay little dog—and the two had great romps together, down in that new, beautiful playground that really seemed to have been made for little boys of six, with irresponsible Irish terrier puppies. There were such splendid places for hide and seek, such jumps, such beautiful little gullies that simply invited you to race along them! Still, there was never a big gum tree that Clyde did not carefully inspect, wandering round and round it in the hope that he might light upon that hidden door which only Santa Claus and the fairies knew how to open. He never doubted that he would find it.

But as the afternoon died softly to twilight, he began to grow a little impatient. He was getting tired. Mick, too, had had enough romping, and looked wistfully at his master with dumb eyes that asked why they did not go home. Clyde knew he ought to go, and yet he could not bear to leave his purpose unfulfilled. So he quickened his steps, and ran from tree to tree, hoping that each would be the object of his quest, and as each proved fruitless he grew more quiet and downcast. "I fink it's not quite nice of Santa Claus," he said to Mick, and Mick wisely wagged an affirmative tail.

At last he knew he must give in. The lengthening shadows had all merged into the dim light of dying day; it was yet bright on the plains, but very dusky in the sombre bush. There was no use in hunting any longer for Santa Claus. Perhaps he was too busy, perhaps he did not like little boys to come and see him; he would not show himself. No chance now of having Captain Alan back for Auntie Jo's Christmas. Clyde choked back a sob. Auntie Jo and Mother must be back by now; they would be wondering where he was. He must hurry.

Not till the darkness in the scrub grew dense, while overhead the stars twinkled one by one into sight, did the little hunter realise how hopelessly he was lost. He had turned naturally in the direction whence he had come, forgetting how many twists and turns his wandering feet had led him. As the light faded he ran on quickly, hoping to get out upon the plain; but there was no change in the far-reaching prospect of trees—they only seemed to grow denser as he went. Mick, trotted gamely after him, a very sorry little dog.

Clyde pulled up at last, for the darkness was before him like a wall. He had fallen many times over stumps and roots; the creepers had caught his feet, and scratched his face. One low hanging bough had twitched off his straw hat, and he had not waited to find it. He was bruised and aching, his feet like lead, and upon him was a horror of loneliness. The bush that seemed so friendly in the daylight had grown great and mysterious and terrible, and he was only a little, tired boy.

He sat down, and caught hold of Mick, as the puppy thrust his nose into his hand.

"Mick, we's lost!" he said.

The little dog crept closer.

"Never mind," the brave little voice said, quivering a little. "Daddy and Auntie Jo will find us; if Captain Alan knew, he'd come."

They nestled together under the lee of a big log. Overhead the night breeze woke, and the boughs stirred and nestled to greet it. Faint sounds broke the stillness, as the night life of the bush roused itself. Lithe bodies slipped past—once or twice the bushes crackled beneath the weight of some heavier animal that plunged past them, suddenly aware of intruders. Far off a mopoke called sadly.

"Mummy said I was always quite safe," said the trembling voice. "I don't 'spect anything would hurt a little boy." A sudden crash made him start, and a sob escaped him. He checked it, and set his lips. "Auntie Jo said it was cowardly to cry," he whispered. "It isn't the straight fing. But Auntie Jo's big." The slow tears trickled on the puppy's rough head.

Clyde did not know what it was that roused him later. He did not think he had been to sleep; but suddenly the grim darkness gave place to a softened pale light, and, instead of being terrible and unfriendly, the scrub seemed quite beautiful and homelike. Overhead the white moon rode high. The boughs above him made a delicate pattern against its white purity.

In front of him was a long green alley, walled with musk and dogwood, and carpeted with orchids—he could see them distinctly in that soft, tender light. There were faint mysterious rustlings coming from the trees. Clyde looked about him lazily, happily. Somehow, he did not seem lonely now. Out of sight somewhere came the sharp crack of a whip.

Then, as he watched with listless, happy eyes, a strange little procession came into view. First of all, some of the wild bush animals, walking demurely and unafraid—wallabies, kangaroos, wombats, and others Clyde did not know. After them came ever so many grotesque little beings; tiny brown and green lads and lasses that, until you saw them closely, looked almost like twigs and leaves and flowers, so quaintly were they dressed. Some were just like strips of bark; others resembled a handful of grey, quivering grass, a pert sharp little face peeping out amongst the nodding balls; others again were all in green, with funny hooded, peaked caps, like the queer green orchids Auntie Jo used to find under the lightwood saplings. Clyde laughed with delight at their antics as they danced along the grass.

Then there came into view the strangest vehicle. It was just a long bark canoe, mounted on four spidery wheels: and drawing it, pacing two by two, were six great black swans. Trailing vines were their harness, and every swan wore a big collar of mistletoe and a pack saddle of clematis. The canoe was so full of beautiful things that it threatened momentarily to overbalance—toys, pictures, books, tools, fruit, all the most lovely things that anyone could imagine packed into a Christmas stocking. And walking beside the car was the driver—the strangest old man. Very tall he was, with a long beard and great bushy eyebrows, beneath which twinkled the kindest pair of keen grey eyes. He did not wear common clothes—Clyde never could describe them exactly, but he knew they were all covered with rough green and grey mosses and lichens, and that on his head was a wreath of mistletoe, while a waggish looking whip bird perched on his shoulder. So Santa Claus came to Clyde.

He watched the little procession as it moved up the glade. No one took any notice of him. The little Bush Fairies capered past him merrily, the animals looked at him gravely without question; even the old man did not speak, but went on slowly.

They were past; then the memory of his purpose came back to the little fellow, and he started up and ran forward.

The swans halted abruptly. Everyone suddenly seemed to be looking at Clyde, and for the first time he felt afraid. But he would not let himself think. He was catching at the old man's hand.

"Oh, please!" he cried, "if you wouldn't mind. Just for

Auntie Jo's stocking—she won't want anything else if you'll only put Captain Alan in!"

No one spoke. Clyde's little voice grew sharp in its anxiety.

"She wants him so dreffuly, I know she does; an' all the time she's so tired in her poor eyes. Just bring him back this once!"

Still the deep silence.

"If you'll bring him, you needn't bovver about my stocking—not even the air gun! That would be a rest for you if you got tired bringing him back, 'cause he's very big!"

The stern old face above him melted into the tenderest smile. A hand was on his head, and Santa Claus's voice was very low and gentle.

"All right, little Clyde, you shall bring him back!"

Then everything melted away—the birds and animals grew dim, the strange car disappeared, the gnarled old man was gone. But the memory of his voice and the infinite tenderness of the smile in his eyes were with Clyde as he sank down on the mosses and slept, with the puppy's rough head against his flushed little cheek.

* * *

Through the long night the dancing lights of the lanterns glowed through the bush like will o' the wisps. The very skies echoed the long coo-ees, the shouts that rang with the despair of fruitless search. Haggard women and stern-faced men—they sought together for one baby form.

Alan Hume had wasted no time from the moment when the alarm had brought him—not pausing for gates—to the muster of searchers at Bargilla. He had been the first into the scrub—love for the little lost lad who had been his friend, spurred by the memory of a girl's white face; of dark, agonised eyes, which even in their pain had rested in his for a moment in sudden relief and trust. The bitterness of weary months fell from him with that look. As he searched through the night, all the old cruel misunderstanding seemed suddenly a little, worthless thing. It was nothing—and love was all.

The grey pallor of the dawn clothed the bush as he came into a green valley, and saw, with a quick throb at his heart, the quiet form by the log. Clyde was sleeping soundly; Mick, wide awake and hungry, was licking his hand.

With a breath of relief Alan saw, as he knelt beside him, the faint color in the boy's cheek; heard the quiet, regular breathing. He put his hand on the cool forehead, and Clyde woke with a little cry.

"It's only me, old chap." Hume's voice was shaking in spite of himself. Clyde met his eyes and smiled.

"Yes," he said: "'course—I know. Where's Auntie Jo?"

"We'll find her soon." He lifted the little fellow up. "Are you sure you're all right, old lad?"

"Yes, sanks." The child was the calmer of the two. "Did that good old Santa Claus bring you, Captain Alan?" His voice broke into a glad little cry. "Oh—there's my Auntie Jo!"

Joyce came slowly into the dim glade. She was ghastly in the half-light—her white frock stained and torn with a hundred briars. She caught her breath suddenly as she saw them—the tall, brown-faced man and the little child in his arms.

Clyde slipped down and ran to her, his face alight with eagerness.

"I've brought him back, dearest!" he cried, and struggled as she crushed him to her with hungry, frantic kisses. "Santa Claus gave him to me—for mine Christmas stocking, 'stead of an air gun! Oh, Auntie Jo, you mustn't mind like that"—as a great sob came from her. He put up his little hand and tried to drag hers from her face. "Captain Alan—tell her she mustn't—tell her you've come back!"

"Joyce—tell me I may stay!"

Hume's hand was on her shoulder. Still kneeling, her arms around the little childish body, she lifted quivering lips to his.

THE VALLEY OF FORGETFULNESS

Harden dropped from the tram as it swung round the corner, waited a trifle impatiently for a motor to dodge a Jersey cow driven by a small boy on a bicycle, and struck off down the cross street that still lay glaring and hot in the slanting sunlight. He pulled his hat lower on his forehead as the rays struck against his eyes. The canvas blinds were lowered on the verandahs of the trim suburban villas on either side. Here and there a man might be seen in his shirt sleeves, just home from the City, and already beginning to potter in his garden. Harden nodded to more than one tired face like his own as he went along. The grateful sound of the plashing of sprinklers at work on the lawns came gently to him, bringing a breath of coolness into the December air; in one garden a bare legged urchin was running back and forth beneath the falling drops, on his face a look of ecstatic happiness that took no thought of the future or of the outraged mother or nurse. On the verandah of one cottage that had for garden only a patch of dusty, dried up grass, a baby wailed fretfully in an old go-cart, too small for it to stretch its hot limbs. The man paused a moment, irresolutely, uncertain as to whether he should go to it; then he shrugged his shoulders and walked on. But the weary little cry followed him down the street, and added another line to the network round his eyes.

The gate at which he stopped presently was high, and built of jarrah boards, set in a closely trimmed hedge of pittosporum, so that the garden within was quite screened from the gaze of passers by. Inside, when the gate had shut out the glaring street, was coolness and green and quiet. A long lawn rose in a gentle slope to meet the verandah of the red-tiled house. Two or three trees dotted its surface, with garden seats and a swing in their shade; and all round, the garden beds were gay with colour and heavy with perfume. Wherever you looked, there were roses in standards and tall bushes, trained against the fence, and climbing up the posts of the verandah. Roses everywhere, crimson, and creamy, and gold, and white; Crimson Ramblers tumbling over an arch-way across the path, Belle Siebreicht lifting her exquisite pink towards the roof, La France filling the air with waves of scent. There were other flowers — tall brown and gold correopsis, masses of phlox and balsams in their parti-coloured daintiness, pansies and carnations and sturdy gaillardias; but always the eye came back to the flower that was queen of the garden. For Harden's wife had once loved roses.

He cast a quick look round as he shut the garden door behind him. There was no one to be seen except a small figure in the swing, attired in the most diminutive of bathing suits. At sight of Harden it uttered a shout, fell with decision from the swing as the easiest way of descending quickly, and, picking itself up, raced across the grass and fell bodily upon the newcomer.

"Steady, old man," Harden said, feeling his small son a trifle dubiously. "Did you hurt yourself? I wish to goodness you wouldn't tumble out of the swing like that!"

"'Twas quickest," said the boy, with brevity. "I'm always in such a hurry when you come, dad. Never hurt, any-how. Has you been very hot?"

"Uncommonly hot," said his father. "Where's the other wickedness?"

"Coming, I s'pect. She went for a dwink; she's been

for forty-'leven dwinks since lunch. Wish she'd hurry up, 'cause she's bringin' me mine."

"While you swing?" said his father, smiling a little. "That's not the way to treat a woman, Teddy. Why don't you go for your own drinks?"

"She doesn't mind," said Teddy, easily. "An' I was pretty busy." He changed the subject with masterly finesse. "Did you bwing home any parcels, dad?"

"I did not," said Harden. "Why should I?" He laughed at the small face.

"I d'no, but it's jolly nice when you do," his son answered. "Here's Tinker."

Tinker was not a puppy of dubious extraction, but something much more exquisite. She came out upon the topmost step of the verandah, and stood there, hesitating a moment; and she was quite beautiful. A small dimpling person, with a mass of loose brown curls tumbling round her head, and soft, rounded limbs, but little concealed by a bathing suit even more diminutive than Teddy's, and a face that might have been the face of an angel, but was something very different, seeing that it belonged to Tinker, and that in Tinker were depths of guile unfathomed yet of man. Teddy was no saint, but his twin sister had been the terror and the despair of a procession of nurses. Seeing her father, she gave a shrill shriek of ecstasy, planted the aluminium cup she carried upon the step with a vigour that spilt half its contents, and fled to meet him.

"Beast!" said Teddy, fervently! "Why couldn't you bwing that cup over?" He gathered himself up laboriously, and marched over to the forgotten vessel, his disgusted expression deepening as he found that only a mouthful of water was left. Returning, he pulled his sister's hair firmly, and the next moment all that Harden could see of his family was a chaotic mass of legs and arms, whirling in wild combat. He plucked them apart, holding them at arm's length, while they spat defiance at each other much after the fashion of tiger cubs.

"You mustn't fight like that," he said. "When are you going to be civilised?"

"Teddy's awfully uncivilised," gasped his daughter. "He pulled my hair!"

"Well, you deserved it," said Teddy, panting also. "An' you're loads unciviliseder than me, anyhow. I'll tell Daddy how you turned the hose on Watkins this afternoon if — ." He stopped abruptly, by reason of a dimpled and exceedingly grimy hand on his mouth.

"Mean pig!" said Tinker.

"Did you do that really, Tinker?" Harden asked.

The wrathful face suddenly brimmed over into laughter.

"I couldn't help it, Daddy. He was lookin' at the nozzle — an' I was at the tap — an ever so far away. It just had got turned. Oh, Daddy, if you'd only seen him! An' I've been punished once, so it's all right."

"Oh, is it?" Harden commented, grimly. "That means another gardener, I suppose — and I'd just broken Watkins in to dealing with aphis. He nearly gave notice after you and Teddy locked him in the tool shed — this will about finish things."

Tinker's small face was faintly pink.

"No — it's twuly all right, Daddy. I — I fixed things

up."

"You!" said Harden. "It's highly probable you've fixed them very thoroughly."

Teddy exploded.

"She fixed him all right, Dad — they made it up. She finished by letting him —"

An avalanche descended upon Teddy, and speech died, muffled; Tinker's face was scarlet now.

"I will tell Daddy myself," she gasped — "he won't laugh. I'll hate you if you laugh, Daddy! I — I kissed him."

Harden compressed his emotions into a blank stare.

"Shut up, Teddy," he said to that un-regenerate youth. "Oh, all right, Tinker— we won't talk about it." He drew his daughter closer to him — her abhorrence of any alien touch was a proverb, and he knew what the amends honourable must have cost her. He cast about for another subject and found one readily. "I say, why are you youngsters in this rig-out?"

The twins contemplated their bathing suits with affection.

"Well, we wanted to bathe — an' it's Nurse's day out, an' there wasn't anyone to take us. An' 'twas hot. Ain't they lovely an' cool, Daddy?"

"Cool, I daresay; but loveliness is a matter of taste," Harden said. "Hasn't any one told you to change?"

Truthfulness was part of the code of the twins. Tinker shrugged an exquisite shoulder.

"Oh, Jane did — lots of times. But we were too busy,

weren't we, Teddy?"

"Rather," said her brother. "Can't we stay like this, Daddy? An' have dinner with you?"

"You can't," said Harden. "Why don't you behave like ordinary kids, I wonder?" He sighed a little. "Where's your mother, Teddy?"

"Dunno," said Teddy, carelessly. "Somewhere about, I expect, Daddy."

"Haven't you been with her at all?"

"Oh, she doesn't come with us," the boy said. "She doesn't want us, Daddy."

"I've told you you're not to say that, Teddy."

Teddy fidgetted on his father's knee, digging a brown toe into the buffalo grass.

"Well — doesn't seem like it, Daddy. She won't talk, 'nor play, nor anyfing.

When's she goin' to get well, Daddy?" Tinker's treble was insistent. "I do wish we had a well muvver, don't you? Will she be long, Daddy?"

"I don't know, Tinker. Go and dress, both of you."

He put them from him and rose slowly from the grass — a tall figure, with shoulders a little stooped, and threads of grey in his dark hair. There was another look in his eyes — the laughter lit by the children, had died out of them. Before that look Teddy and Tinker were suddenly quiet, moving off gently. Outlaws as they were, there was just one person round whom their little world revolved, and he had moods that even they must respect. They walked off soberly, quaint visions in the striped bathing suits. Then their genial personal devils awoke again, and they vanished into the house in a whirl of shouts and scuffling and the joy of battle. Harden followed them slowly.

He passed through a wide hall, carpeted softly, and parting the heavy curtains at the door, looked into the drawing room. It was empty — an unusual thing; generally he expected to find his wife there at this hour. Other rooms proved vacant; and there was a shade of anxiety on his face when at length he came a little hurriedly into his own den, and found her, a tall, slight form in a dress of clinging white, standing by the window. She turned as he entered, greeting him with a nervous, fleeting smile.

"You've come back?" she said, slowly. It was her invariable greeting, and the man winced.

"Yes, I've come back, dear," he answered. Into his voice came the note of complete gentleness which only she called forth. He went up to her slowly, and she lifted her face for his kiss, as a child might. It was only when you looked closely into her eyes that you saw that they were the eyes of a child.

Harden held her to him for a moment, lightly. Then she released herself with a quick movement.

"Hasn't it been a nice day?" she said. The voice was hesitating, uncertain, as though she were repeating a lesson.

"Yes—a bit hot, didn't you think?"

"Hot? No, I wasn't hot."

Harden dropped into a leather armchair and lit a cigarette, watching her keenly.

"Did you see the children, dear?" he asked.

"No — I didn't see any children," his wife answered. Suddenly an idea seemed to strike her, and she flushed painfully, as if recalling something she knew he wished to hear. "Oh — yes, I did see the children. They were playing."

"I like you to see them, you know, Helen," he said.

"Yes — I know. I saw them."

"Town is full of children," Harding went on. "All the shops and the streets — children everywhere. It's getting near Christmas, you know."

She did not know. She looked at him with pain in her eyes — almost fear.

"Don't you remember — Christmas?" he said, slowly. "Try to remember, darling — you loved it so. We used to get Christmas ready for the children — Santa Claus, you know; hanging up their stockings. Don't you remember, just a little, Helen?"

She drew back, her look pitifully helpless.

"I — I can't."

Harding sighed.

"You're paler tonight, dear," he said. "Aren't you quite well?"

"My head aches," his wife said, forlornly. "It hurts me." She looked up with a strained apology in her glance. "I — I expect that's why I can't remember, Jim. I'll try tomorrow."

"Don't worry, my darling," he said. "I won't have you

make your dear head ache. Were you glad to see me come home, Helen?"

"Oh, yes." The gladness was a child's joy. "It is so long when you are away."

"Is it?" he said — and smiled at her. "The day is always long until I get back to you. Were the children good?"

"I — I think so," she said, flushing again. She came a little closer, standing above him, tall and sweet. "Jim —" she said — "Jim, they are not my children, are they?"

Harding gripped the arms of his chair. He steadied his voice in a moment. "Yes, of course, they're your children, dear", he said— "your very own. Always try to remember, won't you? You were so proud of the twin babies once — and they want their mother so badly, Helen. Try to remember, they're your own babies, dear."

She moved away, shaking her head a little. Then Teddy and Tinker came tumbling in, clothed as the lilies of the field, and she looked at them with knitted brows, behind which the sick brain was labouring.

The twins flung themselves on their father joyously.

"Daddy, do you know it's nearly Christmas?"

"I heard something about it," Harding answered.

"'Tis, then," Teddy cried. "Old Santa Claus'll be coming — isn't it ripping? Oh, I do want heaps of fings."

"But does he come for twins?"

"Well, Daddy!" At the world of reproach Harding grinned. "Didn't he always come?"

"But you were only seven last time," Harding said

seriously. “When people get as old as you, he may not bother any more.”

“Daddy, you’re just bein’ horrid,” said Tinker, energetically. “’Course he’ll come — he came last year to Nan Weatherly, an’ she’s ’leven, so there. You was just pullin’ our leg, wasn’t you, Daddy?”

“You’re an inelegant person, Tinker,” Harding said, surveying his daughter. “Where do you get your language from?”

“Heving only knows,” said she.

“Tinker!”

“Well, that’s what Jane says. An’ Watkins says, ‘May the divil fly away wid me —’”

“There’s no need for you to tell me any of Watkins’ remarks,” said her father, firmly. “What on earth I’m to do with you children —” He broke off, staring at the pair before him, then over their heads to the figure of his wife, with her puzzled face. That look of strained inquiry had been more frequent in her eyes lately; it filled him with a vague fear. Always before him was the dread of some thing worse — some development that would snatch from him the little he had left. It caught at his heart now, as he stared at her. Then the bell rang sharply, and he rose to lead her into the dining room.

The meal was as a hundred other meals. He had three children to look after, and he allowed no servant to watch him at his task; so the trim maid withdrew presently, and he watched over his three quietly, aiding each where occasion demanded. And always he talked — talked gently to his wife, trying to draw her out, to make the dormant intelligence respond to the love that never ceased to call for it. The response was pitifully meagre. Lately, since that harassed expression had come to her, it had been less than ever, so that the task was always uphill. It hurt him most of all to see that the children seemed to make her worse; her eyes dwelt on each in turn with a look that was almost distress. Yet it was the only time he could bring them together. During the day she avoided them, and they — poor mites! — shrank from the mother who seemed to have gone away. He dared not give up this hour, every minute of which whipped his heart with lashes of fire.

It dragged to an end at last, and the children went reluctantly to bed, where Harden followed presently, to hear their prayers and have the "five minutes" that were the best of the day. The twins were wholly saintlike then, and — the nightlight being kind — might indeed have been mis taken for infant angels. They clung about him, begging for yet another moment, and after that another; it was easy to give in, with their soft little bodies nestling to him and their kisses on his face. He had fresh strength for his burden, when at length he freed himself, and went back to his wife — to the terrible, one-sided conversations that seemed so hopeless, though the doctors had told him to try to make her talk. It was like training a dull and unhappy child. Presently she was tired, and he helped her to bed, stooping in the darkness for her goodnight kiss that lacked all the fervour of Tinker's. Harden's step was that of an old man as he came back to his den.

He sat down heavily and pulled at his pipe, looking back over the two years that had gone. It was just so long since Fate had juggled so cruelly with their lives — two Christmases ago. The lines set deeply into his face as he remembered. She had been so full of happiness and life — the merry mysteries of Christmas, the joy in the children, the mere delight of living. Not one had ever felt happiness so keenly as Helen — a child always in her thoroughness of enjoyment . . . He had planned the motor drive as a kind of culmination to their busy week of planning and preparation, and had smiled at her as she came running down the garden path to join him at the gate, not then built high so as to shut out curious passing glances. "I never saw such a child to laugh," he had said, caressing her with his eyes. "Aren't you a bit fey, wife of mine?"

She had stepped in beside him, pulling up the dust rug before she answered. "A woman may well laugh, when she owns you and the twinnies, Jim," she had said. "You don't leave me opportunity for anything else." The street had been quiet; he had stooped swiftly and kissed her before starting the motor.

The smash had come two minutes later, the big motor coming down a steep side street like a whirlwind, swinging out, a car of Juggernaut, upon them. There had been no time to think, to act . . . only a moment's sick shock and bewilderment before he found himself in the dust, holding her to him and begging her passionately to look at him. But she — his own woman — had never looked at him since.

The changeling inside her beautiful shell, which was all they had given back to him, used to glance at him. He knew it was not Helen — Helen, whose eyes had been living windows of the sweet soul within. This was not she, this cold, frightened child, whom he had slowly taught to know him as a stranger, and who refused altogether to know the children. They had fretted over it, poor babies;

cried for their own mother, that thing of laughter and love, until time had rendered them careless, and they had turned to give all their love to him. That hurt him curiously, but it did not hurt her.

The doctors had given him a shred of hope. There was nothing to be done; tenderness and ceaseless care might bring back memory and intelligence; the striking of some chord might vibrate in the deadened brain and quicken it once more. It was all uncertain and vague — a glimmer of light in the blackness that had fallen upon him. He had clung to it desperately at first, before the slow procession of the months, without change, had slowly robbed him of it. Now he hoped no more.

And it was Christmas again. She had loved Christmas —

His pipe went out unheeded. Leaning forward he stared into the empty fireplace, while the slow clock on the mantelshelf ticked into another day.

* * *

Harden came home early on Christmas eve. There was much to do, and opportunity for doing it was scant under the raking fire of the twins' merciless eyes. Most of his shopping had been done days before, and the results spirited home under cover of darkness. But there were various parcels that had been left to the last, as Christmas shopping has a way of being, and it took all his adroitness to conceal tell-tale bulges on his lean person from the inquiring gaze of his offspring. He breathed a sigh of relief when an inspiration of strategy sent the twins careering after an imaginary postman, and gave him a moment to conceal his contraband cargo.

It was not a peaceful evening. Tinker and Teddy were wild with excitement, and something of their upheaval seemed to have communicated itself to his wife. She glanced rapidly from one face to another at dinner, eating nothing. There was an unusual gleam in her dull eyes, even though speech seemed harder to her than usual. Harden was vaguely uneasy— a feeling that had grown upon him during the last week. Without doubt there was a difference in Helen. It was with a sick sense of despair that he realised it was not for the better.

He watched her narrowly. Munro, who had attended her since the accident, was out of town for Christmas. To call in a doctor who did not know the case seemed a futile proceeding. After all, none of them understood her as he did — no one else could have the same pitiful comprehension of her prisoned mind, groping in its blackness. Whatever happened, he wanted to manage her himself. He could do no more than watch her.

The twins were uproarious. They quarrelled delightfully all through dinner, made it up with unusual affection afterwards, and forthwith turned the house into a steeplechase course, by way of letting off superfluous steam. The empty rooms rang with shouts and clear laughter. Whatever sadness lay upon the house, it did not touch the babies, thank God — so Harden reflected, watching his wife. She was restless and nervous, moving about in a quick, uneasy way, foreign to her usual slow movements. Her eyes came back to his helplessly every moment.

Harden went to her at last, putting his arms round her shoulders gently.

"Does the kiddies' noise bother you, dear?" he asked her.

She shook her head.

"No."

"What is it? — tell me, Helen."

"Something hurts me," she said, vaguely. "I don't know. What is it, Jim? Can't you stop it?"

That she should turn to him for aid gave him a moment's wretched comfort.

"I wish I could, sweetheart," he said. "Is it your head?"

She nodded.

"It hurts," she said, shuddering a little. "Something is trying to hurt me."

"Nothing can hurt you while I am here, dear," Harden said. "I'll take care of you all the time. Will you come and lie down?"

She yielded to him, and he led her away, talking to her easily while he put her to bed like a child. Gradually she grew quieter. When she seemed to go to sleep, he slipped away.

The twins were growing tired; there was less difficulty than usual in getting them to bed, though both were naturally certain that sleep should not visit them until Santa Claus had made his rounds. Harden tucked them into the little white beds thankfully. Something in the strain of the evening was beginning to tell upon him — he was very tired. He listened awhile at his wife's door before going back to his den.

There, sitting in the silence with only his pipe and his

long thoughts for company, a great drowsiness came over him, and he went to sleep — to dream that Helen was with him again; the Helen of old, with all the weary time between blotted out in the perfect joy of restoration. It was so dear a dream that when he woke, it was some time before realisation came back to him. Then he started up with a bitter groan.

It was two o'clock, to his amazement; he reviled himself for his sluggishness as he hurried anxiously to his wife's room. But she was sleeping peacefully; no harm had come from his dereliction of duty, and he breathed a sigh of relief as he tip-toed away from her door. There was yet much work ahead of him — important work.

The twins were sleeping soundly as he came into the nursery, his arms full of toys. It was a long room, the two white beds at one end, near the open windows. He gathered the limp stocking from the foot of each bed, and then drew a tall screen between the sleepers and the table where he had placed his burden. The twins had the reputation of sleeping through an earthquake; no mere visit of Santa Claus was likely to surprise them. Still the screen was a precaution that did no harm.

He sat down at the table and smiled a little as he looked at its load; just such toys as a man chooses, being generally at the mercy of a shop lady who recognises a lone male shopper as an easy prey. Things useless and gaudy; bright with paint and gay with ribbons. The twins were not likely to be critical; there were unlimited promises of joy in the collection. Harden divided the toys into heaps, weighing the values evenly, after the manner of a man. He took up a necklace of iridescent beads and slipped it into Tinker's stocking.

Then, suddenly, the hopelessness that had gained on him all day came over him like a flood, with a rush of bitter-sweet memories. God! their Christmases together — the simple happiness — the love that glorified each moment! What had he now to take the place of that most dear companionship? The agony of despair that he had fought for two long years mastered him in one overwhelming moment. Still holding the little stocking, his head dropped to the table before him, between the two heaps of gaudy toys. The night stole on while he lay huddled there, struggling with his tortured soul. Once or twice the children stirred; far off a clock struck from time to time; but outside things had no power to touch him now. There was, indeed, but one sound able to penetrate to his racked senses; and that came presently.

A light, quick step. He would have known it among a thousand others — it called to him, and he sat up, blinking a little at the light, his eyes on the doorway. Why should she come here? — she who hated the nursery now, since these two years of hell? Yet she was coming.

And she came — and her eyes were open. The white figure hesitated in the doorway, puzzling a little over the scene — the laden table behind the screen and the haggard man who sat and stared at her as though he could never bear to release his eyes. Then she came to him swiftly and he caught her and drew her to him, his gaze always searching her with a kind of desperate hope.

"Jim!" she said — "Jim — what is it? I woke up feeling so queer — and you weren't there. Are the children all right?"

He tried to find his voice and could not. Only he could

hold her to him, and put his face against her breast.

"Jim — I'm frightened!" she said. "What is it — are my kiddies all right? Why don't you speak?"

"It's — all right, sweetheart." His voice was strained and far away. "Everything's all right, now."

"But what is it? — have I been ill?"

"Yes — a bit ill, beloved. But it's gone now." He felt her shiver, and drew her down upon his knee, wrapping her in his arms. "You've come back to me," he whispered — "You've come back to me!"

The dawn came in at the open window as they clung together. In the little white beds the twins stirred and woke. There was a dash for stockings and a simultaneous howl.

"Santa Claus hasn't never come!"

Two heads came round the corner of the screen.

"Well, I'm blessed!" said Teddy. "Daddy's been and unpacked our stockings!"

But Tinker came past the toy laden table, with great eyes fixed on those who were beyond it. Helen gave a little cry.

"Jim! But they're big!"

"It's all right, darling," he said. "Everything's quite all right."

"Oh!" said Tinker. "Oh! Bovver Santa Claus. Teddy! Don't you see muvver's come back?"

CINDERELLA'S CHRISTMAS

"It's rather hard on Ruth," said Linda Ferris.

"I don't see it," replied her sister, inserting a hot crimping iron into her hair, and holding it with many facial contortions indicative of extreme agony. "She can't expect to go everywhere—and we took her to the tennis tournament and the biograph."

"Oh, but a dance is different."

"Well, if you think it's pleasant for a whole flock of us to stream into a ballroom, it's more than I do," Ida Ferris said irritably. "We look quite enough as it is, with mother persisting in dressing in that ridiculously young fashion. Besides, who's going to pay for ball dresses for Ruth, I'd like to know?"

"We could have fixed up something," Linda said weakly.

"Yes, and have people saying we dressed the poor relation badly!" Ida retorted. She reheated the iron. "You'd just spoil that girl, Linda. Goodness knows, it's bad enough to have her always about."

"I fancy we find her pretty useful," Linda said.

"So she ought to be—and I'm sure we give her plenty of outings."

"Oh, well, I only felt a bit sorry for her," said her sister, apologetically. "It must be hard, especially as she used to go to everything until Uncle George died."

"If Uncle George hadn't been such an extravagant we wouldn't be saddled with his daughter now," said Ida angrily. "I think it's abominable—it would be far better if she'd go out as a governess or lady help, and——"

"Aren't you girls dressed?" asked a plump lady, floating in on an odor of patchouli. "Where's Ruth? I want her to hook me up."

"She's fixing up the chiffon on Ida's skirt," Linda answered, plunging her head into a sea of Nile-green tulle, and emerging like Aphrodite from the waves. "Am I straight at the back, Mother?"

"Yes, dear," Mrs Ferris said, absently. "Where's the powder puff?" She applied it liberally to a large bare shoulder, and risked dislocating her neck in an attempt to see the effect. "How slow that girl is! Oh, here you are, Ruth! Make haste!" She turned her back on the newcomer, and drew in her breath, preparatory to severe constriction.

Ruth Desmond laid upon the bed the pink skirt she carried, and turned to the Herculean task of forcing a large dimension into a small—from which conflict Mrs Ferris emerged breathless and slightly purple, but triumphant. "Ah!" she said, "that's lovely! And now help Ida, my dear. You know, Ida, you must look your very best tonight."

Ida Ferris's languid smile was flavoured with self-consciousness. She accepted her cousin's ministrations without comment—taking in every detail of the tall figure reflected by the mirror, from the elaborate coiffuring of the Titian locks that formed so strong a contrast to the curly disorder of Ruth's brown hair, to the pink slippers peeping beneath the chiffon folds of her skirt. Ida was justly proud of her feet. In moments of sisterly confidence Linda had been heard to assert that they had been given her as compensation for her nose.

Mrs Ferris fluttered about them, exhorting them to haste.

"The Merediths are sure to be early," she fussed. "Willa Meredith always starts at an unearthly hour, for fear they should have a breakdown—and, of course, they never do—but her programme's full before the other girls have a chance! I don't like flighty young widows," said Mrs Ferris, severely. "I'm sure her brother-in-law isn't that kind of man!"

"Mr Rod Meredith is very rich, isn't he, Aunt Alice?" queried Ruth.

"My dear—he's just bought Broadlands!" breathed Mrs Ferris. "Such a near neighbour as he'll be! And he was so struck with Ida at the Hunt Club ball! I feel it's so nice that he would be staying with Willa, when I wanted her to come here for Christmas. I'm sure the poor man will enjoy Christmas week much more in this bright home than with just his sister-in-law at that big barn of a 'Larncuk'. Do be careful, Ruth, that ruching's all twisted!"

Ruth adjusted the ruching with a little sigh. It was not too easy—this decking the bright birds with their finery, while she—poor, plain hedge sparrow—was to stay at home. Mr Ferris's meek voice was heard in the hall.

"We're coming," Ida called. "There, that'll do Ruth—just put my cape on. Gently, you'll crush the sleeves. Ready Linda?"

Linda nodded. They rustled out of the room. Mrs Ferris turned on the threshold.

"Have a final look to the rooms for Willa and Mr Meredith, Ruth," she said. "They'll be back with us—or

Ida may come back in the car with him, while we take Willa—and Sarah's so careless about little things like soap and clean tumblers. And you may cut one of the Christmas cakes for your supper—a plain one, my child. Good night!" She blew a kiss from plump finger tips, and waddled down the hall to the waiting waggonette. "Come on, Linda!"

Linda had turned back an instant to the lonely figure on the doorstep. She gave her a brief kiss. "Good night, old girl," she whispered. "I wish you could have come!"

"Oh—don't!" said Ruth vehemently.

She went back quickly into the house, and sat down in the dim drawingroom, interlacing her fingers tightly in a strenuous endeavour to control a troublesome inclination to cry. Crying was a luxury she knew she must not permit herself—tear marks had proved too ready a target for Ida's wit in the first year of her life in the Ferris household, and that was nearly three years ago, so that in the intervening time she had had much opportunity for learning sense. She did not cry, but, shutting her lips, looked out wearily across the grey flats, timbered with box trees and wattle.

The sound of the waggonette came back faintly from the road. It was a little hard, Ruth thought. She was only twenty-three, passably pretty, with all the love of twenty-three for pretty frocks and dancing, and with a very much deeper longing for a little love and companionship, with a ceaseless homesickness for the happiness that had died with her father three years ago. It was Christmas eve, too, and Christmases had once been so merry. Ah, well, these were dangerous thoughts. She put them from her, going about the house at different tasks. Work was a good thing,

Ruth knew, to keep one from thinking.

It was 10 o'clock when a knock at the front door startled her. The servants were in bed or away at the township, and after a moment's hesitation she answered it.

"Why, Mrs Meredith!" she said.

There were two people on the doorstep. Willa Meredith, dark and plump and pretty, and a tall man, both in evening dress. Mrs Meredith was laden with wraps, and her companion was a mere receptacle for luggage.

"Good gracious—someone else not at the Christmas eve dance!" Mrs Meredith exclaimed. "Or are you Cinderella on your own account, Ruthie? My dear, we've had the time of our lives—that abominable motor car broke down no less than seven times, and at last—here we are! No use trying to get there—we've given it up. What luck to find you! By the way, do you know my brother-in-law?"

"I believe she did—ages ago, when she was in short frocks," said Rod Meredith, shaking hands heartily. "I'm awfully glad to meet you again, Miss Desmond—it was 'Ruth' then, wasn't it?"

Ruth laughed. "It's so long ago, I've almost forgotten," she said. "Come in, you poor lost people. Where's your chauffeur?"

"Gone!" said Willa tragically. "He vanished into the night to seek a blacksmith, and when he finds one he'll bring the car here—which won't be before Christmas! Oh, Ruthie, I'm so hungry!"

"Aunt Alice said I could cut a cake—a plain one!" Ruth laughed, leading the way to the diningroom. "I don't know what else there is, but I'll go and look."

"We'll come too, and help," said Willa. "Rod, put down those things and bring a lamp. When one doesn't know a passage there are always steps in it, and there's nothing so destroying to the temper as a step in the dark that you're not prepared for!" She whisked the tail of her gown over her arm and followed Ruth along the dim hall to the deserted kitchen.

"You poor, lonely little soul!" she exclaimed, as the silent house revealed itself to her. "Surely you're not quite by yourself, Ruthie?"

"Oh, I suppose old Norah's at home, but she always goes to bed early," Ruth answered lightly. "The others will be in the township—Christmas Eve, you know. And anyhow, their quarters are a good bit away and I should hardly know whether they were in or not."

"But why aren't you at the dance? Do you mean to say Grace Harrison didn't ask you?"

Ruth's face was hidden as she explored a cupboard for plates.

"Oh, yes, she asked me."

"H'm," said Mrs Meredith, with infinite meaning, checking herself on the verge of an explosion. She caught the eye of her brother-in-law, in her own a "What-did-I-tell-you?" expression. Ruth emerged from the cupboard slightly flushed.

"Now, if you people would withdraw to the drawingroom and behave nicely, I'll make coffee," she said.

"Withdraw?" said Rod Meredith blankly. "Not much—we're going to help. Personally, I prefer supper in a kitchen!"

"Wild horses wouldn't move me," Willa averred. She perched on the big table and swung dainty bronze slippers to and fro. "Rod, that fire wants wood. You see, I can help from the start!"

"I always said you were a capable woman," said her brother-in-law, stoking. "Which saucepan, Miss Desmond?"

"I'm a little afraid," Ruth hesitated, "Aunt Alice would be awfully annoyed with me for entertaining you here."

"She won't know anything about it," said Willa. "Besides, they won't be home for ages yet—and moreover, we insisted—and I'll tell her so! Now, Ruthie, don't argue with your elders, but give Rod that saucepan—and for pity's sake go and find that plain cake, I'm starving!"

Supper lengthened itself out to an unconscionable extent. The appetites of the belated motorists went beyond and above cake; and Ruth remembered that she had been too busy to go in to dinner, and discovered that she was hungry. So they ransacked the storeroom, and the scratch meal of mixed ingredients was merry and protracted. Willa Meredith, watching Ruth, observed that at first she almost started at the sound of her own laugh, and then that the little wrinkle between her brows, which had no business there at all—at twenty-three—gradually smoothed itself out, as the laugh became more and more frequent.

"I don't believe they let her laugh," she reflected, wrathfully, and straightaway set herself to counteract the supposed influence of the Ferris household. Her efforts were ably seconded by her brother-in-law, and between them Ruth was fast developing into a quite normal maiden, when Willa's sharp eyes caught sight of something on the top shelf of the dresser.

"Ruth," she said, solemnly—"is that a concertina?"

"Where?" said Ruth—"oh, there—why, yes, I believe one of the men has one of those lethal instruments. Did you want it?"

"Don't be disrespectful to a concertina in my presence," said Willa. "Father's overseer taught me to play one when I was twelve, and I love them. Give it me, Rod." She handled the concertina affectionately, and it emitted a long-drawn groan, to the great joy of her hearers. Undismayed, Mrs Meredith persevered, and presently "elicited something resembling an air."

"There!" she said, triumphantly. "I knew I could, if I once got going. Now I'm going to play a waltz."

"She really can!" said Rod Meredith, in affected wonderment, as after various preliminary shrieks and wails, the concertina settled down to 'The Merry Widow'. "Anyone would know it!"

"Then, why don't you make use of it?" snapped Willa, over her instrument.

"By Jove!" said Meredith. "May I, Miss Desmond?"

It was thus upon a strange scene that the door opened a few minutes later, and Mrs Ferris and her daughters appeared on the threshold. Curled up on the table, an incarnate sprite of mischief, Mrs Meredith contorted and swayed over the creaking concertina; while on the linoleum-covered floor a slender figure in a pink print dress swayed and floated in the arms of a tall man. No one saw the newcomers for a few moments, until Mrs Ferris emitted an uncontrollable snort.

"Oh!" said Ruth, who had heard that snort on other occasions. She stopped short and faced the doorway, growing a little pale.

"How refreshing!" said Ida Ferris, in her low drawl. "Don't let us interrupt you—it's quite idyllic."

Meredith flushed angrily.

"Willa and I had a breakdown, Mrs Ferris," he said, advancing to greet his hostess; "several breakdown, in fact. The car proved too much for us at last, and we walked on here."

"Where Ruth took care of us beautifully," put in Willa. "We were famished, and she took us in and fed us."

"But why the kitchen?" said Mrs Ferris, a little blankly.

"Ruth's ideas are a little limited," put in Ida. "She would naturally . . ."

Her voice trailed off into amused silence, and Ruth grew scarlet under her look.

"You're quite wrong, my dear Ida," said Willa composedly. "Ruth wanted to entertain us in much state, but we're homely souls, you know, and preferred the sweet simplicity of the kitchen. We've had a quite lovely time. I hope the dance was as nice?"

"Delightful," said Ida. "Shall we go into the drawing room now—or perhaps Ruth would prefer . . ?"

"I'm going to bed," returned Ruth, "now that I can depute my duties as hostess." She met her cousin's sneering eyes with a level glance.

"Don't run away, Miss Desmond," said Meredith. "It's hardly fair to brand us so plainly as nuisances."

"Oh, it's high time the child was in bed," Mrs Ferris interposed, in what Willa mentally designated her fat voice. "Past twelve o'clock. Say goodnight, my dear, and run off." And Ruth made her escape as speedily as possible.

She was brushing her hair, her cheeks still burning, when Linda entered.

"I'd give something to have hair like yours," said the latter, sinking upon the one uneasy chair the little bedroom boasted. "The dance?—oh, it was simply rotten! Hardly any men, and Ida was too furious for words because the Merediths didn't turn up. We left early, which was rather rough on me, as I did happen to be engaged for the last few dances, and there had been dreary spaces on my programme before; but Ida simply wouldn't stay. She was ready to scratch you when we discovered you waltzing with Rod Meredith in the kitchen!"

"Well. I couldn't help it," Ruth said. "He asked me—and Willa was playing that ridiculous thing."

"Of course, you couldn't," said Linda. "Ida would have been ready enough to dance with him in the kitchen, or any old place he might happen to ask her. It's only her temper—don't you worry. She's making the running with him now in the drawingroom, and Mother and Willa are valiantly endeavouring to conceal their yawns. Well, I'm off —good-night, old girl. Merry Christmas!"

Ruth met the same greeting before breakfast in the garden.

"You're early at work, Miss Desmond," said

Rod Meredith, coming round the corner of a hedge unexpectedly. "Can't I carry that basket?"

"It's scarcely burdensome," said Ruth, surrendering it. "I must cut these roses before the sun is hot, or they won't last an hour."

"I was in England last Christmas—and the two before that, in Canada," Meredith said. "It's quite jolly to see an Australian Christmas—with roses—again. As for you Miss Desmond, you've become a young lady, instead of my friend with a long pigtail, since I saw you last. We had some good rides together—do you remember?"

"That's very long ago," Ruth murmured. "That was before Daddy died. Everything has changed since then."

"Well, friends shouldn't change—and I hope we're not going to," Meredith said firmly. "Let me hold that branch down for you." He bent a great bough, fragrant with dewy crimson buds, within her reach—an action keenly noted by Miss Ferris, who gazed from her window in the wrathful helplessness engendered by dishabille and curling pins, and intensified by the sight of the pair strolling away to a path beyond her vision. Ida did not look a pleasant person when she was annoyed, and as she dressed hurriedly she was very annoyed indeed.

She was outwardly serene, however, and supremely confident of her own attractions, when she strolled into the garden half an hour later and came upon Meredith and her cousin. She gave a little start.

"You here, Ruth. Mother has been calling you. But the morning is too lovely to remember one's duties, I suppose?"

"I didn't think I had left any undone," said Ruth, guiltily conscious of not having hurried as much as possible over gathering her roses. "I'll go and find Aunt Alice. Thank you, Mr Meredith; I'll take the basket." She held out her hand for it.

"I'll carry it in for you," said Meredith gravely.

"Oh, no; let me have it."

"Really, you need not trouble, Mr Meredith," Ida said. "Ruth is quite able to take it herself—aren't you, Ruth?"

"I must complete my contract," Meredith said, laughing. "Now, then, Miss Desmond, are you coming?" He marched off serenely, leaving Ida in a frame of mind that made the prompt annihilation of a clump of lilies a soothing occupation.

That was the beginning of a Christmas week of great discomfort for little Ruth Desmond. She found herself in a sudden atmosphere of suspicion that made all previous coldness a thing pleasant by comparison; and the worst of it was that she could not quite tell why. She was not conscious of having offended any of the unwritten canons that governed the Ferris household; certainly, she worked very hard, and her aunt, who was accustomed to remark in a vague way, in her case, that "honest work always tells," gave her every opportunity of active service. The festivities of the week were many, and it seemed to Ruth that she lived in an atmosphere of cutting sandwiches and compiling fruit salads. Then Rod Meredith developed an alarming way of appearing suddenly, and taking as much of her task as possible into his own big hands, or, if he could not render help, of sitting on benches, or kitchen tables, or haply flour bins, and talking to her while she worked.

It was pleasant, but harrowing, for there was always the certainty of Ida and her mother appearing, and that led to further deepening of the chilly atmosphere of suspicion. Added to which, there came upon the girl a queer fluttering of the heart whenever a certain firm footstep sounded, that made it increasingly hard for her to look up and meet Rod's eyes calmly. It was the hot Christmas weather, she told herself: she was a little overdone with the constant work. When the guests went it would be better. And then a sudden numb feeling made her realise that when one guest went the emptiness of her life would be greater than ever.

"Why don't you come out on these picnics and things?" Rod asked her for the twentieth time.

"I don't want to," she said, laughing at his glum face. "I told you so."

"Then I think you might put your feelings aside for the good of the community, and be unselfish," he said, "I thought all girls liked picnics."

"So they do," said a brisk voice, as Willa Meredith appeared. "They're hunting for you, Rod. My dear boy," she added, as she walked him off, "why do you worry the poor little soul? Don't you know she can't come?"

"Can't? Why not?"

"Because she has neither time nor clothes," said Mrs Meredith. "I knew it was bad, but I didn't know how bad. They pretend she doesn't care to come—the truth is she has far to much to do, and hardly a decent thing to wear. I never saw such a poor little Cinderella. Oh, I've got a lot out of Linda—she's a poor, backboneless thing, but she has a little heart. Ruth won't open her lips." She nodded wisely. "I'm going to alter things."

"How?"

"How? I don't know just yet. Carry her off somehow—if they'll let her come. I must do something Rod. One thing I have done—got her a new dress for their dance tomorrow night. Otherwise she wasn't coming in. I found that out from Linda." At which point they reached the verandah, and Rod found himself detailed for the fifth time that week to drive Ida in the dog cart. He was beginning to loathe with his whole soul both Ida and the dog cart.

Ruth was somewhat pale and heavy-eyed next evening when she came downstairs in the pretty white frock that was Willa's gift. She had been working hard all the hot day. Much of the preparation for the dance had fallen on her, and it had been late before she was able to go to her room to dress. As it was, the first dance was over as she reached the hall, and hesitated, listless and dispirited.

A tall figure emerged apparently from a clump of palms near the staircase.

"I thought you were never coming," Meredith said. "I've got a programme for you and 'made so bold' as to put my own name down a few times. It's our dance now," as the music struck up. "You don't think me too grasping, do you?"

Ruth was too tired just then to cavil at anything. The music roused her a little as they danced up the long room—that, or the arm that held her closely, and the brown eyes that looked straight into hers until she sought refuge by down glancing. Half in a dream she found the waltz over, and Meredith led her to a shady corner of the creeper screened verandah.

"There!" he said. "What do you mean by coming down

dog tired? It isn't fair, Ruth."

Her name slipped from him unnoticed by either. Ruth found herself struggling with a most unusual desire to cry.

"Well," he said, "it isn't fair to badger you, either. I know it's not your fault. Never mind. Let's talk." His quiet voice soothed her imperceptibly as he talked without waiting for her replies, and when at last he jumped up she had forgotten that she was ever tired.

"By George!" Meredith said, "that's the Lancers, and I've shirked three dances, and was engaged for one of them! I must go and make my peace. You'll come in?"

She shook her head.

"I'll stay here during this dance."

"Then I'll find you afterwards." He smiled at her and was gone.

Ruth shut her eyes for a moment, yielding to the strange new sense of happiness wrapping her round.

"Oh, you're here!" said a voice whose languid drawl did not disguise its bitterness. "Actually released poor Mr Meredith for a moment! I wonder at that. How did he manage to get away?"

Mrs Ferris followed her daughter.

"I'm utterly amazed at you, Ruth!" she said. "The talk of the whole ballroom—as if it wasn't bad enough before, your hunting the poor man down!"

"Aunt!"

"Sitting out here with him half the evening," said Mrs Ferris, malevolently, "in a dark corner, where no nice girl would dream of going. I've put up with your conduct during the week, Ruth—always dragging him into places where you were working, until anyone could see how sick of it he was. But this is too barefaced."

"How dare you!" said Ruth, huskily; "how dare you!"

"Dare! My gracious!" said her aunt. "It's you that is the daring one, miss. I can't countenance it any longer—making yourself a disgrace and a laughing stock to him and everyone. Anyone could see he has really no eyes for any girl but Ida—but all men will play with what's thrown at them! You can't blame them," said Mrs Ferris, with the decision born of years and ponderousness.

"Ruth's infatuation's been quite an amusement to Rod," said Ida, using the Christian name with a shy little giggle. "He's been laughing over it to me. He never saw any girl quite so open about it, he said."

"There!" Mrs Ferris began.

Ruth cut her short. "Oh, don't—don't!" she said, choking. Turning, she fled from the verandah into the fragrant darkness of the garden.

There was a big pepper tree at the very end of the garden, close where the creek gurgled outside the picket fence. It was an old place of refuge. She had carried hurts and slights there many a time, but never a heart so torn as now. She crouched against the rough trunk, shuddering uncontrollably, without tears. Tears were dried up in the hot waves of shame that raced over her. He had laughed—he thought her barefaced! The cruel words rang in her ears. She had thought him kind, and all the time he was jeering at her with Ida. Her aunt's malicious taunts were forgotten in the agony of her thought. Later they would hurt. Just now she was conscious of one thing—that he had laughed.

A quick, anxious step came down the path, and Ruth shrank closer to the tree, feeling that above all things she could not speak to anyone then. For a moment she held her breath.

"Ruth—are you there?"

At his voice a cold shivering succeeded the hot shame flush. She kept very still. Perhaps he would not see.

It was the gleam of the white frock that led Rod Meredith into the shade of the old tree. He put his hand gently on her shoulder.

"Ruth!"

"Go away!" she whispered—"please go away!"

A big wave of pity swept over the man.

"I came to find you," he said. Willa heard them talking to you—those vile women. Ruth, you didn't believe them—you couldn't! Damn them!" cried he, suddenly—"I wish they weren't women!"

She faced him, still clinging with one hand to the rough friendliness of the trunk.

"Then—you didn't say it?"

"Say it?—say one word against you to that unspeakable pair! Ah, Ruth, you didn't believe it of me?" His voice faltered and shook. "Ruth—little Ruth—don't you know I love you?"

"I thought," she said, "I thought"—

"I thought it was plain enough," he said. "I tried to hold my tongue, it seemed so beastly sudden; but you had me bowled over from that very first night, when I danced with you in the kitchen on Christmas Eve!"

"They said it was Ida."

"Ida!" he said. "Ida!" And the tone was sufficient. "If she were the last woman alive I'd be lucky to get away from her! Ruth—sweetheart—say you'll marry me!"

* * *

On the front doorstep Mrs Ferris and her elder daughter gazed with wrathful eyes at two figures that came out of the shadows of the garden.

"So it's you, Ruth," said the elder woman, icily.

"Need you ask?" said Ida, with a little giggle. "No one else does quite such peculiar things as Ruth." Meredith's arm pressed more tightly against that he held, but the girl did not flinch.

"So kind of you, Mr Meredith, to bring in my runaway," Mrs Ferris purred. "Come with me, Ruth; I want you." Her voice was full of malevolent intent as she turned. Meredith's cold tones brought her back.

"Ruth has not much time," he said, stiffly—"she returns with Willa and me tonight. She has done me the honor to promise to marry me." He paused, unwilling to surrender the girl for even a moment. Then his brow cleared, as Willa, like a plump mother bird, fussed out on the verandah.

"There's the fairy godmother." Meredith said, laughing; and the Ferris women suddenly realised that for all practical purposes they had dropped out of his world. "I was looking for you, Willa. I want you to take care of my little Cinderella!"

A COASTWISE CHRISTMAS

"It's beautiful, isn't it, darling?" she asked.

"Perfect," he assented; and added a little hastily—"love."

They were sitting in a nook of the hummocks, looking out upon a view that comprehended "the long wash of Australasian seas," the green rollers came tumbling in below them, their crests advancing and creaming upon the hard yellow sand, then slipping back with much haste and flurry into the Southern Ocean. It seemed to Herbert Forester that there was a certain sameness about the breakers. Undoubtedly, what they were doing they did all the time. And though the view was assuredly magnificent, and poet and painter chaps would rave over it—still, when you boiled it down, it was principally water. He had said as much in a tentative fashion, to Joyce, his wife, but she had been distressingly horrified. So he had "crawled down" hastily, making a more or less feeble attempt to assure her that he was only joking; after which Peace had spread her snow-white wings again. There was no doubt that it was peaceful.

It had been a year before that the small god Eros had suggested their present location as an ideal setting for a honeymoon; to be, as all honeymoons should be, Bert said with conviction, absolutely *a deux*. They had been members of a big party camped further up the coast, and in a motor launch trip had found this little inlet, almost land-locked; a long inland strip of water two miles wide, with a tiny fishing village nestling on its inner shore, and dotted here and there with minute islands. It was the outer land wall that appealed to Joyce and Bert—a green solitude of ti-tree, fronting on one side the calm water of the inlet, and, a mile across, the breakers rolling in upon the back beach. "Rolling forever!" Joyce had said. And Bert meeting her shy gaze—the engagement was a month old—had echoed "Forever!" And neither knew exactly what they meant, but they were very happy.

"It would be so absolutely jolly," Bert had said. "We could have all our camping paraphernalia sent to that little place—what's its name?—Shoreville—by coach, and drive down ourselves; then hire a boat and pull across. There's good water, and every acre's full of ripping places to camp. It's only two miles to Shoreville for supplies—nothing of a pull; we could go there twice a week, if we wanted a change." They laughed tenderly at the foolishness of the idea. "Well, once a week. (Can you drink condensed milk, sweetheart?) And we'd have it all to ourselves—the whole blessed landscape: 'Just us two by ourselves.' Beats all your Melbourne and Sydney honeymoons to pieces. Cheap too" said Bert, who was nothing if not practical; "we could have a month instead of a fortnight. A whole month!"

"A honeymoon," said Joyce, very low. And so it was settled.

They had kept to the idea with wonderful persistency, considering that both were young people of somewhat impetuous tendencies, and that once or twice the engagement itself had tottered on its throne. Bert remarked, afterwards that occasionally he had had his doubts as to the permanence of the engagement, but the idea of the honeymoon had never wavered for an instant; a statement which was somewhat ambiguous, and demanded explanation.

Other people had mildly tried to dissuade them, with the annoying cock-suredness of those, who, having gone through the mill themselves, feel it incumbent upon them to instruct the novice. Bert and Joyce declined to believe that they stood in need of any instruction. When George, who was Joyce's elder brother, and married at that, grinned knowingly, and said—"Civilisation's a good old stand-by—take my tip and try Sorrento," Bert was more than a little nettled, and Joyce told him in confidence that it saddened her to think of how much of the poetry of life Mildred and George had missed—a benevolent reflection which would have hugely amused Mildred and George, who were wholesomely devoted to each other, and their three riotous youngsters. Joyce was wearing at the moment a clinging evening frock of soft silk of a die away color, and the quality of appealingness which was the strongest note in her prettiness was never more in evidence. Also, it was moonlight. Bert thought her half divine.

Eventually, opposition to the primeval honeymoon had ceased, seeing that the chief personages were bent upon it, and that they belonged to the genus that finds its purposes increase under opposition. After all, as the father of Joyce had said, it was their picnic. So the lovers studied the questions of tents and flies, and specialised in canned provisions, and made deep and searching inquiries as to the various brands of concentrated milk. Then, the question being settled, all their friends inundated them with advice about camping. Bert calculated that, had they absorbed all the gratuitous counsel offered them, a steamer of great draught would have been required to transport their effects from Shoreville to the Ideal Site. They minimised this difficulty by taking the advice where it happened to coincide with their own intentions. Bert had camped out once—as a guest—and he was morally certain that to teach him anything about the game would be to gild refined gold and paint the lily. Joyce agreed absolutely. Whether in agreement or disagreement in vain, Joyce did nothing by halves.

The day after the wedding saw them chugging into Shoreville in the little motor lent them by Bert's brother. Bert was not altogether expert as a chauffeur, and the last ten miles, which had been principally heavy sand, had been a trifle strenuous. They welcomed the little village enthusiastically.

Shoreville turned out to meet them to a man, and particularly to a child—it was the midday recess, and the State school was conveniently near the hotel, where the bride and bridegroom had thankfully alighted. Not one of the youth or beauty of Shoreville had ever seen a motor, and presently there was a dense and palpitating ring about the car. Bert had some difficulty in penetrating it on returning from arranging with the landlord, about a garage; he had very much deeper difficulty in inducing the car to start again, and Shoreville enjoyed itself hugely. Finally he managed to get going again, and saw, with considerable relief, the door of a rather ricketty stable padlocked upon his unruly responsibility.

Lunch—Shoreville called it, with firmness, dinner—had, been a welcome interlude; after which, it had not been difficult, to arrange with a local, fisherman to convey their baggage, which had previously arrived, to the Ideal Site, and tow them in the dinghy which they hired from the landlord; at a somewhat fancy price. The solatium demanded for his labor by the fisherman was also spectacular, had they known it; however, ignorance is indubitably a factor of bliss, and bliss was certainly predominant as they, glided easily over the blue water of the inlet, which held the reflection of a perfect sky, flecked with white baby clouds. Joyce and Bert wished the voyage had been a longer one, when at length the boat's keel grated on the beach and the dinghy bumped into her stern with sudden force. The fisherman—who plainly thought them mad—assisted Bert to carry their possessions inland, and gave him sage counsel as to the securing of the dinghy. Then, with several backward looks indicative of amazement, he put off. The wind caught his sail as he ran it up, and the boat curtseyed to a gust, and scudded off before it. They were alone—in Eden.

Eden was a busy place that afternoon. After the exact site for the camp had been selected there was a little clearing of ti-tree to be done—foreshore regulations not having penetrated to regions so remote as Eden—and suitable stakes and poles to be found—a matter by no means so easy as it sounds, even with bush on every side. It was late before the tents finally appeared, a patch of startling white in the deep green; and even then an old camper might have smiled at some of the details of their erection. Joyce and Bert were devoutly thankful to see them up at all; a limp parcel of tent is somewhat harrowing for the novice to deal with, and the honeymooners were warm with exertion. Other arrangements were treated as lightly as possible, and the first meal on the Ideal Site, which was to have been dignified by fish caught by the bridegroom, resolved itself into tinned mutton opened painfully by the bride. They did not wash up.

Dawn, however, brought more energy—it also brought little flies, which made sleep an impossibility—and the day went busily and blissfully in establishing themselves with the thoroughness demanded by a month's occupation. Bert freed their little clearing of the tiniest spike that might offend his lady's foot, and masked its only opening cleverly with cut bush, so that no passing marauder might ever dream that Eden lingered there. So cleverly, indeed, was the masking done that when Joyce wandered away in the course of the day she utterly failed to find her way back to camp, and was only rescued after much soprano coo-eeing, and somewhat tearful, by her palpitating lord; an interlude which considerably delayed progress. However, in good time all was finished; the deck chairs unfurled, the hammock slung between two big banksias, the meat safe gracefully dependent from a sheoak limb; even great sprays of snowy Christmas bush festooning the ridge pole of the dining tent. The dwellers in Eden agreed that it was very good; and went forth to fish.

Now, your true camper is born, not made. Necessity and practice may manufacture a very decent imitation out of the spurious article; but the man or woman who thoroughly enjoys camping is a thing apart. To such is given in fullest measure that gift of the gods called knack—which infers capability, adaptability, common sense, readiness, and several other useful attributes; to which should be added, in the case of the camper for pleasure, a sense of humour, without which all the rest were as naught. So equipped, you may camp joyously on a sandy desert, with one lone pack horse to carry your outfit; otherwise an oasis (within handy distance of the railway line), and a train of laden camels were insufficient to secure your happiness; for you have not the heaven-born soul of the camper. It must be admitted with regret that our honeymooners belonged to the genus for whom camel trains would ply in vain.

Just when it came definitely home to Joyce that she was bored, she could never—or would never—tell. Not even to herself would she readily admit the amazing possibility of such a serpent in Eden. By all laws, human or divine, the situation should have been perfect; therefore, she argued, it was perfect, and—perhaps she would feel better to-morrow. The day was hot, and it was depressing that the flies had got to the corned beef. Who, coming from Armadale, would have dreamed that the lone bush would hold so many flies? The little ones woke them with the first hint of dawn, and the big ones rioted round them as they ate, insomuch that you made violent sword play about your face with your knife while you endeavored to convey your fork to your mouth. Bert had been remarkably angry when in the haste of the moment he had put his knife in his mouth and hurled a toothsome fragment of fish from his fork into the ti-tree; and Joyce had cooed over him, immensely concerned. Neither had seen anything, funny in the tragedy. There were other things besides flies; ants of sorts, and lizards, and various creatures that crept and crawled, and that Bert, called collectively—and disgustedly—"wogs."

Neither did the routine of camp life appeal to the bride. On a gas stove, she rather prided herself on her cooking—but this business of black quart pots, slung on a blackened bough, was a thing apart. The smoke had an unholy way of blowing in her eyes, no matter on what side she took her stand; and it was so difficult to tell when things were done; and so often they weren't. Bert was willing enough, but cookery was a sealed book to him, and he was one of those unfortunates who are not brought "up to do things." Office, tennis court, and golf links had rounded out his little life—very comfortably, as far as he was concerned. He had been accustomed to think himself no mean backwoodsman when he split the box blocks in their yard at Caulfield, and received his mother's thanks for the labour. Joyce found him small help, although he ate heroically whatever she gave him, and never betrayed the smallest pang of indigestion which certainly should have rent him. And—there were other things, though Joyce crimsoned at her own scarcely-admitted cavillings; the little make shifts of camp life, the bridegroom who was so different to the spick-and-span, well-tailored youth, she knew. She thought she hid her feelings, but Bert felt her shrink once from his unshaven face, and after that he made heroic efforts to use his razor daily, and to dress his part like—to quote his own phrase—"a blooming Johnny in a musical comedy."

He, too, made strenuous efforts to conceal his boredom. Joyce was altogether sweet, of course, and the honeymoon was perfect—but there was so little to do. The fishing was poor; only flathead came to the hook at all readily and Joyce did not care for flathead; neither were they fishermen by nature, and Joyce was apt to be scared in a small boat. In Eden itself was naught but ti-tree—to their town bred eyes all bush was ti-tree; and wherever you walked there was nothing else to see, save on the ocean beach, where he had once enjoyed one glorious surf bathe—which had been the first and the last because on his return dripping and triumphant like a sea god he had found his bride weeping with anxiety for his sake upon a hummock. They had brought with them but two books, and those under protest, and more to convince other people in the train that they were ordinary travellers. Joyce had brought *Sartor Resartus*. And Bert, *Harry Dale's Jockey*. Having read them, they had exchanged; and then Bert had read his own book again—lingeringly. Bad as he felt at times, he did not again venture upon *Sartor Resartus*.

They were well into the third week of the honeymoon now, and there was no part of Eden that they did not know. Exploration could go no further in any direction. Both loathed the sight and savour of fish, and canned provisions were to them as apples of Sodom. These things they endeavoured to conceal from one another, although Bert had that morning declared, hurling an empty condensed milk tin into the scrub, that he'd give a fiver for a cow; and Joyce had sighed. They had told each other everything they could think of likely to interest or amuse—both playing the game, as was decent; every topic under the sun had been thrashed out. Now they began to shrink a little from discussions, since these had begun to breed a little—just a little—shade of acrimonious feeling, which is against all law and tradition on honeymoons. There were long grey patches of silence—not good, friendly, comfortable silence, but scarred by a horrible feeling of being guiltily dull.

"They put the pantomime on tonight at Her Majesty's," Bert said, suddenly. His eyes rested with weariness on the tossing breakers.

"Oh, so they do! The pantomime!" Joyce sighed. "I do love pantomimes. We'll go when we're back, won't we, dear?"

"Rather. Seems quite nice to think of a theatre again."

"Doesn't it?" She flushed guiltily. "Not dull, Bert, are you?"

"What, an, idea!" He laughed with much vigor. "Nor you?"

"Why Bert!" She slipped her hand into his, and he rolled over on the hot sand and brushed it with his lips, "Dearest!"

He sat up a moment later and began to fill his pipe.

"You're smoking too much, Bert."

"One must do something." He flushed in his turn. "Oh, I didn't mean that, you know, dear; but one smokes without thinking when one's loafing—and the fishing's so rotten, you know." He changed the subject strategically. "To think of its being Christmas tomorrow!"

"Yes. 'Member last Christmas, Bert?"

"Rather!" enthusiastically. "Wasn't there a crowd! Ripping day, wasn't it?"

"Lovely! And to think, now, there's just us two!"

"Heaps better, isn't it?" said Bert, playing the game like a hero. "You—you wouldn't like to go over and have Christmas dinner at the hotel, would you darling?"

The temptation was so great that Joyce knew it should be resisted.

"I'm quite happy here, dear," she murmured. "Unless you—?"

"Oh, not at all," said the bridegroom, hurriedly; "It was only a passing thought." He lit his pipe, and the operation stifled a sigh, "Got to go over to Shoreville in the morning, you know—tucker and mail."

"Yes it'll be lovely to get letters, won't it?" said Joyce, brightening.

Their relations had appreciated the claims of Eden, and

letters had been few and far between.

"You'll come, won't you?"

"Ye-es—if it's not rough." The trips to Shoreville were not joyful expeditions to Joyce—the pull was a long one, and tides had a way of being against them. "It's easier for you if I don't, you know, dear—my weight—"

"Your weight!" said Bert,laughing. "Well, it's just as you like. We'll see in the morning."

The morning broke gusty, with the surface of the inlet whipped into it's weak attempt at "white horses." They wished each other "Merry Christmas" with careful enthusiasm, trying not to remember the distant flesh pots, as they breakfasted upon sardines, and bread of a stupendous staleness, faintly flavored with kerosene. But for the dancing water Joyce might have reconsidered her refusal of the invitation to the hotel dinner; as it was, she urgently commanded her lord to break into the Shoreville emporium and rack it of its utmost in the way of delicacies.

"You bet," said Bert, pushing off. "I've had about enough of this tack."

It was the first time he had hinted at discontent, and Joyce's mouth quivered slightly—it was also the first time he had left her without a prolonged farewell. The boat required some management, and in the flurry of getting away he could only wave his adieus—nearly losing an oar in the effort. Bert's oarsmanship was more strenuous than skilful. The boat made quick progress—the tide was with her and Joyce sat down on the shore and watched disconsolately. It was most "un-Christmassy" she thought; she missed them all horribly—the big home circle, who had made each Christmas in her life. Here there was only

Bert—she started at finding the word in her heart, but it was there all the same. Only Bert, and she wanted them all—she wanted Christmas.

A little island lay across the water, not many hundred yards away. They had landed on it once—it was but a scant acre of sparse scrub, with a shelving beach. Her gaze rested on it idly. Then she stood up.

"Whatever is Bert doing?" she said, aloud.

Bert was pulling for the island with hurried strokes. He cast frequent glances over his shoulder, each time bringing fresh energy to work upon the oars. Looking at him keenly, shading her eyes, she suddenly realised that the dinghy, was very low in the water. "Luckily, there was not time for acute anxiety. The boat filled and went down a dozen yards from the island, and Bert, still grasping the oars, waded ashore.

"G-good gracious!" said the little bride. She sat down on the beach, feeling her knees give way. Across the stretch of dancing waves her husband waved and gesticulated—she heard faint sounds of shouting, but could distinguish no words. This may have been as well. She saw him wade in—try to pull the submerged boat ashore, and fail utterly. He paddled out again, sat down on a log and looked at her. It was amazing to think they could feel so far apart.

It is probable that, had Joyce had time for a moment of anxiety, her every feeling had been swallowed up in thankfulness for her husband's escape. As it was, she scarcely realised it. To her dismay, she found that her chief sensation was indignation. It was so silly of Bert to be cast away on a stupid little island, just for want of a little care in examining the dinghy. What were they to do now? In books people so situated flew signals of distress, remembering which, she procured a white petticoat and, laboriously climbing a tree, tied it to the highest branch she could reach, where it fluttered bravely, and, being seen from Shoreville, was taken as an exuberant decoration in honour of Christmas. There seemed nothing else she could do. She was bereft of husband, home, letters, dinner—of all that makes Christmas. Like the women of Babylon, she sat her down, and wept.

From this distressful, albeit wholly natural, occupation she was presently aroused by a shout.

A smart little motor boat came drifting down upon her. She had noticed it, earlier that morning, churning lazily up-channel, its sole occupant a man in white flannels, whose comfortable position had led Bert to remark that he wished he could borrow that jigger to run over to Shoreville, instead of acting as motor himself. Now the little launch had gone wrong—that was evident. The engine was silent as she came swiftly along—the current ran strongly out to sea round the point towards which she drifted. Her occupant stood upright, a thin coil of rope in his hands.

"Catch, please!"

The rope whizzed past Joyce. She caught it, and, obedient to a quick order, flung the loop in which it ended over a little stump close by. The rope tightened and the boat swung round, her bow in to shore. The man in white flannels pulled in closer and sprang out.

"Thanks, awfully," he said.

He was a tall fellow, with a brown, boyish face, and hands that were lean and capable. Joyce watched them as he pulled the boat further, up the beach and made the rope fast. She decided that he was not an intruder to be afraid of.

"You'll think I'm a fearful ass, to be caught like that without oars," he said, presently turning to her. "Fact is, some blessed boys had taken 'em when I came down this morning, and I wouldn't wait to hunt up another pair—the motor never plays up. Only it chose to!" He laughed boyishly. "Stuck me up altogether, hang it! I'd have drifted out to sea but for you—unless I'd bumped to pieces on the bar."

"Hadn't you an anchor?" Joyce asked.

"A little one only—it wouldn't hold in the channel, with the wind and tide going at this rate. It's quite enough for fishing as a rule, and easier to manage than the big one. I'll be more careful in future, I assure you." He grinned ruefully, and changed the subject. "My name's Garland—I live over there." He pointed vaguely across the inlet. "And I know who you are—the bride, isn't it? Mrs Forester? Shoreville isn't a big place, you know," he finished, apologetically.

Joyce laughed, blushing.

"I saw your husband getting his boat ready as I went up this morning," Garland said. "Going across for the Christmas mail, I suppose? I might have brought it out to you if I'd thought, and saved him a long pull. He'll have a bad time coming, back, I'm afraid."

"He hasn't got very far," Joyce answered. "If you look you'll see him on that island. The boat went down just beside it. I think that Christmas isn't a healthy time for boats here!" she finished. Her lips quivered a little.

"By Jove!" said Garland, blankly. He looked at the disconsolate figure of the bridegroom, alone on his island, and turned back to the more pathetic one of the bride, desolate in Eden. "What a beastly nuisance! You poor little soul! This is a nice way to spend Christmas, I must say."

"Do—do you think anyone will come along?" she asked. "I—I flew a flag!" She blushed, indicating the drapery in question.

"Well done you!" said Garland, heroically grave. "First rate idea! Oh, someone's sure to come along—just as well I've broken down, in one way, as my people will certainly be out to look for me if I'm not home before dark—I promised to be in for a picnic at three. But I'm afraid we can't alter things ourselves; and the township's pretty somnolent on Christmas morning."

"It's worst for Bert," Joyce said. "Poor boy, he has nothing, and, at least, I have the stale bread." She flushed. "I can't even offer you a decent dinner," she said. "Bert was to bring that too. And the bread's keroseney—not very, though. We might toast it."

"Great Scott!" said Garland. "Well, of all the Christmases! I think I'm glad I was wrecked, under the circumstances—I went off breakfastless, and told them to put me up a huge lunch. So you'll be my guest, won't you?"

"It's—it's very kind of you," Joyce answered, hating herself for feeling relieved. "It seems a bit unfeeling—with poor dear Bert there—but I'm terribly hungry—and what I'll be by lunch time—! You truly do think someone will come along and pick Bert up, don't you?"

"Absolutely certain," Garland reassured her. "You really needn't worry as far as his safety's concerned. Let's sit here and watch for a sail on the horizon—that's the correct thing, I believe, isn't it?"

They sat down in the shade and talked. Garland had just returned from Melbourne; he had the latest of news—had been to the theatres, knew the prospects of the pantomimes, and had tales to tell of the Christmas crowds in the shops. The very thought of a crowd was music to Joyce. Her charming, sun-tanned face, her unfeigned interest, led Garland to enjoy his own efforts to entertain; brides, he had thought, were uninteresting to all but one man, but this little bride was of a different type.

Afar, across a strip of dancing blue, the bridegroom tarried under a she-oak, watching them, with sullen eyes.

The sun rose higher. The pair on the sand went further into the shade, and the bridegroom came from under the sheoak. Presently the figure in white flannels moved to the boat, returning, not empty handed. Thereafter a thin spiral of blue smoke, lazily mounting, proclaimed the lighting of a fire, and, to the hungry bridegroom, told in clamant tongues of tea. He swore, low and fervently. They were no longer to be seen, but his mental vision showed them plainly enough. And this was his wife! And he, marooned! Marooned and starving—and on Christmas day! The bridegroom groaned, and cast himself upon the sand. Stirring presently, he tightened his belt.

The lunch was certainly good. There was a cold chicken, and sandwiches of cucumber and tomato; there was cake—home made. More than all, there was a bottle of milk—the real product. Joyce could have sobbed over the milk. Garland pressed her to eat, laughing at her protests.

"I really am ashamed," Joyce said, laughing. "I'm frightfully hungry, really—and if you knew how I hate the very thought of anything out of a tin! There never was anything so good as this chicken—except the cucumber. It's—it's a lovely Christmas dinner!"

"Oh, is it?" said a voice in the rear, bitterly.

Behind them stood the bridegroom—and dripped. The Southern Ocean ran down from his garments—which were few, and clave to him—and formed little pools around him in the dust.

"Oh Bert!" she cried, and ran to him. "No, thank you," said the bridegroom, brokenly. "I see you're quite happy—it doesn't matter about me. I—I'll go and change. Go on with your dinner. Dinner!"

He laughed the laugh of a bruised heart.

"Excuse me—I thought I saw a boat," said Garland, hastily, fixing an interested eye on a blank horizon. "I'll trot off and look." He disappeared through the trees, and the bride wept unrestrainedly on the bridegroom's damp breast.

"I don't believe you cared a bit," said Bert presently. He was on the point of yielding—but not quite. There was a little soreness still. "You were talking away like anything."

"Well, wouldn't you?" sobbed the stricken bride. "He'd just come from town—and oh, Bert, aren't you a bit dull? I am, I know. It—it's a lonely place, even if we are on our honeymoon!"

"Dull!" said Bert, explosively. "Then you don't mind if we go away—darling?"

"Mind!" said the bride—"mind——!" Words failed her. She hugged the bridegroom frantically.

* * *

"If you'd just put us across," the bridegroom said to Garland a little later. He was clothed and in his right mind, and had feasted royally on the remains of the chicken. A motor launch, known of Garland was coming briskly across the inlet, and had flown a signal in answer to the fluttering camp pennon, which the bridegroom had then hastily hauled down. "No, I don't think we're coming back—I'll just slip over tomorrow and get the things." He rammed the tobacco into his pipe, keeping his eyes carefully on the operation. "Fact is, we think of going to the hotel tonight—right out of tucker y'know—and—and my wife's rather keen on having New Year with her own people. Women have these ideas about these occasions—Christmases and—things" he finished vaguely. He stood up and waved an arm of welcome to the incoming boat. "Ready, Joy?—hurry!" he cried.

SANTA CLAUS, HELPER

From the verandah Jock's mother watched the little boy come slowly up the path. She had watched him from the time he had come into view, parting the shrubs that screened the pleasant, untidy part of the garden they called "The Wilderness". He walked very slowly, as though the spade on his shoulder were heavy. When he was near the verandah she stood up, leaning over the low, latticed railing, and called to him.

"Coming for a cup of tea, boy?"

Jock looked up and nodded soberly at her. "Presently," he said. "I'll put this by first." He went on. The little mother sighed as the dragging footsteps went to the tool house door. Then she poured out a cup of tea very carefully, making it a little stronger than usual—at eight years old one begins to think it is time one had strong tea—putting beside it a plate of the little iced cakes Jock was specially fond of, she waited.

When he came he pulled his chair further back into the creepers, and did not look at her. He ate his cake slowly, as though his mouth were dry. Although he talked quite cheerfully, the little mother knew exactly how each mouthful felt. She wished suddenly that he were younger—not so much of a man. It is so difficult to help anyone like that. Then father came home, and they all talked together: after which father asked Jock if he had time to lend him a hand with a new fowl fence that he was building, and if mother would come too, and hand them the nails while they fixed the wire netting. They worked together very hard until it was time for tea, which Jock generally had by himself; but tonight he found his place laid in the big dining room. During tea father talked to him exactly as if he were a man, and Jock answered gravely. He liked it: it made things easier.

When it was bed time, he stood up very straight, looking father squarely in the eyes as he said good night, and gripping his hand hard. Father said “Good night, old son.” Then mother said, “I’ll come up, dear,” just as she said it every night. There was nothing unusual; Jock would have hated it had there been. He said, “All right, mother,” and went out.

When she came into the room he was sitting on the edge of his bed in his pyjamas. He slipped on his knees as she sat down, and said his prayers in the ordinary fashion. But at the end there came a break. For a week there had been a little special prayer that Scamp might get better—he had asked her if she thought God would mind his praying for a little yellow dog, and she had assured him that it was all right. Tonight, for the first time, it had to be left out.

He stopped a minute where he was, and she felt his hands hard on her knee. Then he got up, not looking at her, and climbed into bed. She pulled the sheet up, and tucked him in, and blew out the light. Then as she put her face down to him his arms went round her neck and he held her tight. She felt his heart pound and his breath coming unevenly, and her own tears were wet on his cheeks. But Jock would not let himself cry.

“He—he’s so jolly lonely,” he said brokenly. “He always slept here, you know—wouldn’t be happy anywhere else. I say, mother—I did hate leaving him under the beastly pear tree.”

"I know best-beloved," she said. "I know. But he doesn't feel it, Jock—boy."

The boy choked back a sob.

"He did suffer so." he said. "All the time I kept seeing his eyes—he never made any row, did he? An' he thought I could help him—you could see his eyes asking. An' I—an' I——

His voice died away, and he broke into pitiful, low sobbing—it was not easy for the little mother to hear how he tried to stop it, being very ashamed. She could only hold him tightly and say the little foolish things that mothers always have in their hearts, even for boys of eight, and that even bigger boys than eight like to hear sometimes. After a while he was quiet again.

"Father's jolly good, isn't he?" he said. He understands. I say don't let him ever give me another dog. A fellow couldn't stand it, when he'd had one from a pup, an' he died like that. You tell him."

The little mother told father when she went down, after Jock had fallen into a restless sleep, with the tear stains on his face. Father nodded, looking very like a big edition of Jock.

"That's awkward," he said "I had thought, at Christmas … Poor little son, it's hard on him." Then, seeing the mother's eyes he drew her down on his knee, and they talked.

Jock did not again, in his own words, "make a fool of himself." He went about as usual, making no fuss at all, and never mentioning Scamp. But he was so quiet that the house seemed quite strange, and somehow, he could not eat. Father and mother grew quite worried about him, and he made great efforts to reassure them, even whistling elaborately when he knew they were watching him. The whistle never lasted long. Blue shadows came under his eyes, and the brown began to leave his cheeks.

"He's just fretting inside his poor little mind all the time," mother said to father. "As for Christmas, he isn't taking the slightest interest in it. What are we going to do with him John?"

"We've got to have things right at Christmas, anyhow," father declared. "Let's take counsel with Santa Claus."

The mother shook her head. "Santa Claus can't bring Scamp back," she said.

* * *

Jock woke on Christmas morning with the sense of missing something that had grown familiar to him. His stocking hung at the foot of his bed, and, sitting up, he unpacked it slowly—no boy on earth could have failed to like what he found, but the world was not right for Jock. He had a memory of last Christmas, when Scamp had sat on the foot of the bed, madly interested—his eye wandered to the collar he had found that day, that just fitted Scamp. It hung empty on the wall now. The smile he gave Father and Mother as they came in was a forlorn little one.

"Hullo!" he said. "Merry Christmas."

"Same to you, old chap," father answered. They sat down on the bed and watched him unpack his treasures. When he had finished he looked at them a little uncertainly.

"Ripping lot, isn't it?"

"There's something else," father said. Stooping he drew

a covered basket from under the bed, and lifted it very gently. He steadied it on his knee.

"You open it, sonnie."

Under the lid a small yellow head poked up feebly, and a pink tongue licked at the boyish fingers. But Jock shrank back.

"Father!—I don't want another dog; I couldn't stand it——"

"Steady; don't shake him," father said. "He's a pretty sick little dog, this chap—run over by a motorcycle, and his leg's broken, and he's generally knocked about. I found him abominably neglected in a dealer's back yard. Seemed to me you're about the only one I know who could pull him through. He's the breed you understand, you see."

The yellow head that was so like Scamp's pushed feebly towards Jock again, and the boy's face relaxed.

"Is he—is he very bad?"

"Wants any amount of care," father said. "By Jove, old man, he was miserable when I found him. He struck me as the loneliest little dog I had ever seen."

The brown hand that had been lonely stretched out and found the yellow head, and seemed to find comfort in the touch.

"I don't want to bother you, you know," said father. "If you could spare time to nurse him, we could give him away after he was better."

"I—I guess I'll keep him," Jock answered, his voice low. The basket was on his knee now. "He's got such sorry eyes, hasn't he? 'Makes you feel you want to keep him—

it's jolly hard for a dog to be lonesome."

"Or a boy," said the little mother. She kissed the top of Jock's head, and followed father out.

"Wise old chap, Santa Claus!" said father cheerfully. "Christmas generally makes things right!"

THE CHRISTMAS COOK

"It's the most awful thing that ever happened to us," Ryll said, despairingly.

She was propped up on a cane lounge in the shady verandah. The chequered light, filtering through the tangle of jasmine and bougainvillea, fell softly on her pretty, harassed face, and the riot of tawny curls that framed it. Before her Billy, her brother, balanced precariously on the rear legs of a rickety chair and reflected in his brown sixteen years' face the dismay that reigned in his sister's.

"What's to be done?"

"Meet him, of course. There isn't anything else. But what we're to do with him——!" Ryll spread her hands abroad dramatically.

"I'm blest if I know," said Billy, helplessly. "Englishmen are generally such chumps, and especially when they're brand new. If dad and mother were at home——"

"It wouldn't matter a bit, then," Ryll said. "Or if he were an 'ordinary' Englishman; but they're such terrific swells. I wish he'd stayed in his ancestral halls, or I wish he'd Christmassed at Government House, or I wish I hadn't burnt my foot! Oh, Billy, it's two o'clock. You'll have to hurry or you'll never meet that train!"

"Wouldn't care if I didn't," said her brother, with gloom. "Christmas was going to be sick enough, anyhow, without dad and mother—without this on top. Oh well, cheer up, old girl, I'll put on the pace. You can have your company smile on by tea-time." He crammed his old felt hat over his eyes, and tramped through the house, whistling shrill melodies.

Ryll heard the buggy drive off, rattling down the stony track to the paddock gate. She leaned back, fanning herself; the day was hot and oppressive, and her enforced lameness made her restless and worried. From the back regions came shrieks as of many fowls, and the worry-lines in her forehead deepened. She shut her eyes, opening them later at the sound of footsteps.

Two men were coming up the verandah steps. The first was a short man with the figure of a tub and a face of such abiding good humour that one glance at it made you his friend forthwith.

"Why, Teddy!" said Ryll.

Teddy Crichton pumped her hand vigorously.

"I've brought Darrell over," he said, evidently considering that sufficient explanation. "But what's up, Ryll?" His friendly glance fell on her bandaged foot. "Gout, is it? I always warned you, you know!"

"You!" said Ryll with scorn. She turned a little to greet the tall brown man who stood behind Teddy. "No, it's burnt—Bridget scattered a shovelful of hot coals on it. It's better, but I can't use it."

"Bless the old harridan!" said Mr Crichton, fervently. "Why, you keep her——! No wonder you look bothered, poor little girl!"

"Oh, that's nothing," Ryll answered. "There's heaps worse. We're in awful trouble, Teddy. Dad and mother have had to go over to Kaloolah for Christmas. Grandfather's been ill, you know, and they thought they'd better. And Miss Upton's gone away for her holidays, and Bridget's managed to get some beer from goodness knows where, and she's just happily incapable. It didn't matter for just ourselves, but on top of it all comes a wire from the horrible Englishman dad came out with last month on the *Omrah*, and he's actually coming today! He's the most awful swell you know, Teddy; his people are lords or marquises or some rummy thing like that! And what we're to do with him, or who's going to cook his dinner, is more than I can say." She sighed heavily. "Isn't it maddening, Teddy?"

Mr Crichton's face was a study. There was pain in it, as well as bewilderment, partly due to a terrific kick on the shin, stealthily imparted to him by his friend. He gulped once or twice before replying.

"Don't you know him, then?"

"Know him?" said Ryll. "How should I? Dad and mother are the only ones that ever even saw him, and they liked him, I think. But you know what a brand new Englishman is, Teddy, don't you? They mean well, I suppose, but they're so awfully impossible in the bush. I'm afraid Billy will be just horrid to him; he does hate frills so, and all these marquis-y people are frilly, aren't they? I'd have sent him over to you, Teddy, and chanced your wrath, but, of course, I know you'll be going over to your people for Christmas. So Mr Blake must put up with us somehow." She turned to Crichton's companion, apologetically. "This isn't very interesting for you, Mr Darrell," she said. "We're so accustomed to pouring all our troubles into Teddy's ears that we can't help doing it now."

"Don't worry about *me*," Darrell assured her, smiling. "I'm just as full of sympathy as he can be, anyhow. Perhaps it won't be as bad as you think, Miss Carew?"

"I haven't any hope," Ryll said gloomily. "To tell you the truth, I simply can't stand Englishmen at any time; they always make me feel nervous and awkward and back-block-ish. But it can't be helped. Teddy, I think from the sounds that Eleanor is trying to run down the Christmas dinner. If you could catch her as she goes past you, she could make tea."

The sounds of feathered warfare had been growing more and more apparent. A frenzied squawking heralded a rush of legs and wings, and a big Langshan rooster tore madly round the side of the house, hotly pursued by a long-legged child of twelve. They crossed the lawn at breakneck speed, dodged in and out of several flower-beds, disappeared behind a pyramid tree, and emerged again in full cry. Several times Eleanor was close enough to make a grab at the Langshan's legs, but he managed to elude her. They fled on beside the verandah.

"Eleanor!" said Ryll, weakly; "your stockings!"

"Pooh! said Eleanor, clutching in a futile manner at the disappearing hose. "Can't any of you duffers——!" The remark was lost as she took a sudden header into a bush of New Zealand flax, whence her dishevelled legs kicked dismally.

"Oh, I say!" said Darrell hastily. He covered the lawn in a few strides, coming upon the Langshan just as that deluded bird was uttering sqawks of triumph, which changed to long-drawn notes of woe as his captor's hand closed on his knobbly legs. Eleanor emerged from the flax bush, considerably the worse for wear.

"Thanks, no end," she said, holding out her hand for the bird. "I thought the English Johnny's Christmas dinner was gone for ever when I took that plunge!" She smiled at him in a friendly way. "How d'ye do? I'm Eleanor."

"How do you do?" said Darrell, solemnly, "I guessed you were. Where shall I put him?"

"There's a coop round here; Billy's going to kill him when he comes home." She blew a kiss to the occupants of the verandah. "How are you, Teddy?" she called in her clear voice. "Keep your hair on, Ryll; I'll get tea, and pull up my stockings too!"

Darrell carried the tea-tray out to the verandah a little later, followed by Eleanor with a huge dish of cakes. He had been given the freedom of the kitchen, had received a bibulous greeting from Bridget, and was feeling in some measure one of the family, for Eleanor had a knack of setting those she liked at their ease. Those she did not like were never wholly easy in her presence. She kissed Mr Crichton with some feeling.

"Heard our beastly news?" she asked. "Isn't it rotten? Ryll isn't so badly off, 'cause she's grown up, and she can talk nicely; but just you picture me cooking the dinner! Me! Sugar, Mr Darrell? I had to ask him his name, Teddy, as you wouldn't introduce me prop'ly."

"I'd change places with you willingly," Ryll said; "you don't know how lucky you are, you baby—no responsibilities —"

"No responsibilities!" said Eleanor blankly. "Why I've got the rooster!"

"I'll come over and help you, if you'll have me Miss Eleanor," Darrell said, laughing. "You needn't smile; I *can* cook, really. Teddy's going away, and I'll be all alone at Walmer."

"Will you, really?" Ryll said. "Oh, that's horrid for you. If you think you could stand it here—but it won't be a bit lively, and what the dinner will be like I don't know, unless, as Bridget says, 'The Lord'll be wid it in the oven.' But we'd be very glad if you came.

"But you'll have one stranger already!"

"It's different, somehow," Ryll answered. "Mr Blake's a horrid frilly Englishman, and we've never seen him, but, you see, you're Teddy's friend, and you know after seeing you run down the Langshan there really isn't much stiffness left!" She laughed suddenly at the recollection, then her face changed. "There's Billy!" she said, and became as dignified as a bandaged foot permits.

The sound of the buggy came clearly from the track behind the house. A silence fell on the group. They watched the door as if fascinated.

Steps came up the hall, and Billy stalked out upon the verandah—alone.

"Where—where is he Billy?" Ryll murmured.

"Ask me something easy," said Billy wrathfully. He threw his hat on the floor and fell into the nearest chair. "Didn't come, that's all I know."

"Weren't you in time?"

" 'Course I was in time," said her indignant brother; "ages early, and a nice hot hole it is to wait in, that station."

He became aware of the visitors for the first time, and delivered stiff greetings. "Well the train came but no blessed old Blake. Jolly good riddance, but he might have had the decency to let us know."

"Oh, don't worry about trifles, Billy," Ryll said ecstatically. "Isn't it heavenly! And there's not another train till Monday, so he can't be here before they're back!"

"Praise the pigs!" said Eleanor, "now I can cook that chook with a light heart. I know I'd have spoiled him altogether if old Blake had been here!"

"Eleanor!" said Ryll.

"Well, he is old Blake; I don't care!" said Eleanor. She vaulted suddenly over the verandah railing and rolled joyfully on the grass below.

"You might be civil enough to get a fellow a cup of tea!" said Billy. "I tell you, it's hot!"

"We're all a little upset with joy," said Eleanor, clambering back over the railing. "It's the escape of our lives, and you *will* come over, won't you Mr Darrell?"

"If you'll have me," said Darrell promptly.

On the road back to Walmer Mr Crichton spoke severely. "A nice brute I look!" he said, "to be going off and leaving the guest that isn't mine at all!"

"You'll have to live it down, Teddy, boy," said Darrell Blake, serenely. "You couldn't expect me to stay there as Blake—the reputation they'd fitted me with was too awful. And I could hardly stay there, anyhow. If you don't mind lending me a room, I can ride over every day."

"The house is yours," said Teddy, hospitably. "But

you'll have a pretty miserable time, I'm afraid. Better come with me."

"No, thanks old man," said his friend. "Fact is I'm looking forward to no end of a Christmas!"

* * *

"And he never came," said John Carew. "That's not like Blake."

"Not a sign of him," said Billy. "And I put on a stiff collar to meet him, too!"

It was three days after Christmas, and Mr and Mrs Carew were returning to the bosom of their neglected family. The buggy rolled swiftly along in the grey dust of the bush track.

"I think it's a mercy he didn't, all things considered; though I'll be exceedingly sorry if we miss seeing him," Mrs Carew said. "But poor Ryll, crippled, and that terrible old Bridget! I don't know how you'd have managed, Billy."

"Well we wouldn't have had too rosy a time, anyhow, mater, if it hadn't been for Ted Crichton's chum," her son remarked. "He's a real brick; came over every day and helped no end. Give you my word, he cooked every bit of the Christmas dinner, and most of the tucker since. Of course, Eleanor helped, but she's only a kid. I peeled the spuds, and Ryll mixed up the pudding, sitting down. But Mr Darrell cooked the lot."

"Darrell?" said Mr Carew, musingly.

"Yes; he's a ripping good chap. Ryll and Eleanor are just as gone on him as they can stick," said Billy, with the beautiful frankness of brotherhood. "We reckoned we were jolly lucky to have him about instead of Mr Duke-of-Blake, or whatever he is. But we're jolly glad to see you two home again." He turned off the stones to the soft grass of the paddock. "We'll sneak in," he said grinning. "The train was early. I bet you'll find them in the kitchen."

Things were busy in the kitchen. Ryll, her lame foot extended on two chairs, sat beside the table, deftly icing a big cake. There was a pleasant smell of baking. Darrell, having removed from the oven a huge batch of scones, was in the act of arranging a fresh relay on the hot shelf. His cheerful aspect was not detracted from by the fact that an apron was tied about him, and that a large dab of flour ornamented his nose. In the corner Eleanor washed up dishes with much haste and clamour.

"Well upon my word!" said Mr Carew.

Darrell swung round at his voice, and the scone in his hand dropped to the floor with a little thud.

"Dad!" said Ryll, joyfully. "Mater!" A yelp of joy from Eleanor drowned further remarks. She flung herself on her father, mop in hand, and embraced him fervently.

"How are you, Blake?" said Mr Carew. There was a twinkle in his eye. "Haven't you dropped something?"

"I have," said the cook, meekly, stooping to pick up his scone. "I can't very well shake hands, Mrs Carew—I'm dough-y."

"What are you calling him?" said Eleanor, indignantly. "Blake, indeed! He's worth twenty-seven Blakes. This is Ted's friend, Mr Darrell, Dad. He's been most awfully useful!"

The cook was crimson. Over the table, Ryll, also

crimson, regarded him fixedly.

"Blake seemed somewhat unpopular when I arrived," he said, stammering a little. "I got here by an earlier train, and Crichton brought me over. He introduced me as Darrell, and it seemed easier to stay so." The explanation was ostensibly for Mr and Mrs Carew, but the unhappy cook found himself facing a stern young judge with a bandaged foot. "I—I'm afraid you think it was awfully low-down of me, Miss Ryll," he said miserably. "But how could I tell you I was that frilly beast, Blake?"

"I think it was abominable," said Ryll. "You—you—we said such awful things! And on top of that you cooked our Christmas dinner—and I ate it!"

"You didn't eat it all," said Eleanor, tragically. "I had some—lots. And Billy made a real beast of himself."

"I didn't know you were so accomplished, Blake," said Mr Carew.

"Did I never tell you I was five years by myself in New Zealand?" said his guest. "It's the only thing I can do—to cook! But I'm really ashamed of myself. I'm afraid Miss Ryll will never forgive me."

Ryll's head suddenly went down on the table. Her shoulders shook with emotion. The cook moved forward, miserably.

"Miss Ryll," he said, "don't cry; it isn't worth it. I was a brute."

"Cry!" said Ryll, indistinctly. Her voice was lost in peals of laughter. "I'm sorry to be so rude," she gasped, "but it's too funny!"

* * *

"It's all very well," said Eleanor a month later. Billy and she were in the apricot tree, and she spoke gloomily, partly because she felt that to eat more was imprudent. "It's all very well. You haven't got to be a bridesmaid and wear a rotten silly dress all over lace and doodads and things."

Billy grunted indistinctly.

"Oh, I know he isn't a bad chap," said Eleanor, "and of course, I'll never marry anyone but Teddy myself! But when Ryll goes I'll have to be a young lady, and it isn't in me! I never reckoned because he could cook that we'd have to engage him permanently!"

A CHRISTMAS MISADVENTURE

"But let me just say——" he began.

"I have let you say a good deal too much already," she said frigidly. "And none of it really signified. If—if you will excuse me——" The trembling of her lips threatened the calm words, but she managed to get to the end. "I would really much rather not hear you say anything more—or say any more myself." This was self-evident. "There is nothing to be gained by it."

"Then you actually mean that we——"

"May be quite good friends—in future."

"Oh, hang friendship!" A stronger word just escaped utterance. "Nell, you can't——"

"Oh, yes I can. Goodbye." The swish of her skirts along the verandah followed swiftly, and the wire door clashed after her. She had really gone.

He stared stupidly. Scores of things that he might have said, and had left unuttered, came to him. Above them all the recollection of two cold eyes that would not have softened at any argument. He had not known she could look so icy. And over such a little thing, too! It was so unreasonable.

If he had only not been such a confounded idiot as to keep the programme—that tell-tale slip of blue cardboard that had borne such damning witness against him! He had hated the dance. She had not been there, and he was in the first few months of the engagement, when the absence or presence of the other makes all the difference between boredom and bliss. No one had been at the dance that he knew—only "that little ass Faye Oliver," and though she was unquestionably an ass she could dance, and was pleasant to look upon. Wherefore, at sea amongst a crowd of the strange women who could not dance in the least, he had fallen back on Faye with something like relief. Eight dances was it they had had? Or nine? The programme could tell. It had told—ten—and hence these tears.

He bit his lip at the thought of Nell's amazed face of indignation, that had so swiftly changed to icy impassiveness. It seemed to him such a little thing—conscious though he was that his labored explanation had sounded horribly forced and unconvincing. The figures were against him; also against him were the sly bits of gossip that had come to the girl's ears, and had been repelled with incredulous scorn. He—Stephen—did not know anything of that. There did not seem to be much that he did know, so swift had come the bolt out of the blue.

The ring lay in his palm. He unclenched his hand and looked at it dully—the diamonds he had bought with such happy pride. Happiness was gone now; pride also—no, not pride. He could show her yet he did not care. And to prove that he did not, he whistled, very deliberately, and still whistling, entirely out of tune, marched into the library, with his head well up. He was very young.

The library had but one occupant, a gentleman who sat on the hearth rug and builded him large edifices with wooden blocks. One, designed to represent the Eiffel Tower, was nearly completed as the whistler entered, and the architect glanced up truculently.

"Don't you shake, whatever you do!" he warned.

The intruder made no response, having, in fact, not heard. He walked over to the waiting table, and flung himself down in a chair.

Carl stared. His remarks were wont to be received with a certain amount of deference—absolute indifference was treatment he justly resented. However, the intruder did not look a fit subject for interference just now, and so Carl decided to let the matter slide, and went on with his lofty mansion, piling Ossa on Pelion, until at length the Eiffel Tower collapsed and fell with a crash.

At this consummation of his efforts Carl shook back his curls and sat up with a satisfied sigh. His wandering eye took in his uncle, who was sitting at the table with his head in his hands.

"When I feels like that," said the nephew, after prolonged regard, "Mummy gen'lly gives me lickerish."

There was no response.

"Uncle Steve!"

"What is it?"

"Have you a pain?"

"No—yes, confound it. A bad pain, old man."

"You looked like a pain," said the small observer. "I gets it like that"—confidentially—"you know—just under the wishbone. I had it after I ate the green quince. Mummy fixed me up with lickerish. Would you like some?"

"I think not, thanks," said his uncle, absently.

"Been eatin' green quinces?"

"No—sour grapes."

"That's bad," Carl nodded. He had planted his elbows on his knees, and his small face looked seraphic amongst his curls, filled as it was with concern. "Micky told me green grapes was the dhivil an' all for upsettin' yez inside. Are they?"

"They're all that," said his uncle. "See here, old chap, if you don't mind I'd just as soon not talk just now."

"My gwacious, you must feel bad!" Carl said, deeply concerned. "Mummy says I can' most always make her feel better when her forehead aches. But p'raps your ache isn't the same. My quince ache wasn't. I bathe Mummy's head with odyklone, but I know it wouldn't have done me any good to have my head bathed with anyfing. Would you be carin' to see my pup?"

"Not just now, thanks," Stephen said.

"Micky says he's a tearin' foine pup as hasn't his aiqual this side Galway," said the small man wistfully. "I fink he'd make most anyone feel better. I'd better bring him, bettern't I, Uncle Steve?"

"No—hang the pup!" said his uncle irritably. His mood changed instantly at sight of the grieved little face.

"Never mind, Carl boy," he said, picking up his nephew and setting him on his knee. "I'm a cross-grained brute, and you're no end of a good chap. Only you mustn't mind me just now, because the—the pain's bad."

"Is it, then?" queried Carl, sympathetically, stroking his uncle, where he considered the attention most effective. "I'd rub you for a year if it'd make you better. Say I send Auntie Nell to you?"

"No!" said the other, with such vehemence that the small

boy jumped. "Don't you do anything of the sort."

"Oh, all wight. I don't fink you do know what's good for you, though, Uncle Steve. Auntie Nell is no end clever about pains."

"I don't doubt it," said Stephen grimly.

"Say," said Carl, "I'll tell you somefing, Uncle Steve, just for a treat, to make you better. We're going to have the beautifullest Christmas—all because Mrs Harper got the measles."

"I don't understand, I'm afraid," said his uncle, with weary patience.

"Well, don't you see—Mrs Harper got measles, so she can't cook any Christmas dinner for us; an' she gave them to Bella and Lizzie, an' there's only Kate left; and Mummy says for all the good Kate is she might as well be without anyone at all." The imitation of his mother's harassed voice was perfect. "An' Mummy says there's not any fun in staying in this big, hot old house an' workin' all Christmas; an' Daddy said, 'By George, no!' An' so we're all goin' campin' out."

"The dickens we are!" said Stephen. "Who?"

"Oh, me, an' Mummy and Dad, an' you, an' Auntie Nell, an' Mr Stwatton, an' Kate. Kate's to do the washin' up. An' we're goin' to take three tents, an' ever so much tucker, an' stay away till the tucker gives out; an' we're goin' way up the river to the Big Gully; an' I'm goin' to take my fishin' line, and catch salmons and cods; an' it's just hooroo-for-Casey!" The orator descended abruptly from his uncle's knee and turned irrepressible somersaults on the hearthrug.

"You're not pulling my leg, old chap?" asked Stephen, doubtfully.

Carl looked hurt.

"No, I'm not," he said. "You ask Dad—he'll tell you. You'd have heard all about it if you and Auntie Nell hadn't gone out walkin', an' got losted ever so long. I fink I'll go an' tell Auntie Nell now." He gathered himself up from the rug and marched out with much offended dignity.

Stephen stared gloomily before him. If this yarn of Carl's were true it meant considerable awkwardness. There was no means of escape, for Berrinndool, his brother-in-law's station, was thirty miles from the nearest railway line, and communication was only by means of a bi-weekly coach. There was no possibility of a convenient bogus telegram summoning him to Town, for the mail had arrived the day before, and there would not be another until after Christmas. To announce the sudden breaking of the engagement that had given great joy to both sides of the family would mean a very sorry Christmas for all. Then—what could he do?

Miss Stanton's entrance broke upon his musing. She was pale and intensely dignified. He emulated her dignity if not her pallor, and awaited her remarks in silence.

"Carl tells me," she said hurriedly; "oh, you've heard the silly plan!"

"Yes?" His tone was politely interrogative.

"We can't get out of going," she said. "I don't want to spoil Christmas for Ada and Jim. Do you mind——?" She paused uncertainly, awaiting encouragement that did not come. "What I mean is—suppose we—how would it be——?"

"An excellent plan, I think," said he courteously.

"Oh, you are unkind!" she cried. "It is so hard to say things—some things. And you don't help. What I want to say is, would you mind very much if we pretended that things were as they were before—before——"

"Before this morning?"

"Yes."

"You may remember I never wished to change 'things' at all," he said.

Her head went up.

"There is no need to reopen that discussion," she said frigidly. "It need only be the merest pretence, of course—just to deceive them until we get back from his ridiculous camping out party. Then—one of us can go away."

"Certainly—I can," he said. "It shall be just as you wish, of course. We can keep up the merry farce until after Christmas."

"It is easy for you to joke!" she flashed.

"Happily so," he retorted. "You would not have it otherwise?"

"It does not affect me, of course," she said, icily. "I am only able to consider myself fortunate in my escape!" Then, because she was twenty and exceedingly unhappy she retreated, singing gaily, and dissolved in tears on reaching the safe haven of her room.

* * *

"It's a first rate idea!" Jim Stanton said at dinner that evening. "No end of a saving of work and worry for you girls, and it's always cool in those gullies. We'll all have to smoke cigarettes, for the mosquitoes' benefit, and Christmas dinner will be *non est*—two distinctive gains. The usual Christmas dinner is a weariness of the flesh. I'll send two of the men ahead with packhorses to fix camp. And after that we'll shift for ourselves, with the assistance of the futile Kate. All the most approved attractions—shooting, fishing, free rides, bathing, mixed——"

"Certainly not, Jim!" said his wife, severely.

"Beg pardon, old woman. I meant the attractions, of course!" grinned the offender. "It was ever my lot to be misunderstood. Nell, why don't you take my part? And, incidentally, why don't you eat something?"

"Too hot, Jim." Nell's acting was rather below the level of that of the ladies who compose the back row of the chorus in a pantomime. Her brother looked at her keenly, and glanced at Stephen, who was eating doggedly and with evident disrelish.

"H'm," he said. "You do look warm."

"I was just thinking how very pale she was," exclaimed Mrs Stanton. "Quite sure you're well, dear?"

"Quite, thanks."

"As to going out," Jim said, after a pause. "There's no driving, of course, and its fifteen miles to Big Gully. Not too much for you, girls?"

They disclaimed the suggestion indignantly.

"I don't know about Carl, though," his mother added.

"I fink if you fink you can ride that far that I should fink I could!" said that gentleman, with vigor. "I guess you'll be gladderer to get off than me!"

"It's very probable," said his mother. "Weight, age and decrepitude will tell. Meanwhile, my sonnie, if you have finished your dinner, may I remark that is long past your bed time, and race you to bed?" They disappeared in a whirlwind, and Nell, pleading headache, followed them out of the room, and was seen no more that night.

The afternoon of the next day saw the Berrinndool house party ready for the track, and by the time the fiercer rays of the sun had given place to evening coolness they reached the spot where the advance guard had pitched their tents. The locality was cunningly selected. A little natural clearing, giving ample space for the three tents, was lightly ringed with trees, enough for shelter, without shutting out the evening breezes. Not far off, the river gurgled lazily over its stony bed. The scent of bush flowers was heavy on the drowsy air.

Carl, despite his boasts, was sufficiently tired to fall asleep over his tea, and all were glad to seek the beds of leaves in the tents, for the ride had been rough and the track of the most primitive description—and eucalyptus leaves form a couch of delights to the weary. Waking early, bathing parties were formed, and sufficient disturbance created in the river to scare away every fish within miles, as Jim grumbled. However, after breakfast—a meal which would have been merry enough but for the unaccountable silence of Stephen and Nell—the cheerful host and his wife, accompanied by Dick Stratton, the jackaroo, set off for the river, equipped with rods and lines.

"Coming, Carl?" called his father.

Carl hesitated.

"No, fanks," he said at length. "I promised Auntie Nell to go for a walk with her."

"Oh, have you?" said Jim, blankly. "Well, I hope you won't be in the way!" he whistled softly as he hurried away to overtake his wife.

"Something's up," he said, laconically.

"Something's very much up, dear," said Mrs Stanton, vexedly. "I don't know what that stupid pair have found to quarrel about, but it's pretty serious. Steve is wretched; Nell cried herself to sleep last night."

"Hang them!" said Jim. "They might have let us spend Christmas in comfort. Never mind, old woman, they'll make it up in the good old way if you leave 'em alone. But poor Carl!"

Carl, however, was happy. To his unbounded surprise he found himself the sole object of his aunt's attentions, as his uncle wandered moodily off into the scrub, in another direction altogether. To be alone with Auntie Nell was a very different thing to being a member of a trio which included Uncle Steve, and Carl was duly appreciative of the difference. They roamed into the bush together, and—alone—Auntie Nell was a magnificent companion in the bush. She knew all the trees and shrubs and flowers, and had the quaintest tales to tell about them and the queer fairy folk of the woods. Moreover, she was not in the least "scared" of things that creep or glide, and when they encountered a tiger snake she killed it with as little concern as one might display in despatching a mosquito. They roamed further and further away, finding fresh interest every few yards and had no idea of their distance from camp when Carl suddenly discovered that he was hungry.

"I prepared for emergencies," said Nell, producing a package from the depths of a silk bag. "Sandwiches and cake. I don't know what they're like, as Kate put them up."

"I'm sure I don't care," said Carl. "I'm that dretful hungry I could eat a bunyip, Auntie Nell."

"He wouldn't agree with you, old chap, I'm afraid," said his aunt, arranging the small feast on broad gum leaves.

"Would he give me a pain?"

"A very bad one, I should think."

"But you could take it away, Auntie Nell. Uncle Steve said yesterday you knew all about pains."

"Curing pains?"

Carl hesitated.

"I don't fink Uncle Steve did quite mean that, now I fink again," he said. "I fink he meant giving pain—but that can't be right. Uncle Steve was very funny yesterday. He looked mis'able, and he talked very funny too, only not the sort of funny you laugh at."

Nell said nothing.

"You look funny too," said Carl. "Your eyes is all sorry-looking, an' you aren't pink in the cheeks. I wish you were. Where's Uncle Steve gone?"

"Oh, I don't know, old man," said Nell, wearily. "Come on, if you've finished, and we'll get a drink at the river, and then we'll wander on a bit further."

He scrambled to his feet, and suddenly flung himself upon her. "You are the dearest—dearest!" he said between hugs, and she held him tightly to her, hiding her white face for a moment in his curls. "You're my dearest, anyhow," she murmured, her voice breaking.

They found the river, and shallow rippling pools, where they drank, and then they roamed on and on, until Nell began to think of returning—reluctant to exchange the cool shadows of the bush and the childish companionship for the tents and the weary farce of acting vanished happiness. Very slowly they wandered back. Presently Carl stopped and pointed excitedly to a tall stump, jagged and broken, from which the great tree had years ago been wrenched and torn by some fierce gale.

"See that little hole up there—at the end of the crack?" he cried. "It's a bird's nest. I saw the little bird go out. Oh, Auntie Nell dear, couldn't you climb up an' see what's inside?"

"I don't know, old chap," Nell said, surveying the stump doubtfully. "It's a bit too high to reach. Well—wait a moment."

She found a small log of wood and leant it against the stump, mounting upon it with a quick little step. So elevated, she found she could reach the hole easily, and she slipped her hand in with some little difficulty, and felt about for treasure-trove.

"There's only the remains of an old nest, Carl," she cried; "nothing to show you."

"Allwight—come down," came the clear voice.

There was a pause—silence.

"Auntie Nell, why don't you come?"

"I can't, little chap," Nell said slowly. She was struggling to withdraw her hand from the hole. Her face had flushed with the effort, and with something like fear. She twisted and pulled her hand unavailingly. Carl cried out sharply.

"Auntie, can't you? What is it?"

Nell gave up the useless struggle.

"I'm caught," she said dully. "My hand slipped in from the outside because the entrance was smoothed and rounded, but inside it is a sharp, jagged edge, and my big bangle has caught against it and jammed. I don't know what I'm going to do, Carl."

He cried out in his terror.

"Don't!" she said quickly. "Let me think." And the boy was still, staring up at her with bewilderment and fear in his brown eyes. But thought only ended in a repetition of the futile effort to free the prisoned hand, and Nell paused at last, panting.

"Carl, boy," she said, "do you think you could find your way back to camp?"

"I fink so, Auntie Nell. Can't you come?"

"No, dear. You can't go far wrong if you'll stick to the bank of the river. Promise me you won't go too near, dear, and when you come to the big flat rock we bathe from, turn in, and you'll see our tracks, and it's no distance then. Bring Daddy quickly. Make him bring the axe. Don't frighten him or mother, Carl."

"I won't. Auntie Nell, is it hurting you?"

"Not now, old man. But make them hurry. You see,

dear, if this log I'm standing on slipped, all my weight would come on my arm. Then it would hurt." Her voice trembled. "My little mate, will you be all right? You won't lose yourself or be afraid?"

"No, I won't dearest. I'll run all the way. Oh, auntie, don't let it slip."

Nell laughed down at him.

"Not if I know it, old man. Keep along the river, and hurry, Carl." She kissed her hand to him, and the little fellow turned, and, sobbing, ran into the scrub.

It was all strange to him, poor little lad—almost a baby, for all his seven years, and wild with fear for "Auntie Nell." There were no land marks he could recognise; but at least the line of the river was clear, and he kept along it, though mindful of his promise not to go near the bank. It was rough walking—and Carl tried to run all the time. A tangle of wild raspberries was over everything, and their long stems caught at him and held him until the little bare brown legs were torn and bleeding from a hundred scratches. One branch caught him across the face, like a stroke from a scorching whip-lash. He rubbed away the trickling blood with his sleeve as he ran.

A snake trailed its slow length across his path. He would not stop—a flying leap took him over the reptile, with a moment's childish terror lest the cruel fangs should strike him as he jumped. He did not look at it again. There was no time to look at anything —at the fish that jumped and flashed in the deep river pools, the chattering flocks of parrots and cockatoos that screamed overhead, the wild duck that rose whirring from the stream. All the time he saw but one vision—Auntie Nell, white-faced, helpless, with her hand fast in that terrible little hole.

It seemed so long that he raced through the scrub in the gathering evening shadows. The shade was dense in the deep bush of the riverside, and every dark patch contained a new terror for the little nervous lad. He shut his teeth and clenched his fists to keep down the rising fear. "The only fing I've got to be afraid of is that that old log'll slip before I get Daddy!" he muttered as he ran—and when a black, terrifying shadow lay before him he would not take time to go round it, but drew his breath sharply and ran right through. Creeping plants caught and tripped him. Once he fell so heavily that all movement was impossible for a minute. He hated himself for it, struggling painfully to his fee and stumbling on.

Something rose suddenly out of the shadows—a tall dark figure. He was upon it before he could dodge, and for the first time a sharp childish cry of real terror broke from him. A hand fell on his shoulder.

"Carl! What are you doing? Where's Nell?"

He caught at the newcomer's hand desperately, with a big sob.

"Uncle Steve! Oh, go quick—she's caught in the tree!" The tears were choking him—he gulped them down desperately. "She's standin' on an old log; if it slips she'll be hangin' by her hand—oh, be quick!"

"Where?" Stephen's voice was sharp with fear.

"Right there, along the river—ever so far. In a little clear place—you call. I'll tell Daddy—oh, Uncle Steve, where's camp?"

Stephen twisted him round.

"Look," he said, "just through the trees, little chap. Can't you see the fire?"

Carl uttered a glad little shout.

"Oh, fank goodness it's so close! You go on—I'll find it an' tell Daddy to take the axe."

"You're sure?—don't lose sight of the fire, laddie." Stephen was torn two ways. But Carl did not wait. He was off through the trees like a flash, and Stephen, turning, began to run along the river bank as he had not run since his school days. And as he ran he woke the echoes with his shouts:

"Nell! Nell! Nell!"

* * *

She had found the waiting long. Afraid to move an inch, for fear the stick on which she stood should slip, her cramped position soon became almost unbearable. Two or three times she fancied the stick cracked, and the thought send a sickening thrill of fear through her. She had worked at trying to withdraw her hand until the wrist was so swollen that all further effort was impossible. Inside the hole, creeping things crawled over the imprisoned hand with maddening persistency. She wondered dully would they find her that night—before the stick broke. Again and again she blamed herself for letting Carl go back alone—although she could not see how it would have been better to keep him. But he might so easily be lost; the bush was so vast and dark, and he such a little lad.

Was that a shout? Far off the echoes took it up and bandied it about, and the cries of the birds in the tree tops seemed to mock it. She listened with fluttering breath—long as had seemed the waiting, she knew it was almost too soon to hope for deliverance. If it could be!—then Carl was safe; and her own danger was forgotten in the overmastering desire to know that her little mate had reached camp. Again—it was her own name—"Nell!"

She gave an involuntary movement as she answered, and an ominous crack came from the rotten stick. It was giving; she felt herself sinking a little, and the strain came on the imprisoned wrist, faintly at first, but gradually becoming sharper. She cried out with fear, and an answering shout came close at hand.

"Nell, where are you?"

"Here—quick! I'm falling!"

The stick snapped suddenly. For just a second of agony her weight seemed to hang on her arm, and a cry broke from her—in reality, almost simultaneously with the breaking of the stick, Stephen caught her. He raised her in his arms, gently keeping the strain off her wrist. "You poor little girl!" was all he said.

Pride lived for perhaps half a minute of silence; then she put her face against his hair, and broke into low sobbing. He leaned against the tree, panting with something more than breathlessness. So they stayed quietly for a while.

"I can't get your arm out, darling, you know," he said at length. "I'd need both hands for it, and they're otherwise engaged. I can only hold you as comfortably as I can till Jim comes."

"Carl?" she whispered.

"He's all right, dear little chap. I met him just near camp, and he's bringing the others. I ran ahead. Dear, is your wrist much hurt?"

"I don't think so," she said. "It seemed breaking for a moment; but you caught me so quickly. If you hadn't come——!" She shuddered. "Steve, you can't hold me long like that."

"I'm going to manoeuvre you on to my shoulder," he said; "then you won't have to stretch up your arm to that confounded hole. Tell me if I hurt you," and he lifted the light form slowly until she was seated on his shoulder, and able to lean her own against the tree. "That better?" he asked.

"Much. I'm glad for your sake I'm so little," she said.

"You're just perfect," he said; "you always were. Nell—am I forgiven?"

She caught his free hand and carried it to her lips.

"Forgive me, dear," she whispered.

It was nearly the Christmas dawn before the rescuers found them. They had taken the wrong direction in the darkness, and had wandered through the bush fruitlessly all night. Jim Stanton's face was haggard and worn as he came into the open space by the big stump.

"Thank God," he said, "I didn't know you'd found her, Steve."

"I'm all right, Jim, dear," Nell said. She was very pale, and so was Stephen, but their faces were alight with happiness.

Jim was a man of few words. He put his axe into the crack above the hole in the stump, and wedged it open, and in an instant Nell was free. She slipped from Stephen's shoulder to the ground, but her cramped limbs failed her, and she would have fallen but for his aid. She leaned against him and smiled up at her brother.

"Well," he said, "you both look happy." He stooped to kiss her. "Perhaps it hasn't been experience without its advantages," he laughed.

"Not altogether," Stephen said quietly. Unmindful of onlookers he took the girl's face between his hands and kissed it in his turn.

"A merry Christmas, dear," he said.

THE HAMMOCK

The break-up was over. Parents and friends, boys and girls, were streaming out of the school, talking and laughing. Teachers, looking suddenly young and carefree, were shaking hands all round, saying "Merry Christmas!" to the dunces just as heartily as to the prize winners. Outside the fence, motors came to life, and horses were put into buggies; there were calls of, "Anyone want a lift?" and answering cries as the children ran to pile into every vacant space. They went down the country road in clouds of dust, singing and shouting.

Mr McLeod, the head teacher, was left alone at the school-house door. He stretched himself with a look of relief.

"Well, that's over." he said, half aloud. "And this time tomorrow—the sea! But I wonder where Rob and Phyl Benham went? They didn't come out this way."

As if in answer, a boy and girl, leading their ponies, came round the corner. There was no excitement about this pair; they walked slowly, their young faces grave. The teacher went down the steps to meet them.

"I thought you two had given me the slip," he said. "Not much need to do that, when each of you topped your form."

"Oh, we just thought we'd get the ponies first," said the boy. He hesitated, looking down. "Mother said to tell you she was awfully sorry not to come today, sir. Dad isn't very well, and she didn't like to leave him."

"Of course not—but tell her that everyone missed her.

It doesn't seem right to have a break-up, or anything else at the school without Mrs Benham. She's one of our very best supporters. And I had hoped to have your Dad, too. Well . . . tell them you have both put in a really good year's work. Next year should not be so hard for you; your Dad will be fit by the end of the holidays."

"I hope to goodness he will," said the girl. "But he doesn't seem to get on much, Mr McLeod."

"Give him time, Phyl. A man who has gone through so much can't be expected to snap back easily into ordinary life. Carry on, you two, just as you did all the time he was away, and make things as easy as you can for your mother—but I know you will. Well—a happy Christmas and a really good New Year to you all."

He watched them swing into their saddles and ride away. Usually the Benham twins went off at a hard canter, anxious to be home in time for the evening milking, but today they were early, and there was no need to hurry. They went slowly, and for the first half mile neither spoke. Then Phyl broke the silence angrily.

"I hated the break-up, didn't you? Mother never missed one before, no matter how much work she had to do. She just loves coming. Two prizes—and they

just didn't seem to mean a thing!"

"They'll mean a lot to Mother, though, Phyl," Rob said quietly.

"Oh, I know that. But not like seeing us go up for them. She does get a kick out of that. And she loves the whole show, and being with all the other mothers and fathers . . . and this year was going to be the very best ever . . . with

Dad there, too. And I'll bet she's just patched Dick's pants all day by herself, and Dad's stayed out in the hammock."

"I suppose so." Rob's voice was gloomy.

"'Member what fun we had making that hammock, Rob? Mother working like fury at the netting, while you made the stretchers and I polished them—even Dick and Dumps took a turn at the polishing. All of us mad keen to get it ready for him before he came home so as he could lie out in it and look at the gum trees again."

"He's done that," said Rob grimly.

"Yes, but we never thought he would simply live in the beastly thing! Mother hardly sees him when we're at school—he just lies there and smokes, and if the kids go near him he gets cross with them. Comes in for meals, and then goes back to the hammock. He eats all right—I don't believe there's a thing wrong with him. Why can't he be just ordinary? Bill Rankine doesn't go on that way."

"Bill was younger." Rob said. "I believe it was the older men that had the toughest time when they were prisoners. We don't know a quarter of what Dad had to stand from those beastly Japs. I don't reckon we ever will. Years and years of it—starving and sickness and bashings. I'll never forget his face when that silly woman tried to pump him about it at their "Welcome Home" party. She actually asked him, "Did they ever bash you, Mr Benham?" and he turned his back on her and walked away. Dad was always pretty bossy himself—it must have been just awful for him to take what the Japs gave him."

"Well, I know it must, of course." said Phyl. "I get hot all over when I think of it. But it's over now—and he'll never see one of the little beasts again. I believe he'd be better if he did some real work—goodness knows there's enough waiting to be done on the place. You and Mother and I couldn't do everything, no matter how hard we tried all the time he was away."

"He just doesn't seem to see it," Rob answered. "He does the milking, of course—but that's only because he won't let Mother do it any more. The rest doesn't seem to matter to him. My word, Phyl, I'll be glad when I can leave school next year and put in all my time on the place——"

"Yes, and you know jolly well you ought to be going on to high school!" Phyl cried. "Mother will break her heart if you don't—she's always thinking of it since Mr McLeod said you were safe for a scholarship if you liked to try——"

"Well, I"m not going to try, unless Dad gets better," he said roughly. "I wish you'd stop talking about it. We'd better get a move on, or we'll be late." He kicked his pony into a canter.

There was no lack of welcome when they burst into the sunlit kitchen at the farm. Dinner was ready, but Mother had arranged a dinner that could wait if necessary. She had to hear every detail of the break-up, what the speakers had said, who had won prizes. Mother was little and pretty, with brown eyes that were made to hold a twinkle. Nowadays the twinkle was not always there; but it came back as she listened to them, and she handled their prizes as if the books were living things, things that brought her love and pride. She turned the pages—Phyl on the arm of her chair, Rob's arm round her neck, and dinner might have been altogether forgotten had not Dick and Dumps arrived, indignantly stating that they were hungry.

Dick was six, and Dumps—who had not been born when Dad went away to the war—was five. They were never apart. Like all bush children, they made their own games with the things that surrounded them—the creek, the woodheap, the backyard, the sheds, the clumps of scrub left for shelter in the house paddock. That nobody had time to play with them did not trouble Dick and Dumps at all: their only demand was food, at intervals not too far apart. Their mother looked at them now, somewhat consciencestricken.

"Bless their hearts, it's long past dinner-time!" she exclaimed. "Give them a wash Phyl, while I dish up. Rob, ring the bell for Dad—he's out in the hammock."

Andrew Benham came in slowly. He had put on weight since his release from Borneo and his time in hospital; his clothes no longer hung loosely on his big frame. But his eyes were sunk in dark hollows; the unhappy eyes of a man who broods too much over things best forgotten. He ate a huge meal, listening with some show of interest to his wife's account of the break-up. Phyl and Rob left the talking to their mother. Their tongues had wagged freely enough in the first wonderful fortnight after Dad had come home. Then it had seemed that he could never hear too much of all they had to tell him, and he was full of plans for bringing back the farm into good order. He had ridden over it with the twins, taking in every detail.

"New fencing wanted," he had said. "Drains to be cleared out, thistles and bracken cut, sheds mended—oh, heaps of jobs. You kids and Mother have been pretty marvellous, keeping the dairying going all these years on your own. I don't know how you managed it, and doing well at school, too. Well, we'll make it the best dairy farm in the district once I can get down to real work."

But that time had not come. Within a week he had taken over his wife's share of the milking, saying firmly that she was to keep out of the cow yard in future. It tired him at first, and she begged him to rest after the work; it was wise, he knew. And to lie in the hammock was marvellous, under the gum trees that he had thought he would never see again, watching the birds in their spring plumage—honey-eaters, fly-catchers, thornbills and the dainty blue wrens that strutted so fearlessly on the grass near him.

They had planned carefully where to sling the hammock. Low-growing trees screened it from the gate, so that he could not be seen by callers coming to the house; but from where he lay he had a view down a long slope to the creek, with its line of willows and the green hills beyond it. There were big rose bushes near him; the clean fragrance of the roses came to him in waves, helping him to forget the heavy scent of the orchids in the Borneo jungles. Yes, a great idea, that hammock; just his own corner, where he could be alone, after years of densely crowded prison huts. He could slip away to it when the barking of dogs announced that people were coming up the paddock—people who might ask him the stupid questions he dreaded. They meant well, of course. Only they didn't understand that all a man wanted was to forget bad things.

But just because he tried so hard to forget, he remembered more clearly than ever—but with a difference. The hammock became a place where he could picture the prison camps, the guards he had hated; but now he was on top. Rescue had come; it was no longer necessary to be careful, to watch unceasingly, to bow to bullying guards.

His mind-pictures grew into long daydreams, in which he dealt faithfully with every Japanese who had ill-treated him and his mates. It gave him a grim satisfaction to build his pictures, to go over and over them. A doctor could have told him that he was playing with fire, keeping alive sores that must heal before he could be a fit man. But Andrew Benham kept his grim dreams to himself.

He went back to them today as soon as he had finished his dinner. "Well, I reckon I'll get into the open air again," he said, pushing back his chair. "Be seeing you at milking time, kids. Glad you had such a good show this morning." His slow steps echoed in the narrow passage.

"Mother, is he always going to be like this?" Phyl burst out.

"No, I'll never believe that," Anne Benham answered. "It's something we just can't understand. They told us he was all right physically. It's just his mind; he can't forget yet."

"Does he talk to you about it?"

"No—never. I think he might be better if he did, but he won't say a word about it. I try sometimes, but he stops me at once. And that's not like Dad, for we always used to talk out everything together. He sleeps very badly; I believe he lies awake half the night thinking."

"I don't believe he sleeps much in the hammock either," said Rob. "I've taken a look at him often on Saturdays and Sundays when he didn't know I was there. His eyes were always open, and he had a sort of queer, fierce look. I'll bet he was thinking about knocking Japs out in dozens. Wouldn't blame him either."

"No. But it's not good for him," his mother answered. She did not say how often she, too, had caught that look of brooding fierceness on her husband's face as he lay in the hammock. Always it troubled her; it was so unlike the man he had been. Andy had never in his life harboured a grudge against anyone, even a man who had let him down. He had always said: "A grudge hits you harder than it hits the other fellow; better to wipe out a thing clean." But then he had never been a prisoner among the Japs. Perhaps there were some memories that a man could never quite wipe out.

She said, "Look here, children, if we let ourselves get unhappy about it we'll never be able to help Dad. And we've got to help him. The doctors say it's not a bit of use just to try to drive away unhappy thoughts—you've got to have happy ones ready to take their places. I'm pinning a lot of hope on Christmas."

"That's an idea!" said Rob hopefully. "Dad always thought a heap about Christmas, didn't he?"

"Too right, he did," agreed Phyl. "But do you think he's going to care two hoots about it this year, Mother? He'll like the dinner, of course, but then, food's all he seems to care about now."

"Ah, don't Phyl," said her mother, wincing. "We can't let ourselves think that way. Thoughts are catching things—something like measles. We've got to build up a real Christmas for him, and make him help us . . . let him see we can't do it by ourselves. We'll start making decorations for the house right away—every room. I've mixed the pudding today, and tonight we'll all give it a stir, just as we used to do. The big cake's done—it only needs icing, and I've hoarded icing sugar all through the war for his first Christmas with us. You and I must have a day at baking little things, Phyl, and we'll send Dad and Rob out to get a turkey from the Browns—they've got good ones this year."

"You're a great thinker!" said Phyl, regarding her admiringly. "Anything else?"

"Oh, lots! We'll all have a day in the township and buy presents—every single person in this house is going to hang up a stocking this year. Perhaps we could go on Saturday and finish up with an evening at the pictures."

"And who would milk?" asked the twins, in one voice.

"I've fixed that," said their mother proudly. "The Smith boys will be home. Mrs Smith says some of them will do our milking if we can get Dad out for an evening."

"Gosh, you're a marvel!" breathed Rob. "Pictures! We haven't been for years and years!"

"No, and it's time we went again. I believe we'll get Dad to them. He never thought much of me as a car driver, and I don't believe he imagines I've improved since he went away, so he'll just have to take us in. I must remember," she added thoughtfully, "to drive very badly when he's with me, and then he'll be afraid to trust me with the family."

The twins hooted with laughter.

"Let's hope nobody will tell him about the night you drove Mrs Smith to hospital in the big storm," said Rob. "Floods over the road and washaways, and everything else—and you went like smoke. Keep that yarn dark, mother!"

"And how!" responded his mother inelegantly. "He's got to think I'm a poor weak woman who needs him to take care of me. I'm beginning to believe we're making a mistake in treating him as if he were a sort of invalid."

"But that's the way he treats himself," said Phyl.

"Yes, only he doesn't realise it. There's something in his brain that hasn't waked up—and he'll never be our old Dad until it does wake up. I think it's his sense of responsibility. You see, he hasn't had to be responsible for anything all those years in Borneo—only to do as he was told, and to get through each day as best he could."

Phyl said thoughtfully: "Wonder if it would do any good to have a sad accident with matches and burn the hammock?"

"He'd make another," said Rob. "Come along—we've heaps to do before milking."

Stirring the Christmas pudding that evening was not the jolly business it had been before the war. Only Dick and Dumps were excited. Dad dropped in sixpences and threepences, and stirred hard, but in an absent-minded way, as if Christmas puddings didn't really matter until they appeared on the table. The plan of driving to the township for Christmas shopping fell flat, as far as he was concerned. He flinched at the idea.

"Oh, I don't feel like going," he said dully. "You can manage all right without me. I'm not keen on meeting people."

"Wants you to come, too," said Dumps firmly. "Peoples are nice."

"Some people," said Dad. "Well, you go and meet 'em,

Dumps."

Phyl put in a hopeful word. "You might as well come, Dad. We all want you."

"Well, can't you understand that I don't want to go?" he said harshly. He looked at them as if he was a stranger, apart. Then he went slowly out of the kitchen.

"And that's that," muttered Rob.

But his mother's head was up. She smiled at them. "We won't give in," she said.

* * *

It was the next day that all the children's world seemed to crash suddenly. A hot day; Mother and Phyl were working in the kitchen, Rob mending a broken panel in a fence. Down near the creek Dick and Dumps played under the willows. Everything was very quiet, when a succession of sharp cries came from the little pair by the creek.

Andrew Benham opened his eyes in the hammock and glanced towards them. Fighting, he supposed; kids were bound to fight now and then. No need to interfere. But his wife, who knew that Dick and Dumps never screamed without reason, was out of the kitchen in a flash, calling to them.

"What's wrong?"

He heard one word, in Dick's high treble, "Snake!"—saw him pulling Dumps backwards. At the word Andrew was out of the hammock and running. Before him his wife was racing down the hill. As he gained on her she tripped and fell heavily, rolling over "Oh, quick!" she gasped as he went by.

The snake was gliding towards the creek as he reached the children. He caught up a stick and killed it with two swift blows, twisting back as he flung the stick away.

"Did he get either of you, Dick?" He dropped on one knee, his arms round them.

"No, he never. But I just pulled Dumps away in time."

"Sure?" he gasped. He scanned the little bare legs anxiously.

"Never touched me," said Dumps. "But I yelled hard, 'cause he wanted to."

"Gosh, you scared us!" he uttered. He picked her up, turning to call to his wife "They're all right, Anne!" Suddenly Dumps found herself on the ground, and again her father was running. For Anne Benham lay where she had fallen, and she was very still.

"Anne, are you hurt?"

"My leg," she said faintly. "Don't move me, Andy. I heard it snap as I went down."

* * *

Andrew Benham and Phyl faced each other in the kitchen that evening. The doctor had been, and had gone. Rob was sitting with his mother; Dick and Dumps were tucked up in bed. Phyl, the washing-up finished, was wringing out her dish cloth as if it were a personal enemy.

"Well, we'll have to manage somehow, Phyl," he said. "There's not a corner for her in the Bush Hospital—we must look after her at home. But the doctor says we can't damage the leg when it's in plaster. It's all going to be a bit tough on you, though."

"It wouldn't be so awful if you were all right," muttered Phyl. Her voice trembled.

"Me? But, of course, I'm all right. What do you mean?"

She faced him angrily.

"You're not all right. You . . . you're all queer. You don't care a bit for any of us now. We were planning to have such a lovely Christmas, but you wouldn't take any interest . . . and now everything's smashed up. I could manage somehow if you helped. I can cook a bit. But I don't see how I can do it all and look after Mother . . . and you lying out in the hammock all day. I—I wish to goodness I was a bit older . . ." Her voice broke. She turned from him and stared out of the window.

For a moment her father did not move or speak. Phyl, fighting to keep back her tears, didn't care whether she had made him angry. He must certainly be very angry—but that didn't matter beside the burden of misery and responsibility that lay on her. She wished he would go away—back to the hammock—anywhere, and leave her alone.

Then he was beside her, and his arm was tight about her shoulders.

"I'll show you how much I care," he said. "I've been pretty rotten for a good while, but that's over. It's about time something shook me up, I reckon. We'll see this thing through together, Phyl—I learned a fair bit about nursing when I was in Borneo, and I'm not too dusty as a cook, either. You and Rob and I can run a pretty good Christmas for this family if we tackle the job as a team. I know I wouldn't ask for two better mates—and I'll guarantee to do my share. How about it, old thing?"

She turned to him with a sob and rubbed her face against his coat.

"Will you, truly, Dad? I don't believe Mother'll mind having a broken leg if only we've got you really back," she whispered.

She was shaking as he held her to him, but the grasp of his strong arms was very comforting. All the fear and unhappiness of the months since his return seemed to drain away from her. This was Dad—really back; and Dad meant business.

He put her on the battered old leather couch presently, and sat down beside her.

"We'll have this thing out straight," he said. "Man to man, Phyl—no holding back. Have I been letting you all down?"

"We've been awfully worried," she said. She was suddenly anxious not to hurt him. "We knew it wasn't your fault, of course—it was just that you couldn't forget . . . all the horrible things. But they seemed to be getting right between you and us . . . like a beastly wall that we couldn't knock down. And we knew it was so bad for you. That was the worst part—the part that worried Mother most of all."

"And I was too darned blind to see it," he said. "I was fooling myself with the idea that I'd get fit if I rested. Much rest it was, with my mind going like a mill-race all the time—and feeling sorry for myself. Well, thank goodness this has jerked me out of it. Come along, daughter, and we'll have a council of war in Mother's room. Or do you think she ought to be kept quiet this evening?"

"Not for this sort of council of war," Phyl said. "It's going to cure her."

Mother was lying straight and stiff, her face lined with worry. She looked up as they came in, Dad's arm around Phyl—and suddenly a light came into her eyes.

He smiled down at her.

"Phyl and I reckon we've got to plan things out," he said cheerfully. "You'll have to be commander in chief, Mother, because you've got the brains of the outfit, and this house can't run without them—we three will be the working squad. No more cow-yard work for Phyl. You and I can do the milking on our own if we get up a bit earlier, can't we, son?"

"Too right we can!" said Rob eagerly.

"Well, we're only going to do what outside work is absolutely necessary. Phyl and I will be nurses and cooks, and we'll all keep the house ship-shape. I'd be dead scared to have you see any dust in corners when we bring you out of here—and the Doc says we can put you on the sofa pretty soon. But that leaves quite a lot of time on our hands. And we'll need it, because—leg or no leg—we're going to make this Christmas something pretty special."

"Oh, Andy—Andy!" said Mother, very softly. There were tears in her eyes, but she was smiling.

He sat down beside her and took her hand. Phyl signalled to Rob with her eyes. They slipped out quietly.

* * *

It was as if the whole world had changed over-night. Early as Phyl was up, Dad was before her; when she hurried in to the kitchen in her pyjamas the stove had been cleaned, the fire lit, and the big kettle was singing. Dad was cutting bread and butter. He grinned at her cheerfully.

"Oh!" said Phyl.

"Beat you to it," he said. "Cut along and have your shower. Mother's had quite a good night. Tea'll be ready when you come back."

Phyl slipped in to see the patient first. Mother looked pale and tired, but in her eyes was complete peace.

"Phyl, he's been wonderful," she whispered. "A nurse couldn't have looked after me better. Cool drinks in the night—and now he's sponged my face and hands and brushed my hair, as gently as a woman. Oh, I know everything's going to be all right."

"You bet it is!" said Phyl—and ran for her shower.

Everything *was* all right. The working squad divided the household jobs among themselves in strict military fashion, under the command of Sergeant Benham—who kept the heaviest parts for himself. The doctor came, bringing with him the bush nurse. The patient was doing well, he stated, and the nurse promised to come for an hour every morning. And then, all through the day, came the neighbours, in the way of bush folk, hurrying at the first news of trouble to see what help they could give. Not one came empty-handed; there were jars of soup, jellies, cooked meat, pies and cakes and scones, until the larder began to resemble a provision shop.

"I'll send good soup over every day," said Mrs Smith to Phyl. "Real stickto-your-ribs soup that'll strengthen her. And one of the boys'll come every morning and evening to help with the cows—and if there's any other job your dad wants done, he's just to let them know."

"Oh, but he couldn't, Mrs Smith."

"Rubbish! If soldiers can't stick by each other, apart from being old neighbours, then who can?" demanded Mrs Smith. "And you send for me any hour of the day or night, Phyl, if you want me."

It was Mrs Brown who took responsibility for the Benham's Christmas dinner.

"Better have it cold, dearie. I'll cook my best turkey on Christmas eve, and send it over early next day; and a pudding, too. What, your pudding's made! Well, I'll keep mine for your New Year. And mind you all hang up your stockings, 'cause there'll be things to put in them. I've brought some extra tea—our ration's pretty good now the boys are home, and your mum must have a cup of tea whenever she feels like it."

"Well, people are mighty good," said Dad that evening. "So far as cooking goes we seem likely to have a soft job, Phyl. Let's start Christmas decorations tomorrow."

The coloured paper had been stored for years. They made chains and balls until Dick and Dumps were covered with paste to the roots of their hair and had to be unstuck with much hot water and soap, and the kitchen was so full of coloured scraps that it looked as if a rainbow had gone mad in it. They hung them everywhere, keeping the best for Mother's room; and Mother lay and watched them and beamed. She had an urgent private conference with Dad and Mr Smith two days before Christmas eve. The children heard the result next morning when they gathered in her room after breakfast.

"Early dinner today," said Dad, speaking in the stern way of a sergeant, but with a twinkle in his eye. "All of you to parade in your Sunday kit immediately after. With clean faces, or I'll know the reason why!"

"What for?" said four voices.

"Because Mrs Smith is coming over to sit with Mother, and I am taking my family to town."

"Dad!" The four voices rose in different keys.

"Well, we can only do Christmas shopping once a year, and Mother seems to think it's the correct thing. Can't stay for the pictures this time—but we'll all go as soon as Mother can come too. It'll have to be a quick shopping, but we'll do the best we can. Dis–miss!" said Dad, in his best parade-ground voice: and his rejoicing family dismissed with hoots of glee.

It was a wonderful afternoon. The township was crowded, the streets decorated with branches of gum trees tied to every verandah post. Everyone they knew seemed to be there: people were continually stopping them to ask after Mother and say "Merry Christmas!" And the shops, to the Benham children, were marvellous, glittering with tinsel and full of the most exciting things. Dad grew positively reckless over shopping: the battered old car became so full of parcels that there was little room left for its passengers. They had a magnificent tea in the baker's shop, where everybody seemed to drift after three o'clock. And then it was time to think of the cows and the evening milking and the long road home.

Through her open window Anne Benham heard the car coming up the paddock. They were singing; her husband's deep voice rang out above the others. Then came three long hoots of greeting, and in a few moments they were all in her room, the children flushed and excited, all talking at once.

"Mother, it's been gorgeous!"

"We've got whole lots of parcels, only we can't tell you about them 'cause they's surprises!"

"Can't you, my Dumps? Were they good children, Dad?"

"I didn't notice," he said. "We hadn't time to bother about being good, had we, kids? But we had a great time. What about your patient, Mrs Smith?"

"She'll be hopping round on that plastered leg of hers soon if you don't watch her, she's that well," stated Mrs Smith, gathering up her knitting. "Well, I'll be getting home."

"I'll run you over in the car," he said.

They all trooped out. Only Phyl stayed behind. She looked at her mother and they smiled at each other.

"Was it good, Phyl?"

"Just lovely—if only you'd been there. I hated leaving you. Mother, he was just grand to us. He didn't seem much older than Rob. We're going to have such a gorgeous Christmas!—you on the couch and all sorts of excitements. But having Dad well is the best thing of all." She hesitated, a shadow crossing her bright face. "Mother, he'll never slip back again to the bad time, will he?"

"Never," said her mother firmly. "And if he did—well, I'd just have to break another leg!"

AFTERWORD

You might be interested to know that the story 'A New Year's Dawn' in this book is semi-historical, although most of the characters and places in it have fictitious names. It is a story about Mary Grant Bruce's own parents. Her grandson Ian has identified these aliases:

John Woodward	**William Whittakers**, the squatter of 'Tubbutt' Station
Mrs Woodward	**Louisa Ann Whittakers** (nee Grant)
Lynn Mason	**Eyre Lewis (or Louis) Bruce**, Mary Grant Bruce's father and also the template for David Linton, the squatter of 'Billabong'.
Mary Woodward	**Mary Atkinson Whittakers** (known as **'Minnie'**), Mary Grant Bruce's mother
Lizzie Woodward	**Hannah Louisa Wilmot** (nee Whittakers)
Tom Haviland	**John George Winchester Wilmot**, (known as 'Chester'), who was also a member of Black's Geodetic Survey.
Nell Woodward	**Catherine Whittakers ('Kate')**
Mount Misery	**Mount Turnback**
Wangong River	The **Snowy River** for most of the story, but more likely refers to the **Deddick** or **Jingalalla** Rivers at the start. The Snowy runs to the west of 'Tubbutt' but they got their six-monthly supplies, including their only mail, from Boyd Town which is well to the east, just south of Eden on the New South Wales coast.
Barindah	**'Tubbutt' Station**

More Short Stories by Mary Grant Bruce

We hope you have enjoyed this book. It is also available in audiobook formats published by Voices of Today' narrated by Sarah Bacaller and Denis Daly.

You can find out more about the author at her website www.marygrantbruce.com.au.

Mary Grant Bruce's best story, short or long, is **'Port After Stormie Seas'**. Along with her **'The Women Who Made Us'** and **'The High Sheriff's Table'**, it appears in *The Whittakers Story*, compiled by her cousin Clyde M. Whittakers. Mary Grant Bruce's mother was the first Whittakers to be born in Australia.

The Whittakers Story also offers the best sources of information about the farm properties, and some characters, on which Mary Grant Bruce based her 'Billabong' stories and many of her other books.

This handsome hardcover book has been published by Mia Mia Digital Publishing Pty Ltd and is available from many online booksellers.

ISBN 978-0-06480980-6-5

www.ingramcontent.com/pod-product-compliance
Lightning Source LLC
Chambersburg PA
CBHW020941310726
48980CB00001B/4

* 9 7 8 0 6 4 8 0 9 8 0 2 7 *